# PRIVATE LIVES

# PRIVATE LIVES

## A Bob Robbins Home Front Mystery

J.G. Harlond

Private Lives by J.G. Harlond



*All characters in this novel are fictitious. Any resemblance to actual persons, living or dead, is purely coincidental.*

*Bideford in North Devon is a real place, the farms and some locations, however, are fictitious.*



ISBN-13: 978-84-09-20420-5

BISAC Subject Headings:
FIC022070 FICTION/Mystery & Detective/Cozy/General
FIC022060 FICTION/Mystery & Detective/Historical
FIC066000 FICTION / Small Town & Rural

Cover design by Jenny Quinlan.
Cover photograph courtesy of Helen Hollick.

www.jgharlond.com

For Helen

"I think very few people are completely normal really, deep down in their private lives."

*'Private Lives'* by Noel Coward (1933)

## Characters

Detective Sergeant Edgar John (Bob) Robbins
Police Sergeant Edson (Bideford Police)
Police Constable Laurence (Laurie) Oliver of the Cornish Constabulary
Josiah Slattery, farmer, Ridgeway and Hentree farms
Detective Constable Charles West (Bideford C.I.D.)
Detective Inspector Drury (Bideford C.I.D.)
Ambrose Cummings, land agent
George Hook, solicitor
Nancy and Jack Lee, smallholders at Barley Cliff
Bunty and Cilla, Women's Land Army girls at Ridgeway Farm
Greville Healey, farm worker
Stanley and Sheila Healey, Greville's parents from Exeter
Mervyn Evans, shopkeeper at Larkham
Mervyn Hook, Larkham Cross resident
Dame Selena Candle, actress of Daneman Court
Mr Porter from Ministry of Information

**At Peony Villas**

Jessamyn Flowers, landlady of Peony Villas guest house
Arthur Puddicombe, Jessamyn's husband
Maud Puddicombe, Arthur's sister
Harold Gormley (Mr Pots), cook
Hester Edson, maid of all work
Mrs Lavinia Baxter-Salmon
*The Wayward Players*:
Wendell Garamond
Horace and Estelle Dobson
Suky Stefano
Reg Dwyer
Billy Bryant

# Chapter 1

**Bideford, North Devon, England.**
**A Friday afternoon, late summer, 1942**

The first shot shook a murder of crows into the air. The second shot kept them there. Bob Robbins closed his eyes and lay perfectly still in the tall grass while his heart leapt about in his chest. His new binoculars toppled to one side. Reaching out, he placed a protective hand over them, he didn't want them bouncing down a slippery grass slope then over the cliff onto vicious rocks. He took a deep breath. Time to move on. Someone was out catching rabbits, no point trying to see any wildlife now.

Sitting up, Bob shaded his eyes with a warm palm and gazed out across Barnstaple Bay: nothing moved but the occasional white horse of an incoming wave. With a huff of annoyance – for this was an idyllic spot – he struggled awkwardly to his feet on the steep incline then lifted the small groundsheet he'd been lying on, to shake it free of grass seeds. Turning to face inland, he caught sight of a figure pulling something in the field above. The single figure became two. One man standing, another being dragged along the ground. He lifted his binoculars and focused: a youngish man in brown dungarees had his arms linked under the shoulders of another man. He was pulling him backwards up the field. Someone had been shot. By accident? Bob's inner policeman processed what he was watching.

The same sense told him someone else was watching, too. Bob swivelled to his left. Something moved among ancient oaks and brambles up along the edge of the unploughed field. He adjusted the focus and studied the trees. There was nothing. It wasn't important, the injured man took priority.

Tucking his binoculars into his knapsack and leaving the groundsheet where it was, Bob tried to hurry uphill, not easy for a portly man in his sixties but there had been a shooting accident and he had the training to deliver first aid before the ambulance arrived.

By the time he reached the top of the pasture, the young man had dragged the inert form through a dilapidated gateway into a farmyard and was backing towards the open double doors of a barn.

"Hey!" Bob called. "Wait – I'll give you hand."

The young man's head shot up. "What you doin' here?" he demanded. "This is private property. You're trespassing."

"I was on the public footpath – along the cliff."

"Still our farm. Bugger off."

"But . . ." Bob indicated the fallen man, an elderly man he could see now, despite a lean, farm-life physique. "I can help, I'm a –" he stopped, smiled, changed tack. "Just thought you needed a hand. Shotgun pellets is it? I can do first aid."

"No need for that. None of your business. He was going down to tell you to clear off." The boy's knee propped up the injured man's lolling head. Bob bent down to touch the man's neck. "Leave him alone. Clear off!" the boy screamed.

Bob straightened up, embarrassed and surprised, and now deeply suspicious. He nodded, "As you wish," and gave a harmless grin, looking about him, committing every detail to memory. There was no sign of blood, and if the old chap had been shot in the back by pellets – by accident, from a distance – there was a good chance he was only injured. But in that case, he should have been conscious, and this man was most definitely not. "Are you sure I can't help?" It was a genuine offer.

"No!"

"Well, if you're sure. I'm going into town now, though, shall I send an ambulance up for you?"

"We got a telephone."

"Ah, that's all right then." Bob touched the peak of the helmet he wasn't wearing and turned back towards the cliff.

He took his time putting the binoculars in their leather case, re-shaking the groundsheet and folding it into a neat square before stuffing it untidily into his knapsack then placing the precious binoculars on the top. As he moved, he replayed in his mind what he'd heard and seen: a shotgun; two shots in rapid succession, presumably from the same weapon. A shotgun at close range could blow a man's head off, but in this case, he must have caught the pellets in his back – there'd been no sign of blood on his chest. Bob stared up the field, wondering if he'd got his facts right, then realised that he hadn't actually seen any sign of a shotgun. The boy could have dropped it in a tussock of grass, of course. But it wasn't impossible the shots had come from elsewhere. From the woods along the side of the pasture, for instance.

Had the boy fired at him, as a warning, and caught the old man coming down the field in the back? Bob frowned and rubbed the fingers of his right hand against his thigh: had the boy shot the old man by accident? There was no sign of blood on his front, but a cartridge of pellets in the backside or shoulders might knock him off his feet, cause internal bleeding . . . and being elderly he could have had a heart attack or . . . Bob closed his itchy right hand into a fist. As the boy had said, it was none of his business.

But something wasn't right. Taking his time, Bob closed the canvas straps of the knapsack and swung it over his shoulder, conscious now that he was being watched. Had the farm boy abandoned his father, or grandfather, to make sure he was off their property? Or was it the person in the trees? There had been someone there, he was sure of it.

Bob stared at the trees. A shiver ran down his back. Suddenly he wanted to be away, back in a town, back among shops and people and traffic. Ruffled and nervous, he hurried along the footpath, climbed over the stile and hastened to his old Morris tucked into a tractor lay-by. His hand shook as he opened the door and stuffed the knapsack safely under the passenger seat to protect his binoculars and keep them out of sight. Studying coastlines with binoculars and taking snaps of coastal areas was a criminal offence these days. He wound down his window and took a series of deep breaths. As his breathing calmed, his right hand sneaked up onto the steering wheel of its own accord and tapped a light staccato rhythm against the polished wood. Something was definitely not right. Should he report it at the nearest police station?

The third shot cut through his doubts and had him gasping for breath again. Not with surprise this time, but with the certainty that he'd just heard a pistol being fired – meaning the other shots had definitely been from a farm shotgun. Bob swallowed hard and set his hand to the ignition. He was a policeman and it was his duty to render help – and if not, at the very least to ensure the old man was all right – take him to hospital perhaps. If the boy would let him.

Executing a reasonable three-point turn for a steep, high-banked country lane, Bob raced back to the farm entrance he'd passed earlier that afternoon. The sign on the gate said 'Hentree Farm'. Bob manoeuvred into the yard, parked next to an aged tractor, then took stock of his surroundings before getting out.

People liked their guns on this farm, and they hadn't taken too kindly to visitors.

As he opened the car door, the stench of a filthy pigsty struck him like a physical force. He had been too preoccupied by the injured man to notice before, but now he saw hens pecking around the thin tractor wheels and a skeletal dog at the end of a chain. Holding his breath against the appalling smell, he hurried towards a grey, unwelcoming farmhouse. The porch was overgrown with weeds; the front door evidently never used. He knocked several times then headed round to the back of the house.

The back door had been painted a bright shade of green once – long ago. He opened the latch and called in. The kitchen was empty, with the still air of vacant premises.

"Hello! Anyone in?" There was no reply. He walked through to a narrow hallway, peered into an unlived-in living room then briefly debated going upstairs. "Hello!" he called up the stairwell. The old man was in no condition to get up the stairs unaided, and the silent response to his repeated calls was perfectly clear but he tried one last time anyway. "Are you all right? Can I help?" There was still no answer.

Bob hesitated but he knew he couldn't leave without at least checking the old man wasn't lying alone and injured. With a huff of annoyance, he started upstairs. The landing was gloomy and smelled of damp, the wall green-tinged with mould. "Your roof needs fixing," he muttered, massaging his right knee before starting on the bedrooms. All the doors were shut. Peeking in each, he was struck by the sense of absence he'd noticed earlier. No one lived here anymore. The last door was that of the so-called master bedroom. A shaft of sunlight sneaked in through a tightly shut window, sending a weak beam across a threadbare rug. He stepped back, wrinkling his nose at the stale, sickly-sweet smell and observed the room from the door: there was a lumpy bed covered in a brownish counterpane, but there was no farmer lying on it or sprawled out on the rug. He shut the door, hobbled downstairs and left the way he had entered.

As he walked back to his car, he noticed a stone-built milking parlour and a row of stables that ought to be checked. The milking parlour hadn't been used for many years. "Hello!" he called into the echoing darkness.

The lower doors to the stables were bolted shut. Peering over the first he caught a glimpse of shiny metal. A motorcycle. He opened the door and put his hand on the petrol tank. It was stone cold. He closed the door and checked in the next two stables. Nothing. Nobody.

Anxious to leave now, he forced himself to investigate the barn. The doors were rusted open. Gentle, warm afternoon sunlight illuminated the dirt floor; stray beams peeking through cracked windows turned bits of old farm machinery into instruments of torture. A path of sorts led diagonally towards a side door. He crossed the eerie space. The door opened onto another smaller yard, and the source of the foul odour: the remains of a pigsty. Its brick walls were reduced to rubble; the corrugated iron roof, tilted down to the ground, was being used by four mottled piglets as a playground attraction. Bob started to laugh and moved towards them, then stopped as a twitching snout emerged from the beneath the ruined shelter, followed by a long, sagging body. Bob swallowed hard: the entire yard had become a pig pen inhabited by a gruesome sow and Lord knew how many piglets, all slopping around in their own slurry. The sow looked up and fixed her small, mean eyes on his. Bob backed away. The sow moved towards him. Suddenly, she was joined by half a dozen other sows, teats swinging, snouts and tails twitching. Bob froze, horrified, until a huge male with tusks like a wild boar came galloping around the sty, followed by a good dozen older piglets.

"Gawd almighty!" Fear turned to flight. Regaining the power of movement, Bob turned back the way he'd come, getting to the barn door just in time to shove it closed on a long black-speckled snout. There was a squeal from the depths of hell, but he persevered until the door was fully shut, then he dropped the latch – and it fell off.

Then he was running through the murky barn as fast as his short legs could take him – aiming to get back to his car and as far from Hentree Farm as possible. But that meant crossing the open front yard again and he wasn't certain the pigs couldn't get around the barn to the front of the house. He glanced upwards. Was there a hay loft? Would it be safe? Dare he risk it?

He reached the ladder and, despite various missing rungs, pulled himself up to relative safety. Fearing the wooden-slatted floor would give way at any moment, he stepped onto the platform and turned: could the buggers get up ladders? He'd just seen piglets scaling a roof. Then he began wondering if the ladder were moveable: could they would knock it down and leave him in the loft for ever. Lowering himself onto his stomach, he stared below, but it didn't look or sound as if the pigs had followed him after all.

Where had they gone, though? Taking great care, he crawled across the loft to an open square that overlooked the other side of the yard then lay flat again to see what was outside for fear of toppling through the gap. There was a sort of crane contraption below, an empty wheelbarrow and a pitchfork, but no sign of his four-footed enemy.

A glint of sun blinded him for an instant. He shaded his eyes. From here he could see over the field he'd recently come up and right out across the bay. It was a spectacular view, a pristine ocean beyond a sad realm of neglect and decay. Gazing out, he tried to locate the spot where he'd first seen the boy and the injured man. Then he looked down at the yard again to get his bearings: where had they been when he'd offered the boy help? Between the gate to the field and this barn. So, where were they now? And why had the boy refused assistance?

He listened. There were no grunts or snuffles, but that didn't mean the pigs had gone back to wherever they'd been before. He waited.

He waited for what felt like a very long time, then slowly, very carefully descended the rickety ladder and went to the double doorway, not too fast to draw attention, not too slow to give the old sow time to catch his scent. At the entrance to the barn he paused. In the dark hollow behind a half-open door lay a crumpled figure. He'd walked right past it before.

Two fingers placed on a greasy neck told Bob this time the boy was the victim and he was quite dead. He hunkered down, waited for his eyes to adjust to the gloom. A bullet had entered the boy's chest dead centre. Of the old man there was no sign.

***

# Chapter 2

Bob straightened up and cast about him. The old man had been wearing brown dungarees with a green, collarless shirt: perfect camouflage if he were lying among the accumulated dried mud and weeds in the farmyard. The boy had been backing towards the barn – why not the house? Bob turned and stared back into the shadowy barn for clues, but there was nothing that looked out of place. No pile of straw that would have served as a makeshift bed either, for that matter.

He returned to the boy's body and groped in his dungaree pockets for something to identify him. There were bits of wire and a long nail for planks of wood; a packet of American cigarettes, which seemed odd in such a rural English setting; a filthy handkerchief that had been used on a tractor engine by the looks of it; a length of baler twine. In the bib were four used shotgun cartridges. That at least proved or solved – apparently solved – one immediate mystery: the boy had almost certainly shot the old man. By accident? Why did he suspect not?

Standing up and easing his back, he looked around him for another gun. The missing weapons were important, but he had to deal with this victim first. So much for a quiet day birdwatching along the coastal path.

*We've got a telephone.* He had to call the police and ambulance. But why wasn't there a woman around? No wife or mother, or grandmother even. It was all wrong. The whole place stank of neglect. Neglect and pigs, and something he couldn't name – and didn't want to. It wasn't his business what had been going on here. It wouldn't be his case and he wasn't going to be involved so it didn't matter. All he had to do was report the incident.

As he reached what had once been a kitchen garden in the back yard, the sound of grunting and snuffling started again. Despite the happy hours he spent fishing for trout in streams and birdwatching in woods or along the coast, Bob had no love of animals on the hoof. He quickened his step. Sows with piglets almost certainly meant trouble.

The moment he was inside the house again he shut the back door firmly behind him and called out, "Hello! Your pigs are loose, did you know?"

There was still nobody home. This time, however, a kettle and an empty milk bottle told him someone had been in recently, or had at least used the kitchen to make a cup of tea. He looked for a telephone and found an early model on the hall stand by the disused front door. A dozen or more unopened buff envelopes lay scattered about it. He lifted the handset: the line had been disconnected.

Bob sifted through the envelopes for a name. All but two were typed and official-looking. Utility reminders, by their appearance. Some were addressed to a Josiah Slattery Esq, a couple to a Mrs J. Slattery; one, hand-written, was for a Mrs M. Slattery. He opened the drawer and found two birthday cards with fancy birds and flowers on them. Both said: '*Thinking of you Mum on your special day. Have a big hug from me. Xx Ada*'

As he studied a stylised yellow bird among faded violets Bob gave a long sigh: there was a sad story here. He put it on the stand then pushed a hand to the back of the drawer. There was a wad of yellowed envelopes tied in string, all greetings cards by the size of them; no private letters. He undid the bow and studied the addresses. Each was directed to Mrs Slattery of Hentree Farm, Barley Cliff, Bideford, North Devon; each written in a rounded, schoolgirl hand. He examined the postmarks: between 1919 and 1925 they had been sent from Torquay, Eastbourne, Bournemouth, Guildford, Birmingham; the rest were all from London. No clues to the farmer and his wife here other than that they were called Slattery and had probably had a daughter who had left home. He opened an envelope from the middle of the pack. There was a robin on a snow-laden branch: *'Happy Christmas Mum, I think of you all the time. XOOO Ada'*

Ada – a daughter who'd got away, felt guilty, but wasn't coming back. There was nothing here of any use. He shoved the drawer back the way it was and with a mixed sense of relief left the house via the back door, making an undignified dash for his car to avoid any stray pigs.

The desk officer at the police station took a long look at the state of Bob's straw-rumpled linen jacket then carried on his conversation with the local postman. The fingers of Bob's right hand drummed against the counter.

"Be right with you, sir," the aging policeman said then quipped something private in the postman's ear. The postie laughed and left with a wave of a fistful of letters and a "See you there, then."

The desk officer turned slowly to Bob, "Now then, sir, what can we be doing for you today?"

Bob was so tempted to say, "I'll have a pint of brown ale, landlord," the words were nearly out of his mouth before he realised he had to make a choice as to who and what he was: did he show his police identity card or play it along as a holidaymaker, a concerned member of the public? He settled on the latter. He'd find a bed and breakfast for the night then cross Bideford bridge in the morning and continue what remained of his late-summer break as planned.

"I've come to report a death, officer. An unlawful killing," he said in a dead pan tone.

"An unlawful killing," repeated the policeman with a raised eyebrow.

Inwardly cursing his use of the legal phrase, Bob smiled apologetically and said, "Possibly two," and had the satisfaction of seeing the desk officer's jaw drop open.

***

# Chapter 3

*'Peony Villas, 1901'*. Bob checked the scrap of paper he had been given at the police station and read the inscription across the front of two imposing villas. Identical in construction, they were tall and large, double fronted and conjoined as far as the second floor. A gentleman's demonstration of wealth without unnecessary opulence or vulgarity. Actually, there was a touch of vulgarity but Bob couldn't quite say what it was.

He checked the address the desk officer had written again: *'Peony Villa', Larkham Road*. There was no mention of two villas. And there was no sign on either gate to say which, if either, was a guest house. He walked a few paces up the road to see if there was Peony Terrace or a 'Bed and Breakfast' sign. There wasn't, only a few smaller houses that ran along the river side of the road before it became a country lane.

Gazing at the stucco peony blooms nestling beneath the eaves of each house, then at the name displayed across the front of the joined dwellings, he wondered which house standing high above the road he should approach. Each had a double side gate with the usual 'Tradesman's entrance' notice, each had a brick-built appendage that had once been stabling for a horse and trap and was now a garage for a motor vehicle, but that was where their similarity ended. Number 1 was pebble-dashed in a delicate shade of pink, with white window frames and a deeper pink front door. Number 2 was the standard local grey pebble-dash, its woodwork somewhat distressed, its front door a discouraging black. Then he noticed the steps leading up to the front doors and groaned.

"Neither, thank you very much," he muttered, his thoughts shifting from his aching knees to a growing but less specific unease. He turned back to his car, but as he opened the driver's door a troupe of *artistes*, some still in costume and stage make-up, emerged from a green van and headed up the steps to Number 1. Two men were carrying bulging duffel bags, a woman was carrying a vast, velvet-looking gown; a tall man with a mane of white hair was carrying a baby swaddled in white muslin.

The man with the baby stopped at the front door, shoved out his right hip and said something that made everyone laugh. A blonde girl in some sort of pixie outfit fished in his trouser pocket, extracted a key and opened the front door. They jostled indoors, joking and calling for someone.

A guest house that permitted clients to use their own key – that made a difference. Bob pulled his overnight bag from the back seat, grabbed his knapsack and headed up the steps.

There was a tub of geraniums still in bloom either side of the front door, the wide step was genuine marble; Bob felt his spirits lift and rang a jaunty little bell. A maid answered the door.

"Good afternoon, Miss. Any vacancies?"

The girl gave his appearance a look not unlike the police officer's assessment then managed a polite Victorian bob and without a word went back into the house. Bob surveyed the terraced garden, neat enough for a magazine, then looked out at the surrounding area. The road would have been on the edge of Bideford back in 1901, leading out into the country, a market route perhaps.

"Can I help you?" The voice was light, delightful.

Bob swung round. The woman was considerably older than the sound of her voice, but charming nonetheless. He doffed his summer cap. “Good evening, yes, I need a bed for the night, do you have a vacancy? Excuse my clothing, I’ve erm – had a bit of an incident – with a tent – in the grass. Thought I’d try camping. Didn’t like it.”

The woman’s eyes twinkled with amusement but all she said was, “Oh, dear, that’s a shame. We don’t take casuals, you see. We’re more residential.”

“Ah, pity. Um – can you recommend somewhere else? I’m not keen on pubs these days, too noisy, and not stopping long enough for a hotel.”

The landlady gave him a soft smile. “A short stay. Well, I might make an exception for two nights. But it will be up in the gods, I’m afraid. A room came free up there this morning. An American military man, although I suppose I shouldn’t be telling anyone that.” The lady stepped back saying, “I’m Jessamyn Flowers, welcome to Peony Villa.”

“Jasmine?” Bob queried. “That’s an unusual name.”

“Jessamyn,” the woman corrected him. “It means jasmine, though. How sharp you are.”

There was no sarcasm in her voice and Bob shifted from foot to foot in her clear blue gaze, trying not to look at her left hand as red-lacquered fingers pushed a stray chestnut lock back into place. She was wearing a wedding band and chunk of diamond that would have cost him a year’s pay. As she waited for his expected reply, she gazed steadily into his eyes. He cleared his throat, tried to speak, then something about her name jolted his memory. Jessamyn. Or was it jasmine? His mind somewhat elsewhere for several reasons, Bob stretched out a warm round hand. It was met by a cool white palm. “Bob Robbins, Mrs Flowers. And I’m very grateful,” he added, referring to an earlier part of the conversation.

"According to theatre tradition I am *Miss* Jessamyn Flowers, but I've given up expecting that courtesy down here so *Mrs* it is. This way."

Bob followed the petite woman down a spacious entrance hall tiled in black and white to a table under the stairs, where she opened her guest register and said, "We're obliged to write down given names here, I'm afraid. I assume yours is Robert?" A finely made fountain pen hovered over a new page.

"Oh, no, I'm not actually *Bob* Robbins, no. I have a proper Christian name."

The woman's lifted her eyes to his once more and Bob shuffled from one foot to the other again, trying to decide how best to explain he was D.S. Robbins from the Cornwall County Constabulary, no longer on vacation. So much for a few quiet days to himself.

"Proper names are a legal requirement these days," Mrs Flowers sighed, interrupting his thoughts, "it's this rationing and the war, you see. I have to keep a strict record of people's identities and occupations."

"Yes, yes, of course you do. Quite understand." Then he remembered his ration book, which featured both his name and address. Pulling it from a pocket, he set it face upwards on the desk. "This should do. Shall you be needing it, by the way, for my breakfast and supper?"

Mrs Flowers gave him another heart-melting smile. "I think we can manage without that for two days, Mr Robbins." She wrote *Edgar J. Robbins* in a neat, flowing hand then looked up, "You are from Cornwall?"

"Living there now, yes."

"Occupation?"

Bob grimaced. Experience had taught him that giving his occupation in a guest house could lead to unpleasant confidences – or worse, for requests to investigate something trivial. “Retired,” he said flatly.

“From?”

“Insurance business.” That was true. After leaving the Police in the thirties he’d worked for an insurance company for five years before retiring, then, much to his annoyance, he’d been called back into the Force to replace a younger man who’d gone off to war.

Mrs Flowers entered the words and put the top back on her fountain pen. “Excellent, I think that’s all we need for now. Would you follow me?”

“Anywhere,” Bob murmured under his breath and grinned. Fortunately, the petite yet curvaceous Mrs Flowers was ahead of him and didn’t notice. By the second flight of stairs Bob remembered who she reminded him of: the wealthy socialite and politician Lady Nancy Astor. By the third floor he was out of breath and his knees were giving him gip, but a tiny darn in one of her silk stockings – just to the right of the seam above the left heel – helped him reach the small landing.

It was an attic room, up in the gods as he’d been told. Tiny, but it had a wash basin and a decent chest of drawers, plus a magnificent view over the town and tidal river. “Lovely,” Bob said. “I may extend my stay – if I can?”

Jessamyn Flowers bestowed another warm smile. “Hot and cold here,” she pointed to the basin, “our second bathroom is down on the second floor. Regulation four inches of bathwater only, of course. Bath towels are in the airing cupboard. You may help yourself, but do please use the same towel for the rest of your stay, we are very short-staffed. Washday is Monday.”

“Grand, I could do with freshening up.” Bob suddenly felt grubby and anxious for the woman to go so he could check his armpits, just in case.

"If you would like an evening meal, we serve tea at six o'clock these days, Welsh rarebit, stewed fruit, that sort of thing," she continued. "Except on Friday night, which is our 'Gala Night', when we *dine* at seven-thirty. Our one evening of wicked extravagance, although personally I see nothing wicked in dressing for dinner to cock a snook at that nasty little man in Germany. Thinks he's going to starve us out, does he? We'll show him!"

Bob blinked and smiled but had no time to offer any other form of response, for Mrs Flowers continued, "I planned to offer private suppers on request but rationing has seen to that little pleasure in life as well. There are cocoa and biscuits before bedtime, though, if you like a little something before retiring?" She gave him a knowing look. Bob blinked again in surprise. "If you have access to a bottle of wine or something stronger you are welcome to share it with us – or drink alone, if that is your preference."

Bob found himself nodding gently to the cadence of the woman's voice then realised he was expected to respond here. "Erm, yes. No, that is, no wine or anything like that, not usually anyway. I have a tot of whisky at home of an evening, but I don't carry it with me." He gave an embarrassed laugh then stopped himself and said, "Very nice about the cocoa, though, thank you."

"Anything else?" Mrs Flowers asked, leaving the room.

"No, no, can't think of anything else."

"Oh, but I can!" Mrs Flowers peeped conspiratorially around the door. "Who told you this was a guest house?"

"Desk sergeant at the police station."

Mrs Flower's right hand flew melodramatically to her chin. "Oh dear," she whispered, "they're on to us! That won't do at all."

The door closed on the cramped little room. "Blimey O'Reilly," Bob muttered to himself as he removed his creased beige linen jacket and flung it over a chair. Bone weary, he slumped onto the narrow bed. It creaked loudly under his weight and he nearly slipped off the satin eiderdown. Righting himself, he pushed the expensive covering off the blankets and snuggled into the soft pillow. A lot had happened since he left his cottage on the east coast of Cornwall that morning. His eyes closed and he was nearly asleep before he remembered this was Friday. Gala Night, and he only had a bagful of holiday clothes to 'dress up' in. "I can go as the local tramp," he mumbled to himself and closed his eyes again.

***

# Chapter 4

After showing her new resident to his room, Jessamyn Flowers sauntered down the stairs in a pensive frame of mind. As she reached the hallway her maid of all work, Hester, crossed her path coming up from the kitchen.

"Hester," Jessamyn hissed, "a word." She ushered the girl back behind the service door and stood at the top of the steps with her. "What have you been telling your father about us?"

"Nothing. What would I tell him?"

Jessamyn gave a small shrug, "We have actors from London staying here – you might be telling people about their funny ways, for example."

"No, Mrs Flowers. Have they got funny ways? I haven't noticed."

"Mmm," Jessamyn narrowed her eyes and peered at the girl in the poor light, "so it won't have been your father who gave our new guest Mr Robbins our address?" The girl shook her head, twisting the fabric of her white pinafore with her right hand. "Don't do that, you'll crease it." Jessamyn stayed the girl's hand, then kept it in hers for a moment. Speaking in a gentler tone, she continued, "One more thing, Quentin's here." Hester bit her lip, indicating she already knew, and guessed what was coming. "Remember what I said after he was here last time. You are *not* to go into his room under any circumstances, not to clean it, not even to see if he's there."

"No, Mrs Flowers," Hester shook her head from side to side again.

"Good. He's too old for you and too . . ." Jessamyn paused, searching for an appropriate euphemism, "too worldly wise. Stay away from him. We don't want a repetition of your previous situation, do we?"

"No, Mrs Flowers." Tears welled in the girl's eyes. "But he says he's going abroad and he might not come back and –"

"You've already seen him. Well don't be taken in. That is a form of blackmail, my sweet. If it's true. You know what he can be like as well as I do. Now, back to your chores and we'll say no more about it."

Struggling upright after a short but much needed nap, Bob slowly unbuttoned his shirt and went to the hand basin, musing on whether Mrs Flowers' 'they're on to us' comment was meant as a joke. The hot tap let out a reluctant trickle of brown water then gulped to a halt. The cold tap did likewise. "Here we go," Bob huffed, "here we bloomin' go." He buttoned his shirt, scrabbled for his washbag and headed down to the 'second bathroom'.

Someone had got there before him. Two people by the sound of it, and they'd chosen it as a venue for a full-blown marital row. He assumed it was marital under the circumstances.

"It's always the same," the woman moaned.

"It is." The male voice with a professional actor's timbre bounced off the tiled walls, reverberating around what Bob imagined the bathroom to be. "It certainly is, and you – you don't miss a chance, do you! For once and for all, I'm not interested in her."

The woman said something Bob couldn't catch. Aware that he was eavesdropping, he headed back up the narrow attic staircase just as the door flung open and a somewhat cadaverous featured man in a white towelling robe strode out. “Horace!” the woman called after him. “The bathwater is going cold.”

“Better drink it quickly, then,” Horace retorted and swung into a room labelled ‘Orchid’.

Returning to his eyrie, Bob noticed his room was named ‘Honeysuckle’. “Gawd almighty,” he grunted and went to the sash window, slipped the catch and pushed up the upper pane. Taking a deep breath, he turned back to look into the room, “What d’you reckon, Joan, nice place or too fussy for us?”

Joan didn’t reply. Joan had been dead for nearly three years and she’d stopped talking to him after the business with the nice woman in Porthferris – although that had come to nothing in the end.

After a second, unsuccessful attempt to get into the second bathroom, Bob trotted down to the first floor in search of the first bathroom. That was also occupied so he went in search of Mrs Flowers for an old-fashioned jug of hot water. The ground floor was empty of souls so he knocked at the service door, and on getting no reply went down the bare wooden steps to what he hoped would be the kitchen and scullery. A delicious waft of what he remembered to be the smell of roasting meat confirmed the idea.

The maid who had opened the door was peeling muddy roots at a stone sink. She looked over her shoulder then went back to her task without a word. Bob thought she might be crying. A rotund, ill-shaven man with a completely bald head was whisking batter in a huge basin at an egg-shell littered table.

“Can you let me have a jug of hot water?” Bob asked the maid. She turned to him; her face streaked with dirt where she had wiped away tears. “Never mind, you carry on with what you’re doing.” He smiled at the cook and repeated his request. “Do you have hot running water down here? I need a jug of water, you see. For a wash. There's no hot water – or any cold for that matter – in my room."

The cook had returned to his whisking: the metal implement had been whizzed to a frenzy, sending him into some sort of culinary trance. Bob tried again more loudly. "Mr – erm . . ."

"Pots," the cook announced above the mad whirr.

"Pots? Ah, yes, *Mr* Potts, I need some hot water." The rotund man shook his head. Whether it was because he couldn't hear, or because there was no hot water Bob wasn't sure. "Oh, never mind. Tell me where I can find Mrs Flowers."

The man halted and gave him a vacant look.

"Mrs Flowers? Outside, is she?" Bob started towards a door that looked as if it would lead outdoors. "In the back garden?"

"He means Mrs Puddicombe," the maid sniffed over her shoulder.

"Oh," replied the cook, "through there."

"Puddicombe?" Bob queried, but got no further because as the cook indicated a door to his right using his whisk, the handle rolled on of its own accord – battering his ample stomach and most of the table.

Bob stepped out of reach and located an open door. It led directly into a basement corridor flanked by two plain doors. He opened the one on the left. In the dark space lit only by a high, ventilation window he could just make out various easy chairs and what looked like stacked mattresses: it was an indoor air-raid shelter or refuge room. Empty of people. He opened the one on his right. A storage area with cardboard boxes on metal shelving. He closed the door and groped his way along the corridor, expecting to come out in a laundry area, but instead found another door and a set of steps going up. He was about to turn back – his knees had had more than enough stairs for one day – when he heard a woman's voice coming from further along the ground floor passage. It sounded like Mrs Flowers. Then there was a man's voice. They were arguing.

Bob's rubber-soled shoes made no sound on the bare wooden boards of the steps, nor on the linoleum above. The woman was definitely Mrs Flowers. Each word carefully enunciated, her tone was not so dulcet now. She was angry.

"No, I've told you before, this is NOT the way to go about it. You'll have to wait."

"Wait, wait! How much longer? I could be dead next week the way this war is going and never had what's rightly mine. I want something to come back to and you *owe* me this."

"Oh, Quentin –"

"Ken! Call me Ken for crying out loud!"

There was a pause as if the woman had moved a step backwards or taken a surprised gasp of breath. "I shall never do that," she said quietly. "All I'm trying to say is that your grandfather is getting old – and as soon as he goes – *if* I inherit, I'll make the property over to you straight away. Heaven knows, I never want to live there again."

"*If*? You're his only descendant. Of course you'll inherit. Unless those buggers in Exeter get to him first. Go and see him. Remind him Gran promised that land to me."

"I've tried. He won't see me." Mrs Flowers' voice died away.

"Well, try again! All I need to know is that the land will come to me. That way I can make some arrangements before I go. I need to get it sorted out, and I've only got another few days."

Quentin/Ken mumbled something else and Mrs Flowers responded with something Bob couldn't catch, but then she moved closer to the door. ". . . You don't need to worry about Greville and his family. They're not related by blood: they have no claim."

"Why is that sneak living up there then, eh? Can't you see, this is exactly why *you* need to make your peace with him. He'll forgive you if you try."

"Forgive *me*! He's the one who should be begging for my forgiveness."

"Don't start all that again. He did what he did. It can't be changed so let it go. All I'm asking is that you say something to soften him up."

Mrs Flowers said something Bob couldn't catch before Quentin took up a more hectoring tone: "It's not his money I'm after. You'll get enough off that vegetable upstairs anyway, but what about me? I've got a future to think about." Silence. "You don't give a damn about me. Never bloody have."

"Quentin!"

Bob felt himself flinch as he imagined a raised palm about to slap the lovely Jessamyn. He put a hand on the door handle, ready to rush to the rescue, then took it away. She probably – almost certainly – wouldn't want anyone knowing about her private family affairs. Who was this rude fellow anyway? Her son?

"I'll speak to our solicitor again. Maybe he can do something. I will, I promise." Mrs Flowers' voice sounded so sad Bob imagined her placing a hand against her heart, tears welling in her eyes. He turned to go then halted as she asked more calmly, "Why this sudden rush? What are you not telling me?"

Quentin replied in a much quieter tone and all Bob caught was "embarkation leave . . . Far East, we reckon."

The door handle turned from the inside. Bob jumped away and hastened towards the connecting basement corridor but the voices continued behind him.

". . . we're for the second front out there."

"That means the Japanese, doesn't it?"

"Most likely. That's why I need to get my business matters fixed."

Mrs Flowers said something Bob couldn't hear then Quentin said, "Not to worry, I've been bumped up to Armoury NCO so I'll be looking after the guns and ammo with a bit of luck, not in the front line shooting the bloody stuff. By the way, I'll be staying here a few nights."

"In your room upstairs here? All right, but you'll have to eat with Maud as well, Number One is full to bursting and –"

"And you don't want me spoiling your suppertime fairy tales."

The bitterness and sarcasm in Quentin's voice made Bob shudder. He retraced his steps as quietly as he could, certain that Mrs Flowers would not want him to know anything about this.

The second bathroom was vacant on his way back upstairs, but the hot water tank was empty.

***

# Chapter 5

The dining room at Number One, Peony Villas, reminded Bob of a Hollywood film he'd seen with Joan before she was too ill to go out. Set in a luxury mansion, all light wood with curlicue bits, and women in slinky satin – there had been candelabra on the table in the film with long, tapered white candles. The candelabra here in Peony Villas were on a solid, dark oak sideboard with squat stubs of red candles, but after three years of war and rationing the effect was similar. He paused in the doorway, distracted and confused by the opulence, staring at the single, large oval table, around which was seated a cast of actors who looked for all the world as if he'd interrupted their lines.

Faces turned to him. Mrs Flowers, at the far end of the table, clapped her hands together, "Oh, I do so love it when we achieve this effect."

Bob stayed where he was and garbled, "Sorry, I think I'm in the wrong place."

"No, you are not, Friday night is Gala Night! Come along in, Mr Robbins. Take this chair next to me, I have kept it especially for you." Mrs Flowers wafted her napkin over the seat beside her.

Bob edged towards the chair, passing behind diners who either acknowledged him with a nod or ignored him altogether and continued whatever they had been discussing. Feeling entirely out of place, he pulled out a Chippendale-style chair with a flowered chintz fabric seat and, trying not to think about his weight and casual appearance and trying not to scrape the polished floor at the same time, seated himself at Mrs Flowers' right.

His placement at the table also disconcerted the tall man with the mane of white hair to her left, for he peered around their host both back and front, trying to ascertain who had been given favoured status, and why. Aware of curious stares from elsewhere, Bob focused his gaze on a long-stemmed wine glass, although there was supposedly no wine, then a starched pink table napkin in the form of flower bloom. He hadn't seen a table napkin like that for years.

Mrs Flowers tilted her head as he fumbled with the napkin's intricate folds and with a glint in her eye, said, "We're having a bit of a celebration, Mr Robbins. Mr Garamond has brought home the bacon. And we have raspberries with real cream – clotted cream from . . ." she turned to the man on her left, who Bob supposed was Mr Garamond.

*The man holding the baby – except it had been another ruddy piglet.*

"Where was it, Wendell?"

"Pandy Cross Women's Institute," the white-haired lion confirmed.

Placing her left hand on the man's arm, she cooed, "You are *such* a charmer, Wendell. I bet you had all the ladies offering you *all manner* of treats. I'm never going to let you leave my dear little Peony Villa, we'll starve without you!"

Wendell touched his pink napkin to his fleshy pink lips and raised an eyebrow. "Is that a promise or a dare, *my dear little* Puddi?"

Jessamyn Flowers' cheeks turned pinker than the napkin. Frowning, she shook her head at the suave Wendell and whispered something, to which he gave a lazy shrug. For a few moments there was a tension in the air, then she leaned back in her chair and spoke to Bob. "I think I had better explain," she said, "six of these lovely people," she indicated diners around the table, "are members of a very special troupe of artistes, staying with me to get away from the horrors of London and entertain around the county." With a slight wave of her left hand she indicated: "Mr Wendell Garamond, actor and director . . ."

*Garamond*? Thought Bob, *another name I've heard of and can't place.*

". . . Miss Suky Stefano, soubrette . . ."

*The one in the pixie outfit. Very pretty, and very young. Blonde and definitely not Italian – a stage name for Susan Stephens?*

"Mr Horace Dobson, an extremely fine tenor and *so* versatile – from Henry the Fifth to Gilbert and Sullivan, isn't that right Horace?"

Horace, thin and grey in a Savile Row suit, inclined his head, "Too generous, milady, too generous."

*Second bathroom.*

"And this is Estelle," Mrs Flowers continued, "a celebrated contralto and the Wayward's positively spine-chilling Butcher's wife . . ."

"A butcher's wife?" Bob queried, trying not to stare at the stylishly coiffured, middle-aged woman in a mauve cocktail concoction.

"The Scottish play. They also do scenes from Shakespeare," Mrs Flowers supplied as explanation.

"Ah," Bob gave a knowing nod, although he had no idea who the butcher's wife might be. "Shakespeare. Dead kings and fairies. All Greek to me."

"Precisely." Jessamyn Flowers gave him a forgiving smile then continued around the table, "Next to Estelle is Mr Reginald Dwyer, stage manager –"

"And Banquo's ghost and everything else," the man grunted.

*Grumpy devil with a tippler's red nose. Where does he get the booze from these days?* Bob gave him a closer look and revised his opinion: the oldest of the men at the table, Dwyer's posture and hooded eyelids behind round, tortoiseshell spectacles suggested he was worn out, not tipsy.

"And Mr William Bryant." Mrs Flowers paused and looked at a rotund man in an old-fashioned bookie's loud check suit. "What exactly is it that you do, Billy, apart from that clever tap dance routine with Suky?"

"The money," he said, with a chuckle. "I'm producer, accountant, booking clerk, advertising. You name it, I'll make it spin. Well, I would if anyone had any dosh left to spare."

"Which is why," the wife from the second bathroom sighed, "we are reduced to singing for our suppers."

"With splendid results, I must say," Mrs Flowers added with a convincing, all-embracing smile and bat of the eyelids.

She turned back to Bob. "And sitting next to you, Mr Robbins, is our much-loved, longest-term resident, Mrs Baxter-Salmon."

Bob took in the woman's pasty face and unfriendly expression and gave an inward shudder: *a right old trout by the looks of her*. Giving her a polite 'how do you do', he realised she was staring straight at him through bulbous dark eyes. Her gaze then shifted to his left. He turned to Mrs Flowers, who gave a weak smile but said nothing.

Suddenly conscious he needed to acknowledge all the introductions and painfully aware of his flat Midlander's accent, Bob began to address the table as whole with a "Good evening, everyone," but as he did so Mrs Flowers clapped her palms together twice and said, "And this, dearest friends, is Mr Robbins, who will be staying with us tonight."

He was saved from having to respond again by the door being pushed open and Hester, the tearful maid of all work, staggering in with a heavy tray, upon which lay a suckling pig complete with apple. *The babe in arms . . .*

The Wayward Players all applauded and everyone began speaking at once. Wendell Garamond carved the small beast as if it were a stag caught out hunting, entertaining the diners as he did so with an anecdote about a real hunting trip in France and spearing the grimmest boar one ever dared catch with a single throw of a particularly historic javelin. It was all Bob could do not to roll his eyes.

Mrs Flowers set roast potatoes and parsnips on each plate, which were then passed around the table. Bob gasped when he saw what had been set before him and tried to thank her, but she said quietly, "Oh, no, please. No more Mrs this or that, everyone here calls me Jessamyn, except Hester and Miss Suky Stefano, which is as it should be."

Two hours later, sated with succulent pig flesh, warm and happy on sticky cherry brandy, Bob staggered up the three flights of stairs to Honeysuckle and dropped fully dressed onto the narrow bed.

"What a day," he said to Joan, trying to kick off a shoe without untying the laces. "What a flaming weird day."

He slept badly. The mattress was lumpy and piglets roved at will around the room all night.

***

# Chapter 6

## Saturday

Before Bob had finished washing his face with what little water now dripped from the hot tap, Mrs Flowers' overworked housemaid, Hester, knocked urgently on his door and gasped out, "Beg pardon, sir, there's a man to see you."

Bob knew who it would be instantly: he'd been forced to reveal that he was a detective sergeant when he'd reported the boy's death and now there'd be somebody wanting to learn more about what had happened at Hentree Farm.

"All right, I'll be down in a jiffy," he said, pressing a sixpence into Hester's red palm.

Despite his words, Bob lingered over putting on his jacket, wondering how he could get out of any further involvement in the inquiry. Then with a sigh of resignation he collected his cap, wallet and car keys from the top of the chest of drawers and descended the three flights of stairs.

Jessamyn Flowers was standing by the open door, wearing an attractive straw boater and with a handbag on her arm as if she were going out. She was chatting to a young man. Sunlight caught auburn strands of hair leaking from beneath the hat, turning them gold. Bob had an urge to put his hand on her warm neck but caught himself in time and turned his attention to the plain clothes policeman. A rapid entry wartime recruit, by his youthful gingery appearance, bumped up to Detective Constable well before his time. Bob knew who'd be doing all the work this morning – the same person who was supposed to be taking a few days much-needed leave.

"Ah, here he is. Mr Robbins, you failed to tell me you were a detective sergeant yesterday." Mrs Flowers' tone was jocular but there was a trace of annoyance.

"No, well I'm on holiday, you see. I've got five days – only four left now – or three if you don't count today. I was hoping to get up to Exmoor." Bob gave her an apologetic grin, but the message was for the plain clothes policeman, not her.

She gave Bob a wan smile and turned to the detective on the doorstep, "Use my drawing room, Mr West. I'm afraid I have to go out so let Hester know if you need anything – as long as it isn't coffee or tea, we keep strictly to our rations here, you know."

Bob followed her, saying, "We can talk out in the front garden, it's a nice day," and directed his visitor to a wrought iron table and chairs on the small terrace.

DC West put out a warning hand, "Actually, sir, I'm here to ask you to accompany me up to the farm. Walk me through what happened yesterday. We were up there last night. They got the young man to the mortuary, but there was no sign of a second dead or injured man."

"No point sitting down then, is there?" Bob replied. "Quicker we get there, quicker I can get away again... Sorry, I didn't catch your name."

"Oh, no, sorry, Charles West, Bideford police, Detective Constable. I was out on another case when you reported the incident yesterday, so I haven't been up to the farm myself yet. We're a bit overstretched at the moment and that's putting it mildly."

"Best we don't waste time in idle chatter then. You got a car or shall I drive?"

West had a police vehicle, but didn't seem to know his way around very well. Hesitating at the end of the road, Bob reminded him of the farm's whereabouts and they headed out towards Larkham then up and down a series of winding, high-banked lanes towards Barley Cliff. Bob was directing from memory and, as there were no roads signs because of invasion fears, they took various wrong turns.

"You're not a local man, DC West," Bob commented as the driver struggled to reverse into a gateway to let a tractor pass.

"That's the problem. We're almost none of us locals here at the moment. Our uniform sergeant is a Bideford man, but the rest of us are mostly from elsewhere, if you count Barnstaple as elsewhere. It's only twelve miles away but to hear Bideford locals it's the edge of the known world."

"Barnstaple? I've been through it. There's a big old bridge there as well, isn't there?"

"Yes. We've got a couple of PCs from there, and Inspector Drury, my boss, but he's been sent up to Ilfracombe to help out – just when we need him."

"Ifracombe? Their need'll be greater," Bob muttered.

"You know Ilfracombe?"

"Only from an enquiry a while back. They were . . ." Bob searched for a polite phrase, "let's say 'not used to serious crime'."

DC West gave him a sideways look. "And you are, sir?"

"I am, unfortunately. Slow down. It's that gate down there." Bob pointed to an opening at a dog-leg turn in the lane. "That's the one."

There was a car parked in the farmyard. "Was that here yesterday?" West asked.

"No. No vehicles, only that rusty tractor over there," Bob indicated the agricultural relic. "And a motorbike parked in a stable."

"It's a nice car. New, by the look of it."

"Didn't think anyone was making cars these days, thought it was all tanks," Bob grunted.

DC West drew up beside the shiny black Austin, got out and looked about him then wandered up to the front of the house. Bob waited beside the car keeping a wary eye open for feral pigs, until curiosity got the better of him and he crossed the yard in the direction of where he'd last seen the old man. All senses alert, he noticed the dog was no longer on its chain and retraced his steps to the police vehicle.

He was just opening the passenger door when a burly man, overdressed for the season in country plus-fours, emerged from the back of the house. "Heard the motor, good morning, are you here for the buyer?" he called.

Before Bob could respond, DC West was striding purposefully towards the visitor. They shook hands.

"Ambrose Cummings, land agent and auctioneer," said the burly man. "Cummings and Associates."

"DC Charles West, Devonshire Constabulary."

Ambrose Cummings came to attention. "Is something wrong? I had an appointment with Mr Slattery at Ridgeway Farm this morning and he wasn't there."

*Slattery?* Bob remembered the name on the envelopes in the empty farmhouse and frowned.

"There's been some sort of accident, we think, sir. A young man has died."

'Died' not shot: not as green as he looks, Bob thought with a nod of approval.

"Tractor again, was it?" Cummings responded. "Lethal on these steep fields. "The nephew, I suppose." The man gave a deep sigh. "That's a shame. Too much of a townie to see the risks, I suppose."

DC West looked at Bob then said, "Mr Slattery's nephew is working here, you say?"

"I believe so, yes, and some Land Girls." Ambrose Cummings' response was more cautious this time.

Bob joined the two men and offered Cummings his hand and his civilian name, then mumbled the name of his old insurance company by way of introduction.

Cummings rubbed his hands together again, "That's reassuring. I wouldn't have expected Josiah Slattery to spend a penny on insurance."

"Is the sale of Hentree going through, then?" Bob queried, as if in the know.

"Sale?"

"You mentioned a buyer." Bob studied the buildings as if appraising their worth. "Good-sized property, working farm," he indicated the view. "Prime spot. I should think a place like this would auction very nicely, war or no war."

"Not at auction. Mr Slattery wanted to discuss the acreage and value of the fields." Cummings was selecting his words now. "I'm not sure I should be telling you this without him here, you know. If he's down at the hospital, I'll be getting along if you don't mind."

DC West moved into his path, "Before you go, sir, can you fill me in on a few details about the young man. He's Mr Slattery's nephew, you say. Do you know if he lives here?"

Cummings looked from West to Bob doubtfully. "Here or at Ridgeway. Mr Slattery has two farms. Where the boy bunks down, I've no idea."

"Two farms?"

"This one and Ridgeway. I just mentioned it."

"You did sir, yes. So, Mr Slattery doesn't actually live here at Hentree?" West queried.

"Not as far as I know. Like I said, I was asked to meet him up at Ridgeway. When he wasn't there, I thought one of us had made a mistake and I came down here."

"Two farms: that's a lot of work," Bob commented. "He must be fit and healthy, Mr Slattery."

"For his age, I'd say so, except," Cummings paused, looked at Bob then decided to continue, "I do know he was struggling to cope. There's a lot of land and Old Josiah could barely manage one after his son was killed."

"His son was killed?"

Cummings nodded. "Tractor accident. In all the local rags. After that – so I'm told – Mr Slattery was in a right old state. Only natural, of course. He certainly couldn't manage on his own. That's probably why the nephew's here."

"But he's selling up – this farm or both?" DC West asked.

"Only this one for now. Although it's worth his while working it now, isn't it, with the war on? He'll be getting government payments and incentives for crops. Strange times, when you think how many farmers were going bust ten years ago. He could have sold back in the thirties and had good reason."

"But he's waited until now."

"It seems he's had a good offer," Cummings pulled a knowing, appreciative face.

"Strange times," Bob repeated with genuine feeling.

"The Land Girls, you mentioned," West interrupted, "are they working at Ridgeway or here?"

"I only saw them briefly – at Ridgeway. As to who's been doing the hard graft, you'll have to ask Mr Slattery. He's only got two wenches, I saw them both, but even with them and the boy he's overstretched. Hence the sale, I suppose."

"He doesn't have any other hired help?" West asked.

"No idea. Those girls do what they can, I suppose. What's happened to the boy?"

"Shooting accident, we think, sir." DC West took out his notebook, "Can you tell me how to find this Ridgeway Farm, please."

"Shooting? Ah, the boy. Told you he was a townie – couldn't handle a shotgun, I suppose." Cummings was fishing now. West made no comment so Cummings picked up on his request for directions. "Out the gate, turn right, up to the crossroads then two miles or so on towards Larkham Cross. You'll see the sign on the gate, then there's a longish track uphill to the house. Bit remote."

"And Mr Slattery is selling this farm with all its land?" DC West pressed on.

The land agent grimaced. "I can't say yea or nay to that. Early days. If you'll forgive me, I've work to do in town."

DC West stayed where he was. "Just a couple more questions, sir. Can you tell me the nephew's name?" Cummings shook his large head. "And would this property go to him on Mr Slattery's death?"

Cummings blew through his cheeks then cocked his head to one side with an exaggerated 'oh-all-right-then' expression. "Well, according to my information, and that's mainly what my secretary knows – she's a Larkham girl – this farm, Hentree, technically belongs to the Pascoe family. Mr Slattery's wife's family. Cedric Pascoe left it to his daughter, Martha."

"But the Pascoe family don't live here at Hentree?" Bob queried, wanting clarification and thinking about the hollow, desolate nature of the house.

Cummings shrugged, "There's only Mrs Slattery left, as I understand it."

"Mr and Mrs Slattery don't have any other family?" West pushed on.

"There was a daughter who disappeared under something of a cloud after the Great War. Joyce – my secretary – says she went up to London, which is a ruddy nuisance because we may need to find her. Assuming she's still alive. What with all the bombing they've had."

"Mr Slattery has no other heir?"

"Not that I know of."

"That's very helpful, Mr Cummings, thank you." West closed his notebook.

"Sorry I can't be more of assistance." Cummings sounded sincere this time. "Obviously, I need to know about land entitlements before we get involved in sales. I learned that the hard way. Some people can be very remiss about ownership and the legality of a sale. That's what I was hoping to follow up today as it happens."

"Ah, one thing," DC West reopened his notebook, "the nephew, is he involved in the sales proceedings?"

"I can't say. There's a grandson. The daughter left a son behind when she ran away – according to Joyce that is." Cummings gave an exaggerated grimace, "I'm repeating gossip. You need to ask Mr Slattery about all this, not me."

Nobody spoke for a moment then Cummings rubbed his beefy hands together again and said, "Well, if the owner isn't present there's not much point me staying. I'll be getting back to my desk. Please give Mr Slattery my condolences when you see him. I'll call back in a couple of days. Be a shame to lose the sale."

DC West lifted his hat and let Cummings return to his car. Bob crossed the yard at the land agent's side saying ingenuously, "Only the one offer, then? Nobody else interested?"

"Oh, there's nothing firm about an actual sale yet. As I said, we're walking the boundaries at this stage, that's all."

Cummings opened his car door and eased his bulk behind the wheel. Then he wound down his window and said, "A word to the wise: Old Josiah, as they call him, he's a grumpy old devil, but I wouldn't underestimate him or his faculties." Cummings tapped his head.

"Right you are," Bob replied nodding. "Thank you, Mr Cummings." He touched the peak of his cap out of habit then added quickly, "Oh, one last thing, you say the buyer who's interested, it's a private arrangement, the farm won't go to public auction?"

Cummings grimaced again. "I can't divulge anything about value or price, if that's what you're asking? Like I said, early days. What I can tell you, is that Jack Hoblin has *offered* to buy Hentree Farm outright. That is no secret."

"And Mr Hoblin is another farmer?" Bob had to raise his voice over the sound of the engine.

"Lord, no! Hoblin's Holiday Camps: have you never heard of them? Paignton, Dawlish, now Bideford. They bring charabancs down from the industrial towns for a week in sunny Devon."

"That'll be good for the local economy, give the locals some employment when this dratted war is over. Larkham folk must be pleased."

"Yes and no. There'll be some building work and maintenance, but these camps have their own shops. Holidaymakers won't even go down to Bideford. Hoblin camps have their own cinemas and dance halls; it's 'all inclusive' so local businesses aren't going to benefit much. Right, must be off. When you see Mr Slattery tell him to get on a blasted telephone and call me."

***

# Chapter 7

Bob watched the land agent's car back out of the farmyard and returned to DC West, who was watching from beside the barn. "Caught all that did you?" Bob asked, casting about him warily.

"I did, thank you, sir. Neatly done."

"No need for the 'sir', Detective Constable, Mr Robbins will do. Bob if we get to like each other."

"In that case you'd better call me Charlie," the young man grinned.

Bob gave him a lop-sided smile. "We haven't got any answers, though, have we? Apart from the fact that we need to get up to this Ridgeway farm P.D.Q. to see if the old man's gone back there. Though how he walked three or four miles uphill in his state is anybody's guess."

"Absolutely, but while we're here, can you walk me through what happened yesterday, so I know what I'm dealing with?"

"Yes, no trouble. We need to begin down there by the cliff, though," Bob pointed towards the sea. "That's where I was to start with. We've got to cross that field and walk all the way down to the footpath. Keep an eye open for loose pigs. By the way, where's the mangy dog?"

"They took it down to the kennels last night, poor brute."

"One thing less to worry about," Bob said with relief.

As they walked, Bob said, "Who legally owns Hentree, I wonder: Josiah Slattery or his wife?"

"We'll have to ask Mrs Slattery," Charlie West replied. "Curious she hasn't contacted us. There's been no mention of a wife at all."

"I wonder if she knows her old man is selling her property?" Bob mused. "Not that it makes much difference. She might own the land, but it'll be him who makes the decisions on what and when to sell."

When they reached the cliff path, where he had been birdwatching, Bob said, "Okay, stop here. Turn around and look back up the field. This is where I was and that's where they were, about halfway up. The boy was dragging him as if he'd been shot or had had a heart attack or something. How that old man has disappeared into thin air defeats me – unless . . . Unless he wasn't really injured and it was him that shot the boy. Except where does a farmer get a pistol from in this area?"

"Not so difficult, actually. There are troops stationed all around us. The Navy is down at Westward Ho! and the RAF have got a new airfield across the water. . . But yes, I agree, hardly connections a full-time, overworked farmer is going to have."

"You got a doctor's report on the boy yet?"

"One of my colleagues is organising the post-mortem and inquest today. You'll be called as a witness." DC West walked to the edge of the cliff and pointed at surging waves capping large, craggy rocks. "We better check down there."

"You can, but I really don't see how an unconscious old man could drag himself back down here and fall in the sea."

"Where does this cliff path lead to, do you know?" DC West asked.

"Goes on for another half mile before it slopes down to a beach. There are no dwellings or huts or anything along here, and nowhere he can get to in the other direction – that I've seen anyway."

DC West dropped onto his knees and lay flat, looking at the rocks below. “He could be stuck behind one of those,” he said, indicating a group of large boulders in the restless sea.

Bob sighed and got down beside him. “Doesn’t look as if there’s much beach at low tide here. Why would he come down here, anyway?”

“Perhaps he was pushed.”

Bob shook his head, struggling to decide whether there could have been a third person involved. “He’d have got stuck on one those rocks. Besides, if someone was going to get him all the way down from that farmyard, why push him in here, where we’re bound to look?” He paused, turned to DC West and said, “You’ll have to get your people to check, though.”

West started to get up. “I’ll come back this afternoon, bring someone with me.”

“That would be best,” Bob huffed, struggling to his feet and heading back up the green pasture before West could say ‘come with me’.

Keeping his head down to avoid further conversation about a cliff search, Bob studied the ground for discarded shotgun cartridges then called over his shoulder, “Do you know what sort of bullet it was that killed the boy yet?”

“Pistol as far as we know. You did say the third shot was from a pistol, not a shotgun.”

“Pistol, definitely.” Bob pulled off his cap and ran a hand through his bristly white hair, replaying the shots he’d heard in his head. “I heard two loud shotgun cracks, saw the boy pulling the old man up the field then, when I was in the car, there was a pistol shot. Erm – I didn’t mention this last night, but I had the feeling there was someone over there in the trees.” He pointed his cap at the woods running alongside the unfenced field.

West looked at the trees. "Bit difficult to actually see anyone from this distance."

Making no mention of his binoculars, Bob replied, "I know. That's why I'm saying I had 'the feeling' there was someone there." West didn't respond so Bob continued, "Could there have been troops nearby on manoeuvres, using the woods for some sort of training activity?"

"Using a derelict farm for sniper practice? It's possible, I suppose." West didn't sound convinced. "Not very safe for the boy and old man to be here though, assuming the old man had given permission for them to use his land."

"No, you're right," Bob pushed his cap back on his head. "They wouldn't have been using live ammunition either, I suppose, and there would have been more shots."

"Probably. There are men in uniform all over the town day and night nowadays, only what motive would any of them have to shoot Mr Slattery's nephew? Unless it was accidental, which is hardly likely. We'd have been contacted by the Military Police by now. It was only one shot fired, that you recall?"

Bob ignored the implied doubt and started walking uphill again.

"The main question is 'why'? Why would anyone want to kill a young man on a farm?" West said, following him.

"Or the old man? To stop the sale of the property, perhaps. But we're back to the same old question: if someone – the nephew for example – arranged an accident with the shotgun, why can't we locate the old man? He or they will need a death certificate before anything legal can happen." Bob was getting out of breath and was glad of a genuine reason to stop. "There," he said, pointing to the gateway into the farmyard. "That's where I spoke to the boy."

West walked on then bent down and studied the ground. "No sign of blood, no pellets."

"Did they not find anything useful yesterday?" Bob asked, catching up.

"They found a shotgun. Single barrel Springfield. Didn't I mention it?"

"No, DC West, you didn't."

The two men were silent for a moment, studying the steep, open field, then West said, "If the boy was shooting rabbits from here, and the old man got in the way, or was sitting down there looking at the view, he might not have seen him . . . The pellets could have done Slattery – if it was Slattery? – quite a lot of damage, but I don't think they would have killed him. There was a case a few years ago, a shooting accident not far from here as it happens. Genuine accident: two boys out after rabbits and one of them got shot. He'd got pellets in his hip and groin but it only looked superficial and they managed to get back home. By the time the doctor arrived, though, he was dead from internal haemorrhaging."

"We get a few shotgun accidents where we are these days as well," Bob replied, squinting in the sunlight. "Lads not familiar with guns out for something for the pot. But they're not usually farm boys who've grown up with guns. Have you fingerprinted the Springfield?"

"Today – someone's on that now, I think."

The two policemen stood in silence again looking out to sea. "It is a very fine view," West said.

"Worth more than the farm, by the sounds of it."

West turned around to look at the scruffy farmyard. "Hardly surprising he wants to get rid of this place. Especially if they don't even live here."

"Perhaps he's been letting this place slide on purpose." Bob stopped, recalling something said earlier. "Have your Bideford men got any idea who the boy is?"

"Not yet. I was out on another job last night," West replied then looked away, embarrassed. "The truth is we only had two men to spare to come up with the ambulance yesterday. There's a search on out Weir Byford way for a missing toddler, and what with all our extra wartime duties uniform branch are completely overstretched."

"And your boss wasn't sure if I was inventing a drama."

West cleared his throat. "Well, he did say it sounded a bit fanciful. But to be fair, he had to put the kiddy first."

"The old man must have made it back to Ridgeway or his wife would have been on to you about him. I think we need get over to the other farm as quick as possible."

"Cummings said Mr Slattery wasn't there when he called this morning." DC West looked at his watch. "I agree, but I've only got until eleven-thirty at the latest. I've got to be back at the station before noon for another case."

Bob tried to contain his annoyance and the persistent, irritating idea that someone had been in the trees: whoever it was would have had time to get up to the barn and shoot the boy while he was on the cliff path. "Before we go up to this Ridgeway Farm, shouldn't we at least check over there in the woodland?" he said.

"If you're sure it's worth the time." Charlie West had the decency to take him seriously.

"No, not 'sure'," Bob admitted, "I can only tell you what I *think* I saw. Finding out the rest is your job, not mine, I'm pleased to say. Perhaps you ought to talk to the wife first, after all, ask who had something against the boy and so on. Do you have women officers in Bideford?"

"We do. Two in fact."

"Let them have a chat with her, then."

"I know what you mean but they're both out on the missing toddler case. She's only two years old and the parents are beside themselves. Which search would you prioritise, sir?"

Bob took a deep breath: DC West was right, he'd have done the same, but it brought home to him his own dereliction of duty, he should have made more effort to locate the injured farmer himself. Then he looked back at the young detective constable, aware he was saying something.

". . . and I've still got a mountain of paperwork to deal with before that."

"But you do need to visit the other farm. Find out what the hell has been going on as soon as possible."

"I was hoping you would do all that, sir."

"Me? I'm on leave. I've only stayed the extra night to be a good citizen. This mess is Bideford's, Charlie boy, not mine."

DC West gave an embarrassed cough. "Well, actually, I've been told – asked, that is – to tell you that you've been seconded to us at Bideford, sir. And to pass over the details you need to know."

Bob's heart sank. "I've still got four days' leave and there's a stack of work on *my* desk as well, back in Cready. My boss isn't likely to agree to this."

"I don't think he's had much choice. They were talking about you on the telephone last night and it's been agreed."

"Like hell it has! This farm business is yours, sonny. I'm just a reluctant witness."

"Who happens to be a police detective. I'm sorry, sir, but our Super spoke to yours and they want you here to sort it out. We've got a load on our plates, including a nasty bit of trouble with some schoolboys at the college and a spate of petty theft, though what anybody wants with antiques and useless knick-knacks in wartime beats me, and now we've got to supervise what's going on down at Westward Ho! to boot. I can't be spared, you see."

"No, DC West, I don't see at all. I'd say a murder investigation trumps your entire list combined." Bob turned away and paced up and down, genuinely angry. It took a lot to rile him, he often feigned anger as part of his job to get what he needed, but this wasn't fair. He hadn't had a proper break since he was called back into the Force.

He was so wrapped up in the injustice of it all he had momentarily forgotten DC West, who was now saying, ". . . that's why I have to be back in town as soon as I can, sir. Can we get on to Ridgeway, speak to the wife, then you can ride back with me to the station?"

"Ah, back to 'sir' now is it?" Bob huffed and stomped towards the car in West's wake. They had not been into the barn or the trees, and he didn't care.

***

# Chapter 8

Ridgeway Farm was in a similar state of disrepair to Hentree, although the house was significantly bigger and showed signs of actually being lived in. There were the usual outbuildings, including a large cowshed, but to Bob's relief no pigsty.

The house was a long grey building with a front door dead centre and gabled windows above. Clematis and ivy climbed the walls, relieving its drab aspect, and someone had once planted fuchsia to form a hedge around a pocket handkerchief lawn. The bright flowers moved gently in the breeze and Bob thought that with a bit of care and attention the house could be quite attractive. A chaffinch chortled from among some apple trees in a small, walled orchard to their left, briefly lifting Bob's ill humour.

Nobody answered the door so they went around to the back and knocked there. "Anyone in?" West called.

"Tell them I came and no one answered," Bob murmured, pushing the door open.

"I beg your pardon?" West said.

"It's a line from a poem. I work with a young PC who's fond of quoting poetry. Bright lad. Bit of an academic type, but he's good at his job for his age."

The kitchen was in regular use, but there was no sign of a woman, and nobody answered their calls.

"You go upstairs, see if they're up there," Bob said, taking charge as it was now his case. "The old man might have been too ill to see that Cummings chap – or they didn't hear him. Though Lord knows how. I'll look around down here and then go round the yard if necessary. See you out there."

The kitchen was only marginally more welcoming than Hentree, although people did eat here. A grease-laden frying pan lay on the hob. A chipped enamel bread bin contained the remains of a reasonably fresh loaf. There were breadcrumbs on the filthy tablecloth, and at least two people had left unwashed plates and cutlery in the sink.

The sitting room had once been a tastefully furnished drawing room, judging by the furniture and faded blue velvet drapes. A tall bureau stood along one wall, flanked by two very full bookcases. The fireplace was large and deep with a fancy chimney piece and a full set of brass fire irons. A mahogany china cabinet with oval panels graced the back wall. Bob was no antiquarian but he recognised quality when he saw it. He went to the bookcase and opened a glass-paned door. Running a finger along a row of gold-embossed spines, he saw Shelley and Byron, Tennyson, Blake's *Songs of Innocence and Experience,* and a curious title that he vaguely remembered as being popular with his socialist-leaning colleagues: *The Ragged Trousered Philanthropists*. Two other titles on a lower shelf drew his attention: *The Mill on the Floss* and *Adam Bede* by George Eliot. He'd seen the mill story on Joan's bedside table, he was sure of it. He pulled out the second book and opened it. A woman's signature: *Adeline Howard, May Day, 1862*. Josiah's mother perhaps. Whoever this Josiah Slattery was, he hadn't been raised to be a common country yokel.

Some words on the next page caught Bob's eye: 'printed in Garamond'. That's where he'd seen the name before! It was a type of print. Funny sort of stage name; but then Wendell didn't exactly trip off the tongue either. He reinserted the book, closed the bookcase and looked around him. The fireplace was cold and empty, although it would be at this time of year; the chairs looked undisturbed. There was no sign of recent use: no books left out to read, no knitting basket or sewing box. Another sad house, he thought.

Closing the door, he returned to the chilly, tiled passage and tried another. This opened on to what had been a gentleman's study and now functioned as an office. There was a walnut knee-hole desk under the window, laden with dusty files, and a lopsided armchair by a small black iron grate. A drop-leaf dining table had been set open against the rear wall, with an assortment of biscuit tins and cardboard boxes serving as a filing system. A kitchen chair next to it had been in recent use, a damaged tapestry cushion left skewed where someone had got up and left in a hurry.

Lying on the table next to the over-stuffed boxes was a scattered pile of unopened letters, and Mr Slattery's ration book. His grocery retailers were 'Evans and Hook' in nearby Larkham. There was no book for Mrs Slattery. Bob stuffed the ration book in his left-hand jacket pocket then rifled through a cardboard box containing official-looking correspondence and report cards for milk and root vegetables, none of which had been filled in. He walked his fingers through a couple of tins, but there was nothing to indicate the boy lived here as well, or his name.

Giving a deep sigh of frustration, he moved into the centre of the small room and stared about him. The study was like the rest of the house, lived in but neglected. His eye caught a flash of colour under the door. "Oh-ho, something unexpected," he commented out loud and bent down to pull a woman's headscarf from under the old wood. "What colour's this then,

Joan?" he asked his late wife. "Coral is it? Or what you called 'peachy'?" He sniffed. "Nice scent, whatever it is."

Returning to the kitchen, musing on the age and personality that matched the silky material, the colour and scent, he folded the scarf into a smaller square and put it on the dresser, the tablecloth being too grubby. Then he set to on the contents of the dresser itself, sorting through cutlery and table linen until he came to the one drawer he always enjoyed finding: the jumble-drawer. Rolls of string, wooden pegs for the washing line, a book of crosswords, nearly complete, and – bingo! – a ration book for Mr Greville Healey. It was relatively new, dated April 1942, and the address was Ridgeway Farm. He put it in his pocket with the other one and gave the kitchen another glance round.

Filthy dirty, yes, but everything was of slightly better quality and in better repair than at Hentree. Not that it made much difference, apart from the single relief of the headscarf the entire place oozed despair. With an inward shudder he moved outdoors to check the outhouses and the privy, keeping a watchful eye for foraging pigs or under-fed guard dogs. The privy door hung open. A pile of old newspapers had been dumped next to the toilet bowl. "Waste not, want not," Bob muttered and shut the door.

"Nobody upstairs," West said, joining him later by the vegetable garden.

"Someone's planted stuff here recently," Bob said, indicating an abandoned hoe beside a seed bed. He turned to West, "Any sign of Mrs Slattery upstairs?"

"I don't think there is a Mrs Slattery," West replied. "No sign of a woman anywhere."

"Same downstairs, except for a woman's headscarf, and it's been worn in the last twenty-four hours I'd say. No woman's touch in that kitchen, either. Leastways not the sort of wife I had. What about the boy?"

"He's got a room upstairs. You'll need to come back and go through it properly, although finding the old man is a priority, and I haven't –"

"Got time. Yes, I know. I've found Slattery's ration book anyway, and another for a Greville Healey, so you've got a name to work on." He handed the small, buff, cardboard booklet to West. "This one's new, so you'll have to find out where he was before. Bit of luck, it'll be his parents' address."

Realising the matter of the boy in the mortuary was back in his hands, Charlie West gave a wry smile. "All right, leave this with me and concentrate on finding the old man and what actually happened at Hentree."

"Right you are, sir," Bob said good-naturedly. Ignoring the fact that he outranked DC West in seniority and a life-time's experience. "I know you're in a hurry, but we ought to check the barn and cowshed, in case the old bugger managed to get back here and couldn't get into the house."

The cowshed was empty and no longer in use, the barn was in use but also empty; no one was either working there or lying injured, and DC West, itching to get away, soon had them racing through the high-banked lanes back to town.

Bideford Police Station, Bob decided on his second visit, had been designed and built by a firm that also constructed public toilets. Brick exterior with a white tiled interior and an echoing, sordid atmosphere; the sort of place that made him rush the hand wash and leave with wet palms. The duty desk officer was marginally more agreeable this time, however, and Bob was shown into a vacant office, while DC West rushed into a larger room waving Greville Healey's ration book and shut the door.

Bob took stock of his surroundings. There was a coat stand with mackintoshes for a rainy day, two desks piled with the inevitable stash of paperwork, and the stale fug of an unventilated room occupied by smokers. He went to the window but it was too high for him to see over the ledge so he sat on a spare chair in front of a desk and stared at the telephone. Then he lifted the handset and dialled Cready Police Station to speak to his boss, Detective Inspector Small.

The call didn't go entirely his way and by the end he was forced to say, "All right, but I can't manage on my own. Let me have Laurie Oliver for a week at least. He's young and fit enough to go poking around farm buildings while I go through paperwork and talk to the family." To his surprise, DI Small agreed.

Pleased, Bob felt himself relax. Then he sat up straight. "Why?" he demanded down the handset. "What's the real reason I am to be here; why are you letting me have PC Oliver?"

There was a moment's silence at the other end then DI Small said, "Do you really not know what the military are up to in the Bideford area? No? Well that's as it should be. I don't know details either, so don't ask."

Bob ran through titbits that DC West had let slip about the increasing number of troops in the area, the search for a missing toddler and the petty pilfering antiques thief, but the toddler would be found, happily or otherwise, and the knick-knack culprit apprehended, and they could get back to normal. No, there was something much bigger that he didn't know about.

"Is it to do with what the Yanks and Canadians are up to?"

"Could be. Careless words cost lives, Bob, careless words."

Bob drummed his fingers on the desk and let them wander into a pile of typed sheets as DI Small said, "Let's put it this way: it's quiet here and their need – the local force in Bideford – is greater than ours because of what is going on."

"And you can't tell me what that is?" Bob insisted.

"No, I can't. There's a ruddy war on, Bob! Bideford have got their hands full and can't be traipsing round the countryside verifying a *possible* double murder or go looking for an old man who may or may not have gone missing."

"Nothing 'possible' about it: I was there."

"Precisely! Which is why it's up to you to sort it out. I'll give you a fortnight."

"What about the rest of my leave? I've got four days left."

"Not any more you haven't. Tell you what, keep your receipts and I'll authorise extra petrol coupons for you."

"Thank you very much," Bob replied ironically. He gave DI Small Mrs Flowers' telephone number so Laurie could call him, then the line went silent.

He waited another fifteen minutes but nobody came to brief him, although the constable on desk duty knew why he was there, because as Bob headed for the main door to leave, he waved a buff envelope in his direction. It was a preliminary report on the young man: death caused by a nine-millimetre bullet. A single pistol shot.

But as a result of somebody practising with a new gun, a stray shot or a deliberate, accurate aim? Which? Someone with access to weapons and ammunition anyway. Bob sighed. As Charlie West had pointed out, Bideford was crawling with military personnel from all the Forces. Not to mention the truckloads of American GI units arriving.

Staring at the single typed sheet, Bob cursed his own poor attitude. If he'd had his wits about him and been half-way professional, he would have noticed something – surely?

Annoyed and frustrated, he left the station and sauntered along the quayside. The tide was coming in, lifting trawlers awkwardly from the River Torridge mud. Fishermen were mending nets, a young family wandered by eating yellow ice-cream from crunchy cones. A picture postcard scene; you could almost forget the war.

He crossed the road, and made his way through Saturday shoppers, up the High Street then took a detour and passed through an ancient, covered pannier market. Fruit and vegetable stalls were doing brisk business. He stopped at a confectionery and baked goods counter and bought some home-made toffee and shortbread biscuits, and tried to pretend he was still on holiday.

It took him a good while to climb the steep hill back up to Peony Villas and he made a mental vow to use his petrol ration the next time he had to go down to the station. By the time he breasted the rise into Larkham Road, he was aching in every joint, and there were still the steps up to the front door and the stairs to his attic eyrie to deal with. Arriving at the gate to Number One, he stood for a moment looking up at the large, conjoined houses, trying to get his breathing back to normal. It then occurred to him that his obvious exhaustion was as good an excuse as any to mistake the gates and satisfy his curiosity by knocking at the black door of Number Two.

He had to knock twice, then a third time more loudly. Eventually a gaunt-faced, late-middle-aged, spinster-type woman came to the door. Her hair was grey, her cardigan was grey, her face was lined and grey. She took Bob so entirely by surprise, his reaction to her appearance was genuine, “Oh, sorry. Wrong house. This isn’t the guest house, is it?”

“No,” replied the woman and shut the door in his face.

The door to Number One was open and Mrs Flowers was at her reception desk under the stairs when he finally got in.

“Ah, good, Mrs Flowers,” Bob began, “I need to ask you if I can stay for a few more days and if you’ve got a room for a young const – colleague, friend?”

The lovely woman gave him a warm smile. “You want to stay with us longer, Mr Robbins. I am pleased.”

Bob swallowed and tried to respond accordingly but it came out all wrong. “If you’ve got something on the first floor, I’d be grateful. I can’t stay in that garret room up there for another week, my knees’ll never stand it.”

“Your knees?” queried the light voice. Bob wanted to eat his words. “Oh, dear, I wonder if Rose would help. I could let you have Rose.”

“Rose?”

“I’m sure Rose would help ease your pains.”

Bob blinked hard, “Rose?”

“A double on the first floor. View across the river.”

“Oh, that Rose! Oh, yes, she – the room – will do nicely, yes, thank you,” Bob babbled, trying to overcome his embarrassment.

“I’ve been saving Rose for a long-term resident who said he’d be joining us, but he isn’t here yet so you can have it for a week I suppose. Your young friend can have Honeysuckle.”

***

# Chapter 9

## Sunday afternoon

Police Constable Laurence Oliver arrived at Barnstaple railway station in civvies, along with a crowd of subdued young evacuees carrying small cardboard cases, and exhausted older refugees carrying brown paper parcels or nothing at all. Waiting to board the train for its return trip to Exeter were enough men and women in different uniforms to establish a United Services Club.

Laurie, in cream-coloured slacks and head and shoulders taller than most, was easy to locate. He waved at Bob like a schoolboy coming home for the summer vacation then picked up his bags and pushed through the crowd. In one hand he had a bulging canvas duffel bag, from the other dangled two red string bags containing helmets: one for his uniform, one for his motorbike, which Bob had never seen him wear. Bob couldn't help but smile. One day, and probably sooner rather than later, young Laurie Oliver was going to make it into plain clothes, but despite his academic inclination and fondness for literature he had 'copper' written all over him. His gangling limbs and fair good looks gave him a look of joyful innocence, but Bob had reason to know he had a sharp mind when needed.

Laurie shoved his bags at Bob, saying, "Stay there, Sarge. I've got my motorbike in the cycle carriage."

Bob grinned again: no fool his lad, he'd been told to use the train and it meant saving petrol.

With Laurie roaring behind him, Bob took the coast road back to Bideford then stopped at a picnic lay-by next to a path down to the estuary sand dunes and a stretch of firm, golden sand. While they sat on a bench enjoying the tranquil sea view, he told Laurie about the incidents on the cliff across the water. They were interrupted by the loud chugging and spluttering of a broken-down RAF lorry coming to a lurching halt on the road behind them.

"This area's crawling with ruddy military," Bob huffed "Never seen so many in one place, and that's not counting the Yanks. There's a new airfield in that direction," he pointed across the dunes to his right, "and a new American army base outside Bideford at a place called Bowden Green."

Laurie sniggered, "Bowden Green – sounds like a wireless programme for housewives. What's going on? What's to protect? Hardly the Thames Basin here, is it?"

"There's something going on with Allied navy personnel down at Westward Ho! Mind you, we can mock but the Vikings sailed right up this estuary, murdered locals in their beds and settled on their land. Not much stopping Jerry doing the same."

"This beach is perfect for landing craft," Laurie said in response. "Where were all those poor refugees on the train going, do you think? They were speaking German."

"They'll be in for a rough time with locals if they keep doing that."

"That's what I was thinking," Laurie replied, gazing out across the sparkling blue water. A small fishing trawler was heading up to Bideford with a hefty catch, judging by the cloud of raucous gulls hanging over it. "Westward Ho! with an exclamation mark was a book," he added.

"An exclamation mark, eh," Bob huffed.

"Place is named after the story by Kingsley. We went there on holiday, when I was young."

"You're still young!" Bob laughed. Laurie had left school and gone straight into the Police in a rapid entry programme designed to replace officers who'd joined the Forces. Bob had been drawn back in from the opposite end of the age spectrum for the same reason.

"Nice place was it, Westward Ho with an exclamation mark?" Bob asked as they returned to their transport.

"Super rock pools."

"That's handy to know."

"Are you laughing at me, Sarge?" Laurie asked.

"Course not. Do you want to go straight to our digs, or can you cope with a diversion via the scene of the crime?"

"Diversion is fine by me," replied Laurie, "but I left home at six this morning to get the Plymouth train, then the Exeter train."

"Yeah, takes all day by Sunday service public transport. Quicker to walk. We'll just get a feel for the place and start tomorrow properly."

Despite it being a Sunday, there was a queue at the traffic lights to cross Bideford bridge. Bob stared up at the little white town as he waited. It was an ancient settlement: Grenville's ships had been built and sailed from here for Virginia. "An old town stuck in its old ways," he muttered to himself, thinking that many if not most locals could trace their families back to Tudor times if not before. "All these little white houses . . ." he said, thinking aloud, "centuries of secrets and scandals – the tales they could tell."

Traffic started moving and they were soon heading out of the town and into narrow, high-banked lanes. Bob negotiated the route as best he could from memory and got to Hentree Farm more by accident than mental map reading.

The gate was still closed, the way he and Charlie West had left it, so he tucked his old Morris into the gateway as far as he could and Laurie stowed his motorbike against the rowan hedge.

Handing Laurie his empty knapsack, Bob said, “We’ll just take a shufty but anything useful, anything suspicious, stick it in there. Use a hanky if you haven’t got any gloves. Nothing smelly, mind.”

“What am I looking for, Sarge?” the boy said, pulling the bag over his shoulder.

“Bullet casings. Cartridges for a farm shotgun. They found a single barrel Springfield propped against the gate leading into the field I was in, but there could have been another gun. The boy could have been after rabbits or birds and the old man got in the way – an accident . . . But something tells me the two rifle shots weren’t an accident, not after what happened later. Either way, there could be another shotgun and a bloody nine-millimetre pistol lying around. Look for shotgun pellets, spent cartridges and brass bullet casings anyway. And if you see any girls give me a shout.”

“Girls?”

“Land Army. There are a couple working at Slattery’s other farm apparently. One of them wears scent. Unless the old man’s got a much younger wife.”

Laurie raised a fair eyebrow, “Scent for farm work?”

“Maybe she doesn’t want to whiff of livestock.”

“Guns and girls, right ho,” the boy replied and was up and over the five-barred gate before Bob could say, “Mind the pigs!”

“Pretty rundown sort of farm,” Laurie commented from the other side as Bob pushed the wobbly gate to walk in.

“It is.” Bob hesitated, casting about for his porcine enemies then to see if there was anyone about. There was no sign of anyone or anything so he set off through the yard, heading for the empty field where the first shooting had taken place.

"I was down there," he said when they got to the small gate leading into the field backing onto the cliffs. "There's a public footpath. I was down there."

"'Far from the madding crowd's ignoble strife.'"

"What? No. Hardly: I heard two gunshots so I came up to see if I could help."

"It's a quotation: Gray's *Country Churchyard*. Never mind." Laurie bounded down the tussocky, unploughed slope to the footpath then stopped and stared at the stunning view. Between darkening, ominous clouds, the sun's evening fire cast pink-tinged orange and ochre flames across the horizon. "Next stop the New World," he shouted to Bob, waiting some distance up the hill. Racing back to join him, Laurie gasped, "These cliffs look like fun. We ought to bring buckets and shrimp nets tomorrow. We could get down there onto the rocks and get winkles and crabs as well."

"We're working, lad. You're not here on your hols this time," Bob scoffed. "Dodgy stuff, anyway, shellfish. Didn't your ma ever warn you?"

"On the contrary. That's what I remember. We stayed in an hotel and went to the beach every day with our nets and pails. Excellent fun."

"Excellent fun," Bob mimicked, but not unkindly. "Well, I'm sorry to disappoint you, but we shan't be building any sandcastles on this trip."

"Ah, well," Laurie replied, clearly disappointed.

"Come on Beano boy," Bob said, "plenty of other exciting places to explore, starting with a gloomy old barn. Although," he paused, "I suppose this is why Hoblin's Holiday Camps wants to buy Hentree."

As he spoke, a cloud opened and rain thundered down. Bob scurried up the field, occasionally losing his footing on the slippery grass and stumbling on tussocks. Near the gate he put his foot in a recent mole hill and nearly fell flat. He paused to catch his breath, turned and saw Laurie standing stock still, head back, arms stretched wide like a scarecrow – he was drinking the rain.

"Silly big kid," Bob said to himself. "A silly big kid." The thought made him wonder what the war had done to another kid. Did his son ever get a moment to do daft things in the rain, wherever he was? He felt a sudden lump in his throat and yelled, "Laurie, I'm going, leg it!" His voice was swallowed by the Atlantic squall so he pulled his jacket up over his ears and headed uphill on his own.

When he got to the farmyard, he took shelter in the open barn doorway, shook his cap to dry it then looked to see if Laurie was following. He wasn't, but Bob realised the land dropped away so steeply he couldn't actually see half-way down the field from this position. That meant when the farm boy had said the old man was coming down to warn a trespasser off his land he must have been lying.

And if the old man had been shot – twice – with shotgun pellets, it could have been an accident. The boy could have been aiming at rabbits or pheasant from around the gate area . . .

It also meant that whoever had shot the boy had entered through the main gate, or slipped in through the woods. Either way, that had been no accident.

Musing on this and the lie of the land, Bob called to Laurie and showed him where he'd found the boy now believed to be Greville Healey.

"Was he shot and then moved, or was the assassin waiting in here, do you think?" Laurie asked, hunkering down to look at the dusty floor.

"Can't say yet, but we need to find out."

"But putting him here – that would have been like trying to hide him."

"It would."

"Mmm," Laurie murmured standing up then looking back through the double doors. "Funny place to put a house and farmyard. Right wide open to the wind and weather. Would have made more sense to build on the other side of the lane. At least that's a safer distance from the cliffs."

"Yeah, but it explains why Hoblin's Holidays wants the land." Bob began to tell him about prospective sale of Hentree and what he'd learned from Land Agent Cummings.

"But it can't be sold if the owner's missing," Laurie said. "There'll be no one to sign for the sale. What's up there?" he asked, pointing at the hay loft.

Before Bob could say, "I've checked up there," Laurie was scrambling up the rickety ladder saying, "Unless the owner has awarded power of attorney or proxy, or whatever it's called. My aunt Claudia gave my pa power of attorney over her cottage in St Mawes. He did all the legal signing for her when she swanned off to Capri with a younger man. I didn't find out about this until recently, actually. Turns out that my cousin's son Sebastian is in fact another cousin not a nephew because he's Claudia's son, which makes him Sally's half-brother only she looks after him like her son instead. All a bit weird, really."

"Happens in the best of families."

"I expect so."

Bob looked up at the boy to see if he was being sarcastic, decided he wasn't, and made do with a half-hearted tut-tut. He'd learned not to belittle Laurie's family history lessons because on occasions they led him to interesting facts or possibilities. Even so, this was one of the better ones.

"What's over there?" Laurie had turned on the ladder and was now pointing at the open door at the far end of the barn.

"Pigsty and a smaller yard." Bob then added quickly, "Do you want to see the other farm? We went there yesterday but there was nobody in."

Laurie came down the ladder backwards, checking each rung before he put his weight on it. "Sarge, you're in charge, I know but . . ."

"But?"

"Shouldn't we find the old man first?"

"Oh, blast!" Bob slapped the rough-hewn ladder.

"What?"

"This downpour: we'll never be able to check for footprints now."

"Haven't they already done that, the Bideford police?"

"Amateurs!"

"Amateurs? You? Us?" Laurie queried. "Hardly."

"Not me," although Bob felt a twinge of guilt, knowing he should have been a lot more thorough on Friday. "Not us, DC Charlie West and his Bideford Merry Men. They should've done that two days ago when they removed the young lad's body."

"You mean, nobody's actually registered the scene of the crime?"

"Not like we do at Cready. I was off duty, you see. On holiday. I'd have been tampering with the evidence. I didn't expect to be involved apart from reporting the incident so I didn't bother about anything like that. Wasn't my problem – at the time. Come on, there's nothing more to see here."

As they returned to the yard Laurie said, "It's curious that nobody's found the old man or reported him missing. How hard did they look?"

"Not hard. He wasn't in the house here, or at the other place yesterday, more than that we don't know. Come on, rain has stopped. You see what you can find out here, I'm going into the house again. Let's hope the old duffer is in the kitchen making a cuppa, save us all a lot of bother that will."

But as Bob went in through the back door again, there was the same eerie emptiness he'd noted before. The last he saw of Laurie was through the uncleaned kitchen window as the boy's mop of wavy fair hair bob, bob, bobbed along the roof of an old henhouse.

Leaning across the wooden draining board, Bob tried to open the window. The catch wouldn't budge. He picked up a dented saucepan. Someone had tried to fill it with water from the single brass tap over the stone sink. There was no water now, though. Bob stood back and tried to make sense of that, then wedged the saucepan against the back door to ventilate the stuffy house – and make a noise should anyone try to shut him indoors. Long experience of investigating dubious locations meant he had developed various strategies to keep his claustrophobia at bay; to keep his breathing steady and heartbeat normal in closed environments.

The larder was as good as empty, only a couple of jam jars remained, whose furred contents he chose not to disturb. A marble slab once used for cheese was polished clean by mice. There was a distinct stink of rodents. The kitchen table had been used recently, though. Marks of a cup showed in the accumulated dust. He checked the dresser, but nothing had been disturbed there in a very long time. Perhaps one of the Land Girls had come in out of the rain and used a thermos flask.

The lower part of the dresser contained yellowed tablecloths, serving dishes; all the usual paraphernalia of family life. He moved through to the sitting room, which he'd only glanced in before. It was a very different place to Ridgeway. No bookcases here. No wireless set, either, not even a lump of dead coal in the grate. The chairs were sagging, wooden-armed affairs. A worn, dust-consumed rug offered the barest comfort for a chilly evening. A tarnished silver cup stood alone on the otherwise empty mantelpiece. Bob rubbed it down the side of a trouser leg. 'Best in show, 1912'. Best what?

Still, it was a clue. The farmer or his wife had been productive and proud of their achievement – whatever it was.

A certificate had fallen into the grate. Blackened with fallen soot but just about legible. *Awarded to Mrs Martha Slattery . . .* The ink had faded with the years but Bob thought the next words were *1st Prize: Chutney.*

It was a start, and it confirmed a Mrs Martha Slattery did exist. Or had existed. A normal working farmer's wife; a mother with children, or at least a child who sent her birthday cards. "So where are you, Mrs Slattery? Why haven't you been in touch with the police? And what happened to turn your family farm into a derelict agricultural museum, eh?"

Bob went into the hall and fumbled with the catch on the front door then tried to tug it open. The wood was swollen, but he managed to inch it far enough to cause a sudden draft. The kitchen door behind him slammed and he nearly jumped out of his skin. "Gawd almighty! I'm too old for this lark," he said to nobody. Then, taking a deep breath, he forced himself up the narrow uncarpeted stairs again.

The same pervading odour of damp plaster and four doors, still shut, but now he noticed a fifth – a large walk-in cupboard. There were piles of towels, sheets and blankets on the shelves, but it didn't look as if anything had been disturbed in a long time. He crossed the landing and opened the door to the main bedroom over the front porch and glanced in again. Sunlight filtered through threadbare curtains as before, illuminating motes of dust. The room had a stale, sickly sweet odour but looked uninhabited. There was no sign of the old man or his wife. Was the bed ever slept in? He pulled back the brown counterpane – and found a cadaver with blankets tucked up to the chin.

"Bloody Norah!"

As he backed out of the room a woman screamed. A scream so piecing Bob's bowels nearly gave way. Frozen to the spot, he gulped for breath, then knew he had to find the privy, fast. Dashing downstairs and outdoors, he nearly knocked Laurie Oliver into the cabbage patch. "Mind out!" he yelled and yanked at the door of what had once been the family retreat.

***

# Chapter 10

When Bob returned to the daylight, Laurie was in conversation with a dumpy woman in a floral wrap-around pinafore. She had grey hair like a bundle of cotton reels and was holding a wicker basket containing a few speckled eggs.

"This is Mrs Lee, sir, I gave her a bit of a fright, I'm afraid. She comes here to collect eggs."

Mrs Lee's eyes were as round as her waistline. "'E did give me a start, sir. I don't meet nobody up here as a rule. 'Cept young Greville, but he's a rude young devil, never a 'Good mornin' Mrs Lee', never the time of day. That's a Slattery for you, my husband says. They let me collect eggs, though, and I give 'em a cake or a pudding or two."

Bob half-turned as if to look at something, checking his trousers were buttoned up in the process. All safely gathered in. He turned back and introduced himself.

"Mrs Lee wants to know if there's been an accident, sir," Laurie said. "She lives nearby and saw the ambulance. I told her you'd explain why we're here."

"Has there been an accident, then?" Mrs Lee's eyes goggled. "Can't say I'm surprised. Josiah Slattery's too old to be doing what he's doing every day. That's why young Greville's here, 'cept he's too interested in hisself and his motorbike to be any proper use on a farm like this. Well, not like this. Hentree's been let go. You can see that for yourself. But Ridgeway's bigger.

Where's the pigs, then?" The woman swivelled around like a child's spinning top. "I thought it were quiet. Where's that poor old dog? And they nasty pigs? Where be they, then? Give me the eejits they do. Greville don't feed 'em right if you asks me."

Staggering slightly from the volley of information, Bob put up a hand to halt her flow. "Mrs Lee, I need to tell you something. But first, can you tell me, do you ever go into the house here?"

"Oh, no, never. I only come for the eggs."

"And the gate? Is that usually shut and locked?"

"Is it shut and locked then?" She peered around him. "It's open now."

"Yes, we opened it."

"Did you? I didn't notice. I come in through the side gate from the woods, see. There's a gern great hole down the lane a pace as well, pigs get out there sometimes. Foxes can get in anywhere, o' course. The ones Greville's left alive. He'd shoot a frog if it jumped slow enough."

As she was gathering breath for another volley, Bob turned her to face the house. "You say you do *Mr* Slattery's cooking."

"Oh, well this and that. Buns and milk puddings and the like. What is this? I'm not their housekeeper, oh no, I have my Jack to think of."

"What I want to know is, where does young Grenville –"

"*Greville*. He's a sort of great-nephew but not in the blood. I can't swear to it, but I did hear there was a Sheila who went down to Exeter and married someone in gentleman's clothing. He's their son, though I can't swear to it. It being before our time."

Bob caught Laurie trying not smile, glared at him and ploughed on, "You don't know where in Exeter they live?"

"No! Why should I? None of my business, is it?"

"No – erm," Bob wiped the back of a hand across his forehead, "so, Greville has come up here to help Mr Slattery, who is getting on in years?"

"Well over seventy, he is now. Well over, I'd say. His son, Young Joe – he was a Joseph not a Josiah – he was killed in a tractor accident. That tractor it was, I 'spect. Before our time, but we heard all about it." She pointed at the relic parked by the hedge. "Overturned on that hill up there." She pointed now at a steep green bank across the lane, where sheep were grazing with their rumps to the off-shore breeze.

"And Mrs Slattery?"

"Bedridden."

"Bedridden?"

"For years. We don't never see her about. That's how they don't get any cakes and the like. But give Old Josiah his due, he looks after her all by hisself, won't let nobody do anything for her, he won't."

"And she's 'bedridden' here?"

"No, oh no. Nobody's lived here as in *lived* here since before our time."

Bob gave an involuntary look in the direction of the front bedroom, but before he could ask anything else Mrs Lee was back to imparting local history so he let her get on with it.

"Josiah, Mr Slattery that is, says she specially likes my puddings, which is nice and makes it a bit worthwhile making the extra for them. I wouldn't do it just for that nasty Greville boy, oh no."

"And Greville comes from Exeter, and he's working here – until he's called up, or permanently?"

"Ah, now as to that my husband and me are in disagreement. My husband, Jack, reckons Greville's the daughter's son – the one that got away – but I say no, can't be because he's too young and she's been gone donkey's years, according to what I heard at the W.I. anyway. And that was all long before Jack started working at Ridgeway Farm, so how would he know?"

While Bob tried to extrapolate actual information from what she was saying, the woman nudged him with her free elbow. "What's going on then? You'm policemen, aren't you?"

"We are, Mrs Lee." Bob smiled, "I'm Detective Sergeant Robbins – I should have mentioned that earlier, sorry. And this is PC Oliver, who's working with me. We need to find Mr Slattery, you see. There has been an accident. Possibly two. A boy, possibly the boy Greville you mention, has been shot."

"Shot! Greville!" Mrs Lee's eyes opened wide with delight, then narrowed, "Dead, is he?" Bob nodded his head. "Well I never . . ." She was either lost for words or framing the news she could now impart to her W.I. cronies. Then in a grave, solemn voice she asked, "Did Josiah do for him?"

"As in shoot the boy? We don't think so."

"Ah, well," she responded, standing back and shaking her cotton reel curls slowly with disappointment, "I 'spect he shot hisself by accident. Lethal with a weapon that boy, my husband says."

Bob and Laurie exchanged glances, while Mrs Lee tutted over the sad irony of self-inflicted wounds and Bob started to wonder if that was a possibility. But if so, how had the boy obtained a pistol, and where was it?

"I knew it would be something like this," Mrs Lee sighed dramatically. "They were saying in the village as how police had been up here with the ambulance, and I said they'd be here for that Greville boy. He's a bad 'un, mark my words. What's ak-chew-ably happened then?" she demanded.

"That's what we're trying to find out, Mrs Lee. You don't know Greville's family do you, or at least where we can find his parents – in Exeter?"

"It was all before our time, see, and he don't – didn't – speak to me in conversation, if you know what I mean?"

"But he's a 'bad 'un', you say? What makes you think that?" Bob asked.

"*Because*," Mrs Lee leaned in for another special titbit, "they're a *funny* family, if you take my meaning? Not 'ealthy. Not that it's my place to say anything, but I've heard the talk – 'bout them being *close*." She gave a knowing nod of the head. "I never seen vedi-ance of anything ak-chew-ably peculiar, but they do keep themselves to themselves. If you catch my meaning? There's another boy somewhere but he went away as well. He's not a Joe, but that was all before we bought our smallholding. We're not Larkham folk see, so it's before our time."

"A grandson?"

Mrs Lee's ringlets bounced up and down. "Went up country they say."

"That is helpful to know, thank you, Mrs Lee. And, tell me, when was the last time you saw Mr Slattery?"

The woman sniffed. "Thursday, I think. When I came for our eggs."

"Did you go inside the house here?" Bob turned to the grey building.

"Oh, no. Nobody lives here, I told you, didn't I? T'ain't safe. Old Joe says the top o' the stairs gave way with the rot. Whole upstairs could collapse any minute, he said."

"Ah, I see. And he paid you?"

"Paid me? Who?" Mrs Lee's eyes narrowed suspiciously then she said, "Oh, to collect the eggs. No, I make cakes and puddings with 'em, and share them. The cakes."

"Of course, yes. A good arrangement. So, you saw both Mr Slattery and Greville on Thursday?" Bob was patience itself now he was back in the old swing of an investigation. The woman inclined her head. She's fibbing, Bob thought: she hasn't got permission to collect eggs at all. But he said nothing, only asked for confirmation nobody was 'ak-chew-ably' resident at Hentree.

"No! Look at the place. Don't you listen! Right ol' shambles, it is, the wood's all rotted. Old Josiah stays up at Ridgeway Farm. Round that there hill, past the church and take the lane for Larkham Cross. You can't miss it. Standing on its own it is on the side of a hill. They kept cows. But not now. My husband Jack worked there a while but he didn't get on with . . . Well, you know, Josiah Slattery's not . . ." Mrs Lee had finally run out of steam.

"One last thing," Bob said, "The boy here, Greville, was fond of guns, you said."

"Always shooting at something is Greville. Rats, rooks, crows, blackbirds. It's like the Somme up here some days, my Jack says. Not that he'd know, on account of his club foot, and I don't think it's a nice thing to say either, what with all they poor boys dead in the trenches we heard about."

"Goodness," Bob said with genuine feeling, "hardly a quiet Devon lane, this."

"You're telling me!"

He smiled again and asked gently, "Mrs Lee, given that you know the boy Greville, would you come down to Bideford and identify the body for us?"

Nancy Lee stared at Bob with horror. "In a mor-chew-u-ary? With dead folks? What a thing to ask a body. The very idea . . ." She shuddered, joggling the eggs in her basket.

"Not to worry, I expect we'll find someone. But could you tell us where you live? In case we need a bit of help with our other inquiries."

Reluctantly, Mrs Lee pointed towards the gate, "Turn left and go down the lane there. Smallholding. Holly Cottage. Lettuces in summer, veg in winter. My husband's called Jack Lee. He'll help you I 'spect. If you ask nicely."

A guffaw behind Bob became Laurie sneezing into a handkerchief.

Mrs Lee gave him a black look and exited Hentree Farm with considerable dignity through the main gate.

Bob waited until she was out of earshot then turned sharply on Laurie. "Laughing matter, is it, lad? Well, I've got something that'll knock the smile off your face. Follow me."

The body was female, her skin taut leather. She had been dead for a very a long time. Strands of white hair straggled across a grey pillow led Bob to think it could only be Mrs Slattery; she of the birthday cards and prize chutney.

After the initial shock, Laurie was calm, business-like and thorough. He opened the wardrobe to check clothing for clues, but Bob decided they shouldn't touch anything before contacting Bideford police. On the way out of the room, however, he paused at a small dressing table. It was bare, save for a plain hairbrush and a hinged, two-picture photograph frame that had toppled face down. On one side was a studio portrait of a pretty girl with dark, wavy hair, smiling at the camera; on the other, a chubby little boy holding a rattle in the shape of a baby lamb. Bob handed the picture frame to Laurie.

"She's like Claudette Colbert," Laurie said. "In *It Happened One Night*. But with longer hair."

"If you say so," Bob grunted. "In the knapsack, please. Then on your bike, find a phone box or the nearest pub and call Bideford on this number." He gave Laurie a crumpled scrap of paper from his pocket and a handful of copper coins. "Mention my name and tell them you're from Cready and who you are. I'll stay here in case anyone turns up."

Bob waited in his car. Laurie returned relatively quickly, they then had a long wait for the ambulance to arrive, which they passed in companionable silence interrupted by Bob's identification of wildlife in the hedgerow. A tiny wren hopped in and out of the undergrowth, while a mouse feasted on berries. A dowdy female dunnock hopped out of the higher branches then lifted into the air with a warning chit-chit as a weasel, sleek and stealthy, cut across the road and disappeared under the hedge on an egg-collecting mission. The thought of eggs set Bob thinking about Mrs Lee and her insistence that she was only relaying information about events at Hentree 'before her time'. Meaning Josiah Slattery's family was a subject of scrutiny for the locals . . . but then any family living in a small rural community would be under scrutiny. And every family, whether in the country or city, had its secrets and eccentrics – as young Laurie was so fond of pointing out.

A mortuary van finally arrived and Bob moved his car to enable it to enter the farmyard. Laurie went into the house with the two men to show them which room. It took them some time to get the woman's corpse downstairs. Bob hovered around the van impatiently, not wanting to be involved yet knowing he should.

"Are there any more, while we're here?" the driver asked as he slammed shut the doors of his vehicle.

"Ha-ha," Bob huffed in reply. He watched it go in silence then turned to Laurie, "Right, back on your bike, it's well past nursery tea time. Ridgeway Farm can wait for tomorrow. You must be starving."

"I'll say! All I've had today is two spam sandwiches and a railway spoon-bender."

"Not to worry, you'll soon be settled in Peony Villa."

"Peony Villa! Really?" Laurie chuckled.

"Oh, yes, Peony Villa. You're in for a real treat there. It's owned by a Mrs Jasmine Flowers, who assures me her Honeysuckle is waiting for you with open arms."

Laurie laughed again. "You're making this up."

"Not a bit of it. Flaming little mad-house, it is. Beds are rubbish but the food – oh, Laurie, boy, you'll be growing another inch upward and outward on their grub."

***

# Chapter 11

When they arrived at Peony Villas, Bob said, "Put your bike over there by the garage wall. Should be safe enough. They keep the gate shut as far as I know."

Laurie did as instructed then came to the car to get his bags from the boot, but Bob said, "Leave your uniform there, lad. Stay in civvies. You're acting DC Oliver while we're in Bideford."

Laurie looked at Bob, a frown on his face. "Is there something clandestine going on here as well? Spies, saboteurs?" The boy's plummy voice made him sound naïve, ingenuous. He could have stepped straight out of a boys' adventure story: the blond young Englishman in breeches riding a camel, with pyramids in the background.

"Clandestine?" Bob repeated. "I doubt it. This enquiry's a domestic or I'll eat my cap. It just might be better if we can get by for a few days with as few people as possible knowing what we're doing, that's all."

"Why, Sarge?" Laurie persisted.

"Nothing specific . . ." Bob drummed fingers on the roof of his car, "I've got a bit of a bad feeling. Bideford have made a fist of it so far. No attempt to search the farmhouse on the day of the crime. And that farmhouse . . . There's more to this than an unwanted holiday camp."

"But what's it got to do with this place?" Laurie looked up at the mismatched twin houses. "This pink one looks really nice."

"It does. It is. It's just that there's something here, as well . . . Call it an old man's fancy, but there's something not right."

Laurie waited for Bob to continue. When he didn't, he said, "So we have our work cut out. Which farm should we start on? Or do we check who actually owns them? Slattery could be a tenant farmer, and he must have family somewhere."

Not so naïve, Bob thought. "Done that," he said. "That's what's buzzing round my head right now. I got information from the Registry Office this morning. No easy task on a Sunday. According to the register, Hentree Farm belongs to a Mr Pascoe, who has been dead and gone since 1914. I'm thinking maybe Mrs Slattery was his daughter – need to get that confirmed though. Whether she is or isn't, the fact is, the farm and land aren't Slattery's to sell, unless he was doing it on behalf of his wife – who's been dead a good long time without anyone knowing about it – or worse, *doing* anything about it."

Laurie whistled through his teeth then said with a wry grin, "So that's why your fingers are itching, Sarge."

"Correct. Oh, and drop the 'Sarge', will you?" Bob said as he opened the gate to Number One. "While we're here, I'm plain Mr Robbins."

"Wouldn't 'Uncle Bob' explain me better?"

Astonished, Bob looked up at the boy's face, "Wherever did you get that idea?"

Laurie gave one of his Stan Laurel coy shrugs and Bob shook his head with mock despair.

But as he laboured up the steps to the pink front door, Bob remembered that the lovely Mrs Flowers now knew who and what he was anyway. He'd soon find out if it mattered, who she'd gossiped to, and whether her comment about not wanting to be too popular with the local force had been a joke or not.

Leaving Laurie to find Honeysuckle with Hester's help, Bob located Rose on the first floor and made himself at home. Hester had brought down his bag so he set about unpacking his few possessions then washed his used underwear in the sink. This being a superior room in every way, it had both hot *and* cold running water. As he was rubbing at a sock, he wondered who it had been promised to. There was a double bed with a fancy headboard and matching wardrobe, a good quality desk and chair, thick pale blue carpet and curtains with red roses on a pale blue background – plus a splendid view over the town rooftops of the river.

But why had he been given this address at the police station? There were dozens of holiday guest houses in the area to choose from. Why Number One Peony Villas, because this was no ordinary bed and breakfast by a long chalk? Jessamyn Flowers' mock horror at finding he had been given the address by the police had amused him, but what lay behind it nagged at him. That, and who and what Quentin/Ken was. Unless he was the reason Mrs F was wary of the rozzers . . . Probably. Not that she had reacted badly to DC Charlie West . . .

Bob rinsed the socks, wrung them tight and hung them over the towel rail then went to the window. Some words from a story book his son had been given by an aunt – a story he thoroughly disliked – came into his mind: 'Curiouser and curiouser'.

Laurie knocked at his door and they went down for the evening meal together. Bob was placed once again at Mrs Flowers' side. She was every inch the film star again this evening, too, in a ruby-coloured silk frock and ropes of pearls, despite it not being a Gala Night. Bob stole a look at Laurie to see his reaction to their landlady and the dining room and was disappointed. Then he remembered Laurie's 'people', as he liked to call them, probably dressed for dinner every evening.

Mrs Flowers introduced Laurie as Mr Laurence Oliver, which brought a spontaneous round of applause from the Wayward Players. Laurie was then placed facing Suky Stefano across the table.

It wasn't such a feast as the roast pork, or the previous evening's game pie, but it was the best cottage pie Bob had tasted since Joan had passed away. As they all tucked in, he said, "You'll be needing our ration books now, Mrs Flowers."

"Oh, do stop the 'missis' you make me feel positively matronly! Call me Jessamyn the way I asked, please. I'm sure we are going to be tremendous friends so I am going to call *you* Bob. Is that acceptable?"

Bob looked at her sideways. Was it genuine? Did women really speak like this off screen or stage? Was she an actress as well? And then a name popped into his head: Pascoe. It wasn't an uncommon surname in the West Country, there were dozens of them in the Cready area, and he'd just read it in a land registry after all, but now he had a visual memory of seeing it on a theatre bill. Where? Somewhere in the London area, years ago. Pearl Pascoe. He closed his eyes and saw a darkened stage lit with gaslights and a pretty girl dancing in nothing but ribbons. There was something about her . . . Dark hair, an oval face . . . Something had jogged his memory.

"Jess-*a*-*myn* . . ." Bob faltered over the name, "can I ask you a private question?"

"You may."

"Were you by any chance – and please don't take offence – but were you, once, a few years ago, the 'ribbon dancer'?"

Jessamyn shot a look across the table at Mrs Baxter-Salmon then said in a very low voice, "Good heavens! I was. Fancy you knowing that."

"I didn't know it, not really. Just a guess – a sort of connection. I saw you on stage. I thought you were wonderful .

. . ." he flushed, tongue-tied with embarrassment as he remembered he'd seen the act twice, and why.

Jessamyn gave him the full force of a wide, blue-eyed gaze. "I was a dancer in those days, yes. Only for a year or two, though. Pearl Pascoe was talent-spotted and whisked off to the West End to be a proper actress and renamed Jessamyn Flowers. I was in *Happy-go-lucky Days*. Did you see it? We had such a long run. Absolute box office fortune-maker it was. Not my fortune unfortunately, thanks to a rogue agent, but there we are, I was exceedingly naïve in those days." She passed him the gravy boat. "I rather had to learn the hard way."

"You gave up the stage when war broke out?"

"Not exactly. The stage gave up on me a few years before that. Age. It's terribly cruel to us poor women. We reach what is called a 'certain age' then it's bit roles as the housekeeper after that. An East End grandma for Ealing Studios or a dowager cameo in a Wilde production, if you're *very* lucky, but that won't feed the cat." Jessamyn went quiet, as if lost in a private memory.

Bob waited, the gravy boat poised above his plate, then said, "Well, on a purely selfish level, I have to say I'm exceedingly pleased you opened a bed and breakfast. This is splendid grub. Food," he added hastily. "And the rooms are nice, too."

"I really don't think we qualify as a bed and breakfast outfit, but if we are . . . well, that's all down to Mr Puddicombe, to dear Arthur, my late husband. He rescued me from dying prematurely on stage, and now he is no longer at my side." She gave a long, sad sigh. "I had a good career while it lasted, but I was *in-finitely* lucky that Arthur found me again when he did. I couldn't have gone back to matinées in the provinces, not after my West End success." She fixed Bob with a melancholy gaze. "So now you know all about me."

Bob stared at her as gravy glugged into a glutinous pool in his mashed potato. Jessamyn touched his hand in warning. Embarrassed again, he righted the gravy boat and returned it to its special saucer.

"Is that what you wanted to know?" Jessamyn asked, dabbing her napkin at a brown spot on his linen jacket.

"I hope you don't think I was prying."

"No, silly. I think you are very clever to have made the connection, I was a lot, lot younger in those days."

Bob waited a few moments, searching for a way to move the conversation onto another topic. Wendell Garamond, sitting next to Jessamyn on the other side, was involved in a conversation with Reg or Bill – Bob couldn't remember who was who; the act*orrr* and ten*orrr*, Horace Dobson, was busy sparring with the butcher's wife across the table about where they had been in the summer of '38, and which of them had been top of the bill in Southend; and Laurie was too far away even to speak to. Not that he would listen; he was too far gone gazing at sweet Suky, who was telling him something that required frequent giggles.

When Jessamyn turned back to him, Bob said quietly, "I don't see you playing a grandma," referring to her comment on roles for older women.

"Oh, heavens, me neither! Hence my Peony Villas."

"You own both houses, then?"

"No." The answer came too quickly and in a different tone to the previous banter. "My sister-in-law has Number Two." The accomplished actress then gave him a cheeky smile and whispered, "I was fully dressed under those ribbons, you know. Flesh coloured tunic and leotard covered in ribbons: they were the very devil to sew on. Costumes are designed to be deceptive."

Bob was amused but he wasn't fooled. Number Two Peony Villas involved or perhaps contained something of a scandal or a secret. Suddenly, he wanted to know more about Jessamyn Flowers, starting with her real name and how she had gone on the stage: how she'd started as a chit of girl in scanty clothing called Pearl Pascoe, become a West End diva then ended up as a landlady in a minor Devonshire town. But that was the end of their conversation because Wendell now had everyone's attention as he explained the delights of the Wayward Players' new Shakespeare production to Laurie.

". . . after which we open with tragedy depending on the majority age of the audience: if they are younger it's Juliet's balcony scene with *our* Romeo going off to war. Burma or Borneo – somewhere distant like that. Or it's a scene from the Scottish play, with me as Adolf Macbeth and Reggie as the ghost, showing dictators have their weaknesses. Sometimes, if we've got a longer programme to fill, we do an earlier scene with Estelle showing him up as a feeble, hen-pecked excuse for a man. Estelle is *mag-nif-icent* in a farthingale. Then there's a short break and we switch to comedy and give them something from *Much Ado* and end with *Twelfth Night* cross-garters – only they're puttees that get wrapped round both legs. Then Suky gives a heart-rending version of *Hey Ho the Wind and the Rain*, Horace sings something stirring, and we end with Estelle as Good Queen Bess singing *There'll Always Be an England*, which gets everyone on their feet, and they all return to their humble abodes in happy frame of being."

"Bit cultural for Devon villages, isn't it?" Bob said, wondering simultaneously about Garamond's wording: a 'happy frame of being'.

"It is and it isn't. Apart from a '*bit* of culture'," the actor-manager mimicked Bob's Midlander's flat vowels perfectly, "one should never underestimate farming communities, Mr

Robbins. There's precious little for them to do in an evening except read, and read many of them do."

"They can listen to wireless programmes," Mrs Baxter-Salmon cut in.

*Unless you live at Hentree Farm,* Bob mused. The thought took him back to what he'd seen in the house, or rather what he had not seen. There had been no wireless set. "Nobody has lived there for years," he said to himself.

"Nobody lives where?" Jessamyn asked.

"A farm I saw today. Sad place."

"Ah," she replied and turned to listen to Estelle Dobson.

The bathroom contralto was saying, "Daneman Court is famous for its Shakespeare. Dame Selena Candle owns two of his folios."

"Written on her very own typewriter," Horace quipped.

Estelle scowled. "Don't mock what you don't understand."

As the Wayward Players continued their in-fighting and Laurie continued to gaze at Suky Stefano, their empty plates were removed and replaced with pretty glass dishes. Bob turned back to Jessamyn. "Who's Dame Selena?"

"Oh, the dearest old diva in the world. She's under contract at Ealing Studios. You must have seen her. She's tremendous in comedies. Tremendous all round, actually. Her late husband was a collector of – well, I'm not sure entirely what it was he collected, but they have a famous collection of it at Daneman Court."

"Daneman Court?"

"Dame Selena's family home. She used to be the Honourable Selena Worthington, but she grew rather large for her debutante tiara and didn't conform to expectations so she escaped. Rather like me. She married a distant Worthington cousin then he got bitten by a snake or something in Egypt. It was a marriage of convenience anyway. She's only ever known as Selena Candle nowadays. Dame Selena, I should say."

"I've seen her: she was the clairvoyant in that film about rescuing a steam engine, wasn't she? Made me laugh."

"That's her. She's being a terrific sport now for the Ministry of Information." Jessamyn leaned in towards Bob so their shoulders were touching and lowered her voice, "Between you and me, I don't think she's coming to see the Waywards about their Shakespeare. She wants them at Daneman Court for a war effort special they're making for the Home Front. One of those informative shorts telling us how to turn a ball gown into a pinafore or a sleeve into a sieve, and dig for victory, that sort of thing, but I haven't the courage to tell them."

"They will be lodging there, then?"

"For the duration of the film, yes, probably. Not sure. There may not be space. She's taken in a group of Austrian refugees, some poor Jewish children and their parents – they got to France and then walked right over the Pyrenees into Spain. Can you believe that! She says they are very cultured people and include two opera singers and a musician she met in Vienna before she stopped being a debutante. It's such a small world."

"It is," Bob agreed with a smile, thinking about Pearl Pascoe. "Be nice to everyone, you never know when you'll meet them again, that's my motto." He then became distracted by the aroma of cinnamon and cloves as Hester placed two large bowls of crisply-topped apple crumble on the table. "This is wonderful," he muttered. "Three years of world war and you still have cinnamon and cloves."

Jessamyn smiled then leaned in even closer to whisper in his ear, "I think Dame Selena has *plans* for me, too."

"Really!"

"I think she may be *e-stablishing* a film company of *her own*." A pause was followed by a long sigh, "But I'm not sure it's the right thing for me at the moment. It means all change here at Peony Villas, anyway. Not that we can go on like this much longer, I'm pestered weekly to take in evacuees and now we are on the council's American GI billeting list as well."

Despite the theatrical stresses, Bob heard a genuine sense of concern in her final words. He also heard the plural 's' on villas. "You mean both houses could be requisitioned?"

Jessamyn either didn't hear or ignored the 'both' and continued, "I sound so heartless, and I know it wouldn't be *en-tirely* a disaster, but if *I* have to take in evacuees or refugees . . . No! Cancel that, it makes me sound too, too horrible. I know what it is like to be in need of a home. A room even. I shall do it with a willing heart, but I do need paying guests to keep our cook, Mr Pots, and Hester employed, you see."

Bob nodded. "Difficult times."

"Indeed." Jessamyn sipped from her water glass then said, "Come and take a night cap with me later. I have to sort out the shopping list for tomorrow – I check each evening in case we're in need. Mr Pots is a terrific cook and gardener, but not so good at remembering we also need to buy goods from shops. Then I like to enjoy my evening if I can."

Surprised and not altogether sure how to respond, Bob delayed his response by saying, "Mr Pots? He's the cook."

"Yes. His real name is Harold Gormley but the Great War made him forget that. He forgot everything except that he could cook. He was my late husband's school friend – Arthur's best friend, actually – until the trenches. We took him in when we moved here. When Arthur and I married and came here to live, that is. Nobody else would have him. Not even his own sisters. One day, while he was absolutely *en-tirely* surrounded by saucepans, I called him Mr Pots'n'pans in fun, and it made him laugh. Which was lovely because he never laughed, you see. So now he's Mr Pots. Poor Mr Pots, he has had a sad life and it's made him a bit – daffy," she tapped her forehead, "but he's all right here. He looks after me and I look after him, and we get along just fine."

Bob leaned back in his chair, that little speech made him want to ask half a dozen questions but they'd keep until later. Instead, he said, "Which flower are you?"

"Jasmine, of course. Oh, but no. I didn't mean that! I have a tiny sitting room down the hall. The door marked 'Private'. No flower at all."

Bob flushed scarlet from throat to bushy white eyebrows. When he could speak again, he said, "Actually, if you don't mind, I'd rather turn in early. Got a busy day tomorrow."

"As you wish," said the delightful, kind-hearted Jessamyn, her eyes betraying a wicked twinkle of amusement.

Sometime during the night, nearer midnight than dawn, Bob left his room for a nuisance visit to the lavatory. Blackout curtain draped the landing window but with his door left ajar there was sufficient light from his bedside lamp to make his way there and back without switching on a torch and alerting anyone to his weak bladder.

As he crossed the thick-piled carpet on the return to his room, he heard a door handle and speeded up. Then, curious to see who was also wandering about at night, he waited behind his door. Light from a briefly opened door across the landing illuminated a tall, elegant figure in silk dressing gown and cravat. Bob gave a silent tut-tut, then froze. It was Wendell Garamond, and the door being closed so carefully behind him was the one decorated with a pretty ceramic tile depicting a twig of jasmine.

***

# Chapter 12

## Monday

Lavinia Baxter-Salmon set a tall vase of wilting chrysanthemums on the scullery draining board next to where Jessamyn was washing a cut-glass jug. "This is the last," she said. "I'll get some more this afternoon if it stops raining." There was a pause. "Or we could take a walk later, Jessie, if you like, gather some autumn twigs and berries instead."

"It's a bit early for that. I have to go into town, I'll get some flowers while I'm out." Jessamyn dried her jug, not looking up.

"He's a policeman, isn't he?" Lavinia kept her voice low.

Jessamyn's profile tensed. "Yes." There was another brief silence then she said, "But he's only here for a couple of nights and I can't imagine it is anything remotely to do with your secret."

"*My* secret? It was your idea!" Lavinia hissed.

"Idea? It wasn't an 'idea', it was an option: a means to the end of a horrible situation." Jessamyn stored the jug on a shelf, saying, "And who benefited, hmm? Who has had twenty peaceful years because of 'my idea'?"

Lavinia bit back words and busied herself picking dead leaves out of the sink. When she turned, Jessamyn was drying a clean vase. "You told him you were a widow," she said, taking the vase and storing it next to the jug.

"Well, I am. As good as."

"You were flirting."

"Oh, for heaven's sake, Vinny, don't start that again!"

"Then tell me," Lavinia's voice was sharp with hidden meaning, "if you are so anxious to be a widow, why don't you help along Arthur's suffering as well?"

"That's a dreadful thing to say!" Jessamyn gasped. "I could never do a thing like that. Arthur has been good to me. Letting him persuade me to come back here was foolish on my part, but he meant it for the best. Besides, Maud's life will be meaningless without him."

"And you don't want Maud Puddicombe hanging around you being critical . . ."

"No, no, I don't, thank you very much, I have you for that. Now, if you will excuse me, I have a business to run. I fear I shall be occupied all day, so if we have callers please tell them I'm not available and deal with it – if you can."

"Occupied? With what? Where are you going?"

Jessamyn flung her tea towel on the draining board and strode to the scullery door. Holding it open, she said, "First, if you must know, I shall be seeing my solicitor. I shall be out all day so don't plan one of your private country jaunts like last week. Anything else? No? I will see you at supper then."

Lavinia Baxter-Salmon waited until the door was closed then gathered up her slimy stalks and wilted blooms and headed up the yard steps to throw them on the compost heap at end of the long back garden, where nobody would see her tears.

The compost heap stank to high heaven and the fox had been at it again. Egg shells lay scattered across the path, yesterday's vegetable waste dug aside to reveal what lay below. Tears welling in her eyes, Lavinia threw on her offering. Some stalks landed neatly; others joined the egg shells. She didn't care. She stared unseeing at the heap, wondering if it was a metaphor for her life to now.

*Up to now*. She could leave.

"I can leave," she said aloud. "I can leave any time I choose." But she knew she wouldn't.

The compost heap moved.

Something below the surface definitely moved.

Lavinia gave an unladylike screech and shot into the garden shed where no one would see her and laugh.

The shed smelled nearly as bad as the compost heap, but there was a chair by the bench under the grubby window and she sank into it gratefully. Leaning forward, she put her head in her hands and gave way to heaving sobs. Hoping, begging that Jessamyn was right, that the policeman wasn't interested in her.

Gradually, Lavinia got herself back under control. She stood up, her head touching the slats in the roof, straightened her spine and edged a corset bone back into place. As she did so she noticed an old picture frame resting against a wall. There was no picture in it, but there was something else. Something . . . she bent down to look and screeched again. It was a cat's skin. A ginger tortoiseshell cat-skin. Each leg was stretched out and tied to a corner with string. "Mr Pots," she murmured, "whatever are you doing with your cats?"

Then she recalled the game pie he'd served the night before and her stomach churned. Mr Pots had spent three years in a prison camp during the Great War: they could be eating anything.

Lavinia left the shed, closed the door tightly and returned to the house. Still not quite in control of herself, she was dismayed to find Mr Pots in her path. He was sharpening two knives on a stone step. This way and that, his hairy wrists stroked each long blade alternately over the granite, this way and that, this way and that, this way and that. Lavinia was just about to faint when he noticed her.

"You want a come down?" he asked.

She swallowed hard. "Yes."

He stood back and Lavinia turned sideways to avoid getting any nearer to him than necessary. But before she could get around him, he said. "That bay's yer."

"Bays year?"

"That's what I said."

"Ah – boy – the boy is here."

"'E's in with Arthur. I don't like it."

"No. Well, I'm sure . . ." Lavinia had no idea how to respond.

"E's a baddun, that bay."

"You mean Quentin?"

"Who else?"

"Oh, yes. No, that is, I agree. But what can we do?"

"Look after her. That's what you can do. Look after her like I promised Arthur. That's what we're yer for, in it?"

Lavinia closed her eyes. Had she ever promised? Perhaps not, but she owed Jessamyn her life. At least a decent, respectable life. "Yes," she sighed, "I suppose it is."

***

# Chapter 13

Jessamyn hurried up to her room, angry with both herself and Lavinia. Why couldn't she just let the past stay in the past? With a slightly shaking hand she dabbed powder to her pink cheeks then, more calmly, neatened her cupid's bow with a twist of scarlet lipstick. Satisfied her face betrayed no hint of her troubled thoughts, she smoothed her skirt, picked up the list she had taken so long to write the previous day, popped it into a compartment of her capacious handbag, and as calmly as she could, went downstairs.

Hester was on the front steps with a bucket and scrubbing-brush. "I have to go into town. I shall be out all day," Jessamyn said without further explanation, and set off for a potentially awkward interview with her solicitor.

She had rehearsed what she was going to say numerous times, but she knew she was also going to have to improvise. Past experience with George Hook, who knew more about her family background than even Lavinia, suggested there would be some tricky questions to negotiate.

Giving herself a reassuring smile in the car's rear-view mirror, she backed her Austin out of the garage and set off down the road then turned left to go down the steep High Street. Passing Chippenham's Upholstery, Scrope and Sons the Outfitters, and various other shops, all of which knew her as Mrs Puddicombe, who had married Arthur Puddicombe *in*

*London.* Alderman Puddicombe, that was – who'd been married to Mary Bennett – such a nice lady, such a shame her getting so ill so young. Arthur Puddicombe who'd gone a bit off his head and went up to London and came back with that actress – famous, they say – and beautiful, you had to admit, although not as young as she was. Fancy him bringing someone like that into the Puddicombe family – local benefactors, they are and she's got a past. Born in Larkham, or so they do say . . .

What that 'past' involved, she doubted any of them could even guess. George Hook knew though, which made their interviews a matter of unspoken tension for her: she couldn't play her Jessamyn Flowers role for him and get away with it for very long. George Hook had an unnerving way of seeing the person she used to be. And he knew it.

The offices of Didcot, Lissman, Lester and Hook were on the first floor of a red brick building on the quayside. Jessamyn ascended green-hued linoleum-lined stairs, gave her name to the receptionist and sat down to wait. The receptionist, a new acquisition, disappeared. Jessamyn picked up an old copy of *The Field* and leafed through it. Horses, guns and dogs – *hounds*, not dogs. Nothing related to her life and she dropped it back on the neat pile and stared at a watercolour of Bideford Bridge. George Hook's wife was an accomplished artist. Were they a normal couple: did they love and respect each other and have normal conversations about paying the milkman and what to do on Sunday afternoon? Did couples like that exist?

The receptionist reappeared. "Mr Hook will see you now, Mrs Puddicombe."

George Hook, a middle-aged man with wire-rimmed spectacles and a paunch but otherwise not disagreeable, came to the door to greet her. Jessamyn sat before his desk and he resumed his seat.

"So, Mrs Puddicombe, how can I help you?"

"I wish to make some bequests. If that's the right word?"

"Bequests. You want to change your will?"

"No. That is, yes, I should, but for now I want to give certain people something *before* I die."

George Hook looked confused, as she'd feared he would. "You mean you want to give them gifts?"

"Yes, except I'd like these gifts to be noted down and witnessed and signed by you in the form of a legal document. For each of them. To protect them – the people receiving the gifts – so nobody can take what has been given from them, or query why they have received it."

George Hook frowned. "Substantial gifts, then?"

"Yes. Could we call it a 'deed of gift'?"

"If that is what you would like, of course. What is it you want to give?"

Jessamyn opened her handbag and extracted the folded sheet of foolscap paper. "This is my hand-written list." She placed it on the desk. "I wrote it last night in the dark so it may be a bit wonky." It was the best excuse she could think of to cover her poor handwriting and spelling. She hadn't attended school on a regular basis, and hadn't learned much while she was there. "Except, please, the information must not leave these premises."

"You can rely on us, for that." George Hook picked up the sheet of paper and read aloud: "To Harold Gormley: the right to live at Number 2 Peony Villas for as long as he so chooses. To Mrs Lavinia Baxter-Salmon – ditto. To Miss Hester Alice Edson – ditto until her marriage, if she wishes. To Miss Maud Puddicombe of Number 2 Peony Villas, an annual income of £1,000 to cover utility bills for Mr Gormley and Mrs Baxter-Salmon." He looked at Jessamyn. "You do know Maud will inherit Number Two from Arthur?"

"Yes, but I want her to provide food and lodging for Mr Pots – that's Mr Gormley – and Mrs Baxter-Salmon. They will need somewhere to live until the war is over, at least. And Hester – she may need a safe haven, I fear."

"I think you'd better tell me what's on your mind, Mrs Puddicombe. Has Arthur taken a turn for the worse?" George Hook's Devonshire burr gave the words a gentle sense of genuine concern, but then he and Arthur had been school-fellows.

Jessamyn sighed, "In some ways I wish he had. I do confess watching his suffering is becoming a torment."

"He's in pain? I thought he was paralysed."

"Not altogether. He can digest soft food and beverages, but he can't speak or move otherwise, except for his eyes, which tell me he's trapped in his body and it is heart-rending, truly it is. Maud does all she can for him, and so do I, obviously, but . . ."

"But you think his end may be near and . . ."

"And when that happens, I want to be free to go back to London or, depending on how the war is going, elsewhere. I don't want to have to worry about people dependent on me for a home and livelihood." She paused, gave him one of her brave smiles then said quietly, "I'm trying to do my best for when the worst happens."

It had the desired effect, George Hook nodded and leaned back in his chair. "I see. That is most commendable. But under the terms of your husband's will your future is perfectly secure. There are investments that will bring in a sound annual income alone. There is no need for you to return to your – er – previous occupation or live abroad more cheaply. We drew this all up before your marriage. Arthur was most insistent, him being so much older than you. Your situation is quite safe. Comfortable even. There'll be no need to sell Number One, either, unless you absolutely want to."

"Yes, I know all that," Jessamyn gave him the grateful smile and re-assessed the script she had in her head, wondering if he suspected her difficult relationship with Quentin. Arthur could have mentioned it, probably had after the first showdown with his new stepson. "And you are right," she said, looking innocently at George Hook, "as soon as I am back in London, I'll see my lawyer there and adjust my own will regarding Quentin. But please, I do want to ensure the people on that list will have a roof over their heads should I choose to leave."

*In case my son Quentin decides to move in and kick them out*, she added silently. *In case whatever he's up to doesn't go in his favour; because Quentin is so much like his grandfather, he frightens me.*

George Hook indicated the list on his blotter with a stubby thumb. "If you'll permit me, Mrs Puddicombe, I suggest that if you are seriously thinking of selling Number One – in the relatively near future – that we value the property as a business first. Selling the house will be easy enough, but have you considered selling it as a business enterprise?"

"No, no I hadn't. But there's no hurry to sell the house at all. I can leave it until the war is over. I was approached by an American Army billeting man last week: they need accommodation for officers. The council have been around asking for rooms for evacuees as well. My preference is for the Americans. That way Hester can keep her job and possibly Mr Pots – Harold Gormley – as well."

"How is Harold?" George Hook asked, a smile on his face. "Still a bit potty?"

"Oh, yes. He's taken to rescuing kittens, for heaven's sake. I found another box of strays in the kitchen yesterday. I don't want to hurt his feelings, and I know he likes having little pets, but they smell, they really, really smell. I told him to let them go. Cats can fend for themselves. By the way, why are there so many Americans coming into the area?"

George Hook tapped his beaky nose, "Preparations for the invasion. Secret preparations," he confided.

Jessamyn put a hand to her mouth in a genuine moment of shock. "Oh, my Lord, they're expecting Germans to land here!"

"Always have been, but this is," he leaned across his desk and mouthed, "the *other way* around. *We* are going to be doing the . . ." he nodded his head to one side to finish the sentence for him. "That's why it's all so hush-hush. They were talking about it in the Black Stag yesterday. Bideford has an important role in this war, you mark my words. If you're missing a faster life in London, Mrs Puddicombe, don't worry, it's coming to us."

Jessamyn stared at him. "You mean the troops in camps around here – they'll be sent on an invasion mission?"

"I expect so. Yes. They're doing manoeuvres on the sand dunes across the water every day."

"And the troops all know about this?"

"Must do. Except we shouldn't even be discussing it, not even here where no one can eavesdrop."

"No, obviously." Jessamyn opened and closed the catch on her handbag. Was this why Quentin wanted to get his hands on the farm? To lease it out and make money? She blinked, "That must be what it's about," she said, feeling a lot brighter. "I'd better do my bit then, offer Number One to the U.S. Army as requested." She grinned, thinking about Detective Sergeant Robbins, "I'll have to give my new arrivals their marching orders before they can get settled in," and got up to go. "I'll leave that list with you, Mr Hook, for the deeds of gift. Shall I come back in a week?"

The solicitor got to his feet, confused by his client's comments and change of mood. "You won't be closing down as a bed and breakfast yet, then?"

"It's *not* a bed and breakfast! Heaven forbid I'd have to stoop to that. I opened it as a residential guest house for London *artistes*, opera singers and retired actors." Jessamyn paused, remembering how the notion had come to her when Wendell had written to her with his idea for a group of travelling players. For him it had been a means of getting away from London; for her an end to turgid boredom. They had had a summer of fun, but she'd always known it wouldn't last.

Looking at the kindly, boring solicitor, Jessamyn gave one of her emotive little sighs, "Yes, I shall be closing down the business side as you put it. As soon as I can. Under the circumstances. And this makes my request somewhat more urgent. In case I have to leave as well."

"But you have your sister-in-law's house. Maud won't want to see you homeless."

"Won't she?" Jessamyn laughed. "I wouldn't be too sure about that, Mr Hook. Which reminds me, can you tell me exactly what is in my husband's will regarding his sister and I?"

George Hook pursed his lips. "I can tell you that you have nothing to worry about, either of you. Miss Maud Puddicombe's house will be registered in her name. And yours will be in yours."

"There is no mention of my son Quentin?"

George Hook inclined his head, "A reasonable bequest."

"I see. Thank you." Jessamyn started towards the door then turned back.

"There's something else you want me to do?" the solicitor asked.

"Yes. Are you allowed to tell me the legal situation with my mother's family property? Can my father sell it or give it away?"

"I shouldn't think so. I don't know the actual terms of ownership, though."

"It was entailed in her family line. Her family were significant landowners once."

"Oh, I know all that. My family live up that way, too, remember."

Jessamyn had become so used to keeping her origins secret over the years she tended to forget some people actually knew her parents and family. "But who legally owns – or will own – what's left?" she asked.

"Mmm, tricky. Entailment as such was abolished in 1925, but your mother technically owns the property so, unless your father has power of attorney, as far as I know, it can't be sold without her consent. Why are you asking?"

"I want to waive my right to the inheritance. My son wants it, and . . . I know my mother is unwell and . . . Basically, I don't ever want to live there again."

"Prime bit of land that, Mrs Puddicombe. You should inherit it by rights. I wouldn't let it go too fast if I were you."

Jessamyn peered at him, "What are you trying to say, Mr Hook?"

The solicitor grimaced and came around to her side of the desk. "Let's just say that once this war's over there'll be changes around here; the council's already talking about creating new housing estates. Long-term planning. There's also the possibility your land could be sold for a holiday camp. There are rumours Hoblins want to set up around here. A better possibility, if you want to avoid that, would be for your parents to let the council rent the farmland, if it's not being used – which as far as I know, it isn't – for wartime installations. Those could then be developed at a later date. There are a lot of changes in the air: agricultural land being made over for other uses, housing developments for bombed out victims. Prices will change accordingly, if you follow me?"

Jessamyn considered the implicit content of the solicitor's advice. The farm itself was near derelict and worthless now, but the land could be worth a lot of money. George Hook had just confirmed her suspicion: this was why Quentin was so eager to get his hands on it. She shook her head, "Even so," she said, "my son can have it – when the time comes. He lived there as a child you see."

"Of course: I expect he has a sentimental attachment." George Hook was a generous man. It was a bald-faced lie and they both knew it.

***

# Chapter 14

Bob and Laurie set out for Ridgeway Farm early on Monday morning. It was a glorious day: golden leaves were beginning to drift along the lanes, hedges were alive with birds gorging on berries. As they got further away from the town, the lanes narrowed and the tree canopies became denser.

"It's like driving into a secret country," Laurie mused, opening a window to touch a low bank of ferns.

"I'll say," Bob grunted, manoeuvring around two cyclists on an awkward bend. "And let's hope we uncover at least one of those secrets before the day's over." Despite the beautiful morning, Bob was out of sorts.

Blithely unaware, Laurie commented on a group of magpies he didn't have time to count, then a milk churn that had fallen from its roadside stand and attracted the local cats. Nearing Barley Cliff, they came upon a herd of red cows lumbering out of a gate, a black and white collie at their heels. Bob switched off the Morris's engine to coast down the hill behind them.

"Funny things, cows," Laurie said, studying the angular hip bones of the beasts in front of the bumper. "Like leather boxes on legs."

"They are," Bob laughed. It was hard to stay grumpy for long with Laurie for company. Setting aside his ill-humour, he started to hum his personal theme tune: 'When the red, red robin goes bob, bob, bobbin' along . . .'

The two cyclists Bob had overtaken followed his black Morris up the lane then through the gate to Ridgeway Farm and up the steep, rutted track into the farmyard. They were wearing Women's Land Army working gear. Watching them through the rear-view mirror, Bob noticed how they exchanged glances as they dismounted. The taller of the two said something and the small one shrugged. They parked their cycles against a wall while Bob manoeuvred his car alongside a farm truck.

"How rude," Laurie said, watching them disappear without a word.

"Mmm," Bob muttered. "Find them, Laurie. Find out what's spooked them. I'll check that truck, it wasn't here before – then I'll be in the house, if I can get in."

Laurie loped off and Bob stood on tip toe trying to see through the wooden slats in the back of the truck. It was empty save for a thick layer of sheep dung. There was a greasy cap in the cab, though. He flipped it over with a finger to see if by chance there was a name in it. There wasn't and the maker's label was too worn to read. As he climbed out, he noticed a woman's handkerchief had fallen to the floor by the handbrake, along with an empty bag of what smelled like strong mints.

Bob left them exactly where they lay and turned his attention to the house, wondering what nasty surprise he was in for this time: from the exterior Ridgeway Farm bore a formidable resemblance to Hentree. Not in its layout or content or size – as he'd noted before, it was a better residence by far – but in its general atmosphere. Each was covered in dingy grey pebble-dash and in need of new guttering; each had wooden garden gates swollen and wedged open in dry mud; weeds from the hedgerow had occupied each small front garden.

No one answered his knock on the front door, but the back door was open. "Anyone in?" he called, walking into the kitchen. "No, but make yourself at home, Mr Robbins. Make a pot a cup of tea if you fancy it. Ta, thank you very much," he replied, "I don't mind if I do."

"You'll find the tea caddy over there," said a woman's voice, making Bob jump. He turned and found a diminutive, dark-haired girl in rolled up brown dungarees pointing a finger at a shelf.

"Sorry, I didn't think anyone was in."

"There isn't."

"You're one of the Land Army girls that followed us up," Bob said.

"Well done."

"Have you been using the truck outside over the weekend?"

"We might have been. Slattery doesn't care as long as we supply the petrol."

"And Slattery is?"

"Geezer who owns this dump. He never goes anywhere. We've been doin' the market runs for him. We did one on Saturday and kept it for a picnic then brought it back yesterday. Why? You from the Ministry or something?"

Bob scratched his chin, wondering if this was why the girls had wanted to avoid him; why this girl was on the defensive before they'd even exchanged names. She brushed past him to put on the kettle. It was a very large kettle suggesting that at one time a family had lived here – a family who made tea for their day labourers. But not anymore.

"I'm Cilla," the girl said over the noise of the juddering tap. "You can call me Priscilla if you like." She pronounced the word 'like' with what Bob thought of as an 'Essex whine'. "Bunty's gone to check the last of the sheep. Your Ag Committee want them sent to market so we're sending them, all right? Slattery doesn't like it, though."

"Fond of them, is he?" Bob queried.

"I doubt it. He doesn't like taking orders that's all. Who does?" she challenged.

"There's a war on," Bob replied blandly. "What is Mr Slattery objecting to exactly?"

"Turning the farm to arable. Means he's got to hire help." She lit the gas then checked how many matches remained in the box and muttered something under her breath.

Bob was about to say something along the lines of haphazard housekeeping but the girl said. "Is that why you're here? To check up on him?" She leaned back against the draining board, arms folded across her body.

"In a manner of speaking. You haven't seen him since Friday – morning or evening?"

"Morning, why?"

"I need to find him."

"He's probably gone into hiding. It's what he does when there's visitors. Specially now, with people coming up from the council."

Now it was Bob's turn to ask why.

"To avoid doing what he's been told, don't you listen? He's furious the War Ag Committee want his grazing pasture ploughed up. Wasn't too happy being sent two Land Army girls, either. Some daft biddy came up about refugee labour, she couldn't get away fast enough. He stands to lose his farm, though, doesn't he?"

"Doesn't do what?" Bob asked, realising he'd missed something important.

"Do what your lot are telling him. He could lose the farm, couldn't he?"

"That's a bit harsh," Bob heard himself say.

"There is a war on," Cilla quipped back at him. She went to the dresser and took down two cups, no saucers, then rinsed them under the tap, saying, "Personally, I can't see what he's got to moan about. He gets a fair subsidy for every new grain field, and it's Bunty and me doing all the work."

Bob nodded and took a chair by the square kitchen table. The threadbare red gingham tablecloth looked as if it hadn't been shaken, let alone washed, in years. Cilla must have been following his train of thought, for she pulled it from under his elbows like a magician and shook it vigorously outside the back door. When she came back, she took a look at the table and said, "Bare table's cleaner," and shoved the offensive cloth under the stone sink.

"So, Mr Slattery is your employer, then?" Bob queried.

"Not bloody likely!" Cilla retorted. "We're part of a mobile Land Army unit. We go where we're most needed for a month or two at time."

The kettle started to rattle on the hob. Cilla went to adjust it, then moved towards an open pantry and emerged with a tin. "Mr Slattery likes biscuits. Only eats biscuits, as far as we can tell."

Bunty arrived in the kitchen with Laurie. Cilla took one look at Laurie's height and demeanour and slapped a hand to her mouth. "Bloody hell, coppers! I was only joking saying he's gone into hiding. Have you come to take him away?" she demanded.

Laurie straightened his shoulders and forgetting that he was not uniform replied, "We are seeking Mr Slattery's whereabouts, yes, miss."

Bob shook his head in mild despair and caught the two girls exchanging warning glances again. When he turned back, he met Cilla's accusatory gaze.

"You didn't tell me you're Police."

"I didn't, and I'm curious to know how you have guessed."

"Oh, that's easy. He *looks* like a bobby," Cilla pointed Laurie, "and you *sound* like one."

*And you've got a family with form.* "Fair cop," Bob laughed. "I'm Detective Sergeant Robbins, and this is acting DC Oliver. Suspicions confirmed."

The young women adopted identical blank expressions, despite being physically different in every other way. The kettle came to their rescue and Cilla filled the tea pot while Bunty opened the biscuit tin and handed it around. "Mostly broken bits," she said, "but mustn't complain."

"Story of my life," muttered Cilla, setting a jug of milk on the table.

"You two have made yourselves at home, I see," Bob grinned.

"Hardly!" Cilla retorted. "We're billeted in town, thank God. Means a long cycle ride twice a day, but believe me it's better than having to live with that miserable old bastard. No wonder he's got nobody working here."

"And no wonder he's had an official warning," Bunty added, smoothing back her auburn hair and re-pinning it.

"Official warning?" Bob queried, pretending he didn't recall what he'd been told earlier and making Cilla indignant yet again.

"I've just told you!" she huffed.

"He should have retired years ago," Bunty said and reached for another broken biscuit. "He should be grateful we're even here."

"Doesn't his grandson help out?" Laurie asked quietly from his standing position by the draining board.

"No grandson here – that we know of," Cilla replied. Bunty looked meaningfully at her. "Oh, him," Cilla sighed.

"You've seen the grandson? He's been visiting, has he?" Bob asked.

"There's an Army corporal. He's been up a few times. I'm not sure if he's actually a grandson, but he's *very* interested in the farms. You saw him in town as well, didn't you, Cilla?"

Cilla glowered at her and Bob pretended he hadn't noticed. "Date was it?" he asked. "Instant mutual attraction?"

"It was only once. And no, nothing mutual. He kept on asking questions about the farm, then he turned all octopus on me. When I pushed him off, he flew into a right one. Went all red in the face and started getting handy with his fists. I didn't like him after that."

"Ah, shame. What did he want to know?"

Cilla pulled a tea cloth from a drawer. "He kept asking what we were doing up here and if Ridgeway was making money. As if I'd know that. That, and who was working here. I told him it was just us and Greville."

"And this Greville, is he another grandson?" Bob asked.

"He's a sort of nephew. He lives here now," Bunty supplied.

"You've not heard what's happened to the nephew, then?" Bob waited for a reaction. The girls maintained a studied disinterest so he said, "He's been killed. Pistol shot. Pre-meditated murder as far as we can tell."

Cilla's mouth dropped opened in surprise and Bunty's eyebrows shot up behind her teacup, but there was a combined loaded silence.

"Cilla, love," Bob said, indicating her vacant chair, "come and sit down and tell us what you know about the nephew, will you?"

It took a while and the results were relatively disappointing. The nephew – definitely not a grandson as far as they knew – was called Grev. He'd also made unwelcome advances to Cilla. After a long day picking root vegetables, she had been at the sink washing her hands when he'd come up behind her and made his advances more physical. Bunty had come up behind him, swivelled him around and given him what for. He'd fallen backwards on the stone flags and bashed his head.

"Which day was this?" Bob asked.

"Thursday," Bunty mumbled, setting down her cup. "We didn't see him on Friday and . . . we thought . . . He wasn't here when we brought the truck back, either."

Bob gave Cilla a long look, wondering if she thought they had come to arrest them for GBH.

Cilla stared back at him, challenging, then said, "Where did it happen?"

"The shooting? Hentree Farm. Do you work there as well?"

The girls shook their heads in unison.

"Do you think the Army corporal's involved?" Bunty asked.

"Do you?"

"Glory, I've no idea. All we know is that he's called Ken and stationed somewhere towards Barnstaple."

"How old?"

"Older than us. Early thirties perhaps."

"And . . .?"

"That's all. Cilla told you the rest."

Bob waited a few moments for further revelations then said, "As you both know the boy you call Greville, would you come down to Bideford with us to identify the body? Just to confirm we've got the right man."

"Why can't Slattery do it?" Cilla snapped.

"Because we don't know where he is," Bob replied quietly.

Cilla bit her lip and Bunty said, "Heavens! You don't think it was him who shot Greville?"

"It's not impossible."

Cilla and Bunty exchanged glances again then Bunty nodded.

"All right, we'll come if we have to," Cilla said reluctantly.

"We need to do a few things before we can go," Bunty added. "The ewes are penned ready for market. We'll have to let them out again if Mr Slattery or Greville aren't going to take them tomorrow."

"By the way," Bob said, "whose scarf is it? I put it on the dresser there."

Cilla picked it up. "I wouldn't wear a thing like this if you paid me."

"Not mine," said Bunty. "Wrong colour for me."

***

# Chapter 15

Once they were out of the way, Bob looked at Laurie and said, "Right, time for a shufty upstairs, see if the old devil has sneaked back in without anyone noticing. Ready?"

There were five bedrooms. Two on the front were occupied – or had been. Laurie went into the room the boy had been using. It had always been a boy's room by the look of it: *A Boys' Compendium of Adventure Stories* and copies of Ballantyne and Stevenson on the shelf over the bed were old editions. He pulled them out one by one, disturbing years of dust, and flipped to the fly leaf of each looking for a name. The first page of the compendium had a space for the owner to write in his name: 'This book is the property of: *Josiah Slattery*'. The next book belonged to a Joseph Slattery; the son killed in the tractor incident.

Laurie put it back and crossed the room to the window. Something clicked under a foot. It was a metal bib clip on a pair of dungarees left dangling over a chair. He checked the pockets: a filthy handkerchief in the trousers, and four used shot gun cartridges in the bib. He tucked them into one of his own pockets, then turned to some clothes dumped at the end of the bed. A bus ticket for an Exeter omnibus company and a ticket for an Odeon Cinema, nothing else. Nothing with a name on it. On the bedside table there was a motorcycling magazine, though. Under that, bingo! a postcard of Dawlish Warren for Mr Greville Healey.

*Having a lovely day on the sands. Wish you were here, Mum.*

"We've got him, Sarge," Laurie called. "The boy here is definitely Greville Healey. He likes shotguns and motorbikes, and he's got a mother, too. Somewhere."

Bob joined Laurie on the landing and studied the postcard, which he stuffed into his jacket pocket before returning to the main bedroom, looking for signs of a woman, in case the female corpse they'd found wasn't Mrs Slattery, although he knew in his gut she was. The big question was how had Josiah Slattery kept his wife's death secret from the boy, who was apparently related to the family? Or was it that, being young, he simply wasn't interested in an absent elderly wife?

There was only one pillow on the bolster of the double bed, but a chest of drawers contained female underwear and cardigans, confirming his worst fears. Old man Slattery had either left his wife to die alone at Hentree, or moved her body there to avoid losing his claim to her family's property.

"Anything for you, Sarge?" Laurie asked as he exited a small room over the kitchen.

"Nothing much, except Josiah Slattery lives here. You?"

"The room over the kitchen was a girl's, I think. But there's nothing there now, no clothes, no books, dolls or anything like that."

"But you think it was a girl's room, once?"

"Flowery curtains." He shrugged, "Only a feeling."

"Feelings are good enough for me. Fits with the Ada cards at Hentree, anyway. Except," he paused, remembering the cards were addressed to Hentree Farm, not Ridgeway. Had Mr and Mrs Slattery maintained separate households?

"Except, what, Sarge?" Laurie queried.

Bob scratched his chin then said, "Nah, I'll work it out later. You reckon there's a missing girl as well then, do you?"

"Maybe."

"Perhaps that was her room before she got married. I'll give it a glance over, see if you missed anything, not that I think you have but I'll double-check. You go down and make a start on the outhouses, and if Bunty or Cilla want to tell you anything, let them. I'll have another look at Slattery's paperwork downstairs as well, so take your time."

Laurie left and Bob had a nose around the girl's bedroom, but there was nothing there of any use – except perhaps that the room had been deliberately stripped of her belongings. He went to the window to have a look below. Behind the left-hand curtain was a china figurine: a girl dancing with a small dog at her heels. Bob felt a tug of abject sadness. It didn't do to get involved emotionally – ever – under any circumstance. But this, for some reason, touched a heart string. He glanced out of the window and saw Cilla pulling up radishes in the kitchen garden. "Something tasty for supper, eh?" he said, and went downstairs.

The study was exactly as he'd last seen it: tins and cardboard boxes containing unpaid bills going back months, numerous buff envelopes from the Ministry of Agriculture and a series of increasingly demanding letters from the local Agricultural Committee. All emphasising what Cilla had told him. Then he noticed a long, thick envelope stashed behind a box for shotgun cartridges. He pulled it out. In the top left-hand corner was a firm's name: Didcot, Lissman, Lester and Hook. It was addressed to Josiah Slattery Esq.

There was a noise from outside. Bob slipped it back, intending to return for it later, and wandered into the yard to see what was going on. Laurie was emerging from a wooden lean-to structure against the large barn.

"Come and look at this, Sarge," he said.

Bob followed him into an ill-lit, tumbledown tool shed. Once upon a time it had been an organised workspace with a bench for cleaning implements and stones for sharpening scythes. The scythes now hung at odd angles from loose hooks; spades without handles and broken tree-branch hay forks had been left propped along a wall. There was an ancient wooden wheelbarrow wheel but no barrow; two steel bands from a barrel but no barrel; the head of an axe but no means of using it.

"What a shambles," Bob huffed. "What am I supposed to be looking at?"

"All this." Laurie stretched a hand to indicate the tools.

"So – bad management. What?"

"Look closer, Sarge. Bunty says she told Slattery about the 'saucepans for Spitfires' initiative, how everyone is being asked to hand in any old, unwanted surplus metal goods to be melted down in factories, and he flew into an absolute rage. She says it's like he doesn't participate in our world at all."

Bob was silent for a moment. The girls here knew him, had talked to him: he sent livestock and produce to market, and must occasionally do food shopping, but that was the limit of his social existence. At least, Bob thought, with a small jolt of satisfaction, at least it proved the man was real – that he hadn't imagined the incident at Hentree Farm. "Still no sign of the farmer, I suppose?" he asked, leaving the shed.

"Not a hint, Sarge."

As they crossed the yard, Bob caught a sound. "Was that a car?" he asked.

Laurie frowned. "Might have been Bunty with the tractor and trailer."

Bob listened again. "Maybe. I've got the fidgets, that's all." Casting about him, he realised he'd forgotten to ask about hungry dogs. "What are we missing here, do you think? Where's Slattery got to?"

"Must have gone to relatives." Laurie replied. "If he was injured, maybe he went to someone who'd look after him."

"'Course he would, yes! But have you seen any cottages between here and Hentree?"

Laurie shook his head. "The nearest place is Mrs Lee's."

"That's what I'm thinking. Go and find those girls again. Ask them about any relatives in the area."

Laurie loped off in the direction of bleating sheep and Bob wandered back into the house. He checked the drawers in the kitchen dresser, then went back to the sitting room, hunting for photographs or greetings cards. In the bureau drawer there were three sepia tinted photographs, each featuring a tall patriarch standing beside a good-looking woman in Edwardian clothing. In one she was holding a small boy on her lap. Bob peered at the father figure, upright, austere; an educated man, no country bumpkin in his Sunday best, this. There was no suggestion of relatives anywhere.

He went back to the office for the solicitor's envelope.

It wasn't there.

He reached around the edge of the table, looked to see if it had fallen on the floor. Double-checked behind the cartridge box. There was nothing there. The letter from Didcot, Lissman, Lester and Hook for Josiah Slattery Esquire had disappeared.

Bob checked his jacket pockets. Had he picked it up? No, he hadn't picked it up, and it wouldn't fit into a jacket pocket anyway. He lifted out the cartridge box and looked underneath it. Not there. He went into the kitchen, retraced his steps upstairs. Nothing.

So, it wasn't a question of short-term recall – he hadn't picked it up and put it down somewhere, like mislaying his car keys – the envelope and its contents had been taken. He *had* heard a vehicle when he was in the yard. His thoughts flew to the army corporal, but as he raced through the house looking for Cilla, Laurie came in through the back door with Bunty.

"Have you been back in here?" he demanded. "Have you taken anything from the office?" He pointed behind him.

Bunty looked at Laurie, confused. "No. We've been busy outdoors. You know we have."

Ignoring her, Bob rushed towards the front door and yanked it open. It opened so easily he nearly fell backwards. "Someone's been in," he said. "Just now. Some bugger's used a key and come in through the front door!"

"It might have been that lady," Bunty suggested.

"What lady? The egg woman?"

"Egg woman? There's no egg woman that I know about."

"What woman then?"

"I really can't say," Bunty responded primly, standing to her full height and remembering her social class and upbringing in the face of rudeness. "I only saw her once. Well dressed. Parked a car down the track. Probably someone from the council, or one of the women who organise the evacuees. God help them if they send children here, poor little mites."

Bob turned and scuttled into the kitchen. The headscarf had gone too.

Bob waited impatiently while the Land Army girls climbed into the back of his Morris, and Laurie, playing Lochinvar, closed Bunty's door. As he manoeuvred out of the yard, Bob peered over the steering wheel for any signs of a vehicle that might have come only so far up the track, and had to do a sharp three-point turn to get back to civilisation. The track was littered with puddles and shiny damp stones but there was no readily visible sign that a car had pulled off the track or had even reversed back the way it had come. "Bugger, it's open," he said as they reached the gate to the lanes, thumping a fist against the steering wheel.

"What's up, Sarge?" Laurie asked quietly.

"I thought I heard a car on the track earlier."

"Maybe you did," Laurie replied. "Did you shut the gate behind you when you followed us up?" he asked, turning to the girls in the backseat.

"There's no need to," Bunty replied. "No livestock can get out this way."

"We might as well leave it open as well, then," Bob grunted and drove out onto the tarmac.

The two girls sat in grim silence all the way down to Bideford. When they got there, Bob drew up in a side street and tapped Laurie on the arm. "You get out here. Go into the council office and ask for Births, Marriages and Deaths. Get in there yourself and look up Slattery while I take the girls up to the hospital mortuary. Go back fifty years, maybe more. Find Josiah Slattery's marriage and see what you can find about the wife and any relatives nearby."

Laurie scrambled out of the car, and Bob and the two young women continued their sombre journey. Identifying Greville Healey took only a matter of minutes but left the girls a lot more distressed than Bob had expected.

***

# Chapter 16

After leaving two very subdued Land Army girls back at Ridgeway Farm, Bob returned to Bideford Police Station to write up his day's report. Half an hour later, Laurie joined him.

Bob was examining their finds from his knapsack and pockets. Two metal buttons, dented; a suspender clip for dungarees; a strip of torn green cotton material; one jointed photograph frame containing two studio photographs; a postcard from Dawlish Warren. Laurie added the used shotgun cartridges and the cinema and bus tickets from his pocket, then picked up the double photograph frame. "She is you know, like Claudette Colbert. Very attractive. Probably a bit younger than me when it was taken. Shouldn't we find the photographer, see when it was taken?"

"We should. Go on," Bob said. "What else?"

"Well, I don't know about the clothes, but she took pride in her appearance judging from her hair. And what a smile. It reminds me of someone: a girl at a dance perhaps. The baby's a boy. Plump, well-cared for, well-fed; looks normal to me. Dark hair like his mother. Dimples."

Bob stared at the young mother, but the stark bones of an old woman's face were seared into his eyelids. He sighed and pushed the evidence to one side. "Right, DC Oliver, tell me what you've learned about the Slattery clan."

Laurie frowned. "Nothing much, to be honest. There's no local clan anyway – that I could find."

"Never mind, run through it. I need an idea of the Slattery family tree to start with."

"There are no records for Josiah Slattery's parents, but his marriage to a Martha Pascoe was registered in May, 1890. They had a son called Joseph, 1893 and a daughter called Ada, 1895. I think the son is the one whose books I found at Ridgeway – along with some that might have been his father's when he was a boy. Joseph Slattery died in 1930. He must be the one Mrs Lee said was killed in a tractor accident, although . . ."

"Although?"

"Well, the farms look so mean, like money's never been spent on them, yet they had a modern tractor with an engine in 1930."

"Perhaps the son was a modern, forward thinking type.

"Any marriage certificate for Joseph?"

"Not that I located, no."

"Hmm – go on."

"The daughter Ada married a David James Beere in 1914. There's no more mention of them, and there's no record of Mrs Martha Slattery after that either."

"But we think she's the one in the bed."

Laurie nodded, "The age matches. She had white hair so she must have been old."

"Or old before her time. That Hentree farmhouse feels like Misery Mansion to me. Any indication that the Pascoe family still own Hentree Farm?"

"Not that I saw, but a Mervyn Pascoe passed away in 1910 and his wife two years later, so unless there's offspring I haven't found, it looks as if their daughter Martha inherited Hentree."

"Meaning Martha's husband got two farms to work. Can't have been easy with only one son and then all the local boys off to war and not coming back. So why don't the Land Girls or Mrs

Lee have any respect for Mr Slattery? They all despise him from what they've been telling us."

"But that's only hearsay, Sarge, we can't use that can we?"

"We can while we've got nothing else. Hearsay usually carries a lump of disagreeable truth. Never overlook hearsay, even when you can't use it in evidence. Anything else?"

"No, sorry, that's it, more or less. It's like that tool shed, isn't it?"

"Eh?"

"Everything shoddy and jumbled together. Nothing that's of any real use." Laurie caught Bob's expression and gave one of his embarrassed shrugs. "It's a sort of metaphor, Sarge."

Bob got to his feet, "If you say so. Anything else?"

"Only that . . ."

"Mm?"

"That shouldn't the police here start a proper search for Mr Slattery? At least find evidence that it was him at Hentree?"

Bob squinted at the boy, "What are trying to say?"

Laurie cleared his throat, "Well, how can we be sure the old man you saw at Hentree was actually Mr Slattery?"

Bob looked up at Laurie with quiet respect. "You're not wrong, lad: he's the likely owner of two farms and can't be located in either, but will finding him help us find the boy's killer, eh?" Bob huffed and shuffled his handwritten report pages into a cardboard folder. After a moment or two he said, "Hentree – seems like a good name to me. Whole bloody thing is chicken and egg."

"That's a metaphor, Sarge," Laurie grinned.

Bob deliberately ignored him. "The boy, Greville Healey from Exeter, did you find anything on his family? Were his parents local?"

Laurie bit his lip, "Sorry, Sarge, I was focusing on the Slattery connections."

"And the name Healey doesn't link to it? Well that tells us something, I suppose. Healey doesn't match the daughter's husband so he's almost certainly not a Slattery grandson. Ada Slattery married David James Beere in 1914, you say."

"Yes. His home address was Barnstaple, occupation carpenter. Perhaps he was killed in the war and she re-married a Healey. No – no wait, Sarge. *Healey, Healey*: I wasn't taking notes, but didn't Mrs Lee say something about a sister-in-law who moved to Exeter?"

"She did and we need to talk to her again anyway. That lady wasn't giving us an altogether true account. There was something missing, something not right in all that bluster."

"How do you know, Sarge?"

"Years of bloody experience," Bob grunted and propped the folder against DC West's typewriter. "Right, shove all that stuff back in the knapsack and let's get on our way."

As they were leaving the empty police station Bob went up to the desk, "Any news on the kiddy?" he asked.

"Not yet," the uniformed sergeant replied. "But the older brother has confessed that she wanted to play with him and followed him down to the river with his pals, so they've ruled out foul play or an abduction – for now."

"Small mercy," Bob replied. "Tell DC West we were here. I've left my notes on his desk." Then he added meaningfully, "He knows where to find me," and watched the uniform sergeant respond with a very small twitch of his lips.

As they walked along the quay Bob said, "I'll go out to Larkham Cross and find the grocers for Slattery's rations this afternoon. Village shopkeepers usually enjoy a chat about their customers. Then I might go to church and have a peek in the marriage and funeral registers. You get your bike out. Check doctors' surgeries and chemists, see if anyone has brought Slattery into town for treatment. I asked at the hospital while we were there earlier. Nobody knew anything about an injured farmer. If you don't get any joy, go and talk to Mr and Mrs Lee. Get them to tell you everything they know about the grandson and the nephew. Find out how long Jack Lee worked for Slattery, why he left and what he knows. See if the wife has a key for either or both of the houses, and if she can drive a car."

"That's proper plain clothes stuff, Sarge, I'm –"

"Old enough and ugly enough."

"You want to know where Mr Slattery might have gone to, what family are around –"

"And who should inherit the farms," Bob added.

"Got it."

"But whoever it is, they'll need Mr Slattery's death certificate first."

"For which they need a body."

"Exactly. Right now, though, *we* need some food. Let's see if Mr Pots can rustle up some sandwiches for us."

Mr Pots greeted them with his usual vacant expression but became markedly more genial when they requested sandwiches.

"Got some meat paste like pat-tay chilling on the slab in the pantry. Made it this morning," he said in his gruff Devonian accent. "Like proper French stuff, it is. Left-over pork bits and a special secret ingredient –"

"That's fine," Bob held up a warning hand, a sixth sense telling him he really didn't want to know what was in the pâté if it was like 'proper French stuff'. "We'll go and sit outside, give us a call when it's ready."

Mr Pots delivered their sandwiches to them on the front terrace along with home-made ginger beer and stood gawping at them as they took their first bite.

"Delicious," Bob confirmed. And it was. Freshly baked bread with a soft, savoury filling.

After they had finished, Bob went up to his room 'to check a few things', but in reality, to take a short nap. He was worn out. The nap took a little longer than he planned and then it took a few minutes more to get his bearings. Still feeling groggy, he opened the sash window and leaned out to get some fresh air. Someone was parking a car behind his. The lovely Jessamyn Flowers. Banging his head on the window frame, Bob got out of sight as fast as he could then stayed behind the curtain, noting the manner she stood at the open gate staring up at the Edwardian houses as he had done a few days before. She then went up the steps to Number Two and disappeared from view.

Bob tugged on his creased linen jacket and trundled downstairs. Lanky, lean and hatless, Laurie Oliver was still at the outdoor table. Sitting in the chair Bob had vacated was the very pretty Suky Stefano, wearing a neat flowery dress with a little pink hat and matching gloves. Seeing his boss, Laurie jumped to his feet. The girl touched his arm and he bent down to hear what she wanted to say. Whatever it was it made him smile. Bob thought he might be blushing as well, but was distracted by the minx in the pink hat sidling past him into the house with a carefree "Have a pleasant afternoon, Mr Robbins."

"Been to a wedding, has she?" Bob asked.

"No, to the bank, she's been to collect her allowance," Laurie replied. "Do you know, the theatre group only pay her board and lodge; she relies on an allowance from her grandfather."

"Because her parents don't approve of what she's doing."

"How do you know that?" Laurie asked watching Bob search his pockets for his car keys.

"Would you, if you were her papa?"

"She's following her dream. She wants to be in light opera."

"Following her dream!" Bob scoffed. "The world's at war and she's singing in village halls. She ought to be doing something useful – ATS, ambulance driver, school teacher. They're an odd bunch, these theatricals. I wouldn't want a daughter of mine mixing with them."

"They are being useful. They're entertaining folk around the county, bringing smiles to faces, raising morale. Village people can't get to the cinema here, not like in a big town. She says I look like Jimmy Stewart, the Hollywood actor."

"Does she indeed? Tell her how much a British bobby earns, see if she changes her mind. Before you do that, though, nip up to Rose and get my keys. I think they're on the wash stand."

Laurie grinned and raced up the steps after Suky Stefano. It took him a while to find the keys and come back downstairs.

***

# Chapter 17

The village of Larkham Cross huddled around an ancient Celtic cross at the junction of three roads going nowhere in particular. Thatched cottages, their roofs reaching down to the pavement in some places, lined the streets for a short distance before the streets turned back into country lanes. It was postcard picturesque.

Bob parked his Morris near the cross, went up to it to take a closer look then wandered into the tiny church. There was an attractive horseshoe porch, and a sturdy arched door opened into a welcoming gloom. The nave was ancient and empty. Picking up a pamphlet from a folding table by the main door, he wandered down the aisle, staring up at the roof beams with their carvings of angels and demons, oak leaves, acorns, small birds and vipers; here and there a sheaf of wheat, a branch of apples, sheep and lambs, then more grotesque faces.

This was what medieval worshippers gazed at during incomprehensible Latin services then, later, during Protestant vicars' sermons in English. Had the men who carved the figures been thinking of Heaven and Hell, or of the countryside around them? Had they been told to do this, or was it their way of warning their loved ones that in among the good things of life lurked temptation, sin and diabolical trouble?

He turned his attention to the pamphlet. The church had been *rebuilt* by the Normans in 1120 because the original wooden structure was burnt to the ground by Vikings, who subsequently adopted Christianity. Larkham fields had been growing food for local families for centuries upon centuries. In the village itself there would have been a blacksmith for their workhorses; a stonemason for their tombstones; a baker providing food for the table and the soul at Mass; a candle-maker to light their prayers on winter nights . . . century upon century. The families lying under the sanctified ground outside had been here then, and as sure as they prayed to God on the sabbath, many names lived on nearby. Bob gave an involuntary sigh. This was the problem with small rural communities: everybody knew everybody, and squabbles could continue through generations, but when it came to telling an outsider what was going on, they'd clam up as one.

Bob went back to the pamphlet: 'The rood screen is unique in Devonshire. It escaped destruction by Cromwell's men during the Civil War. . . The aisle floor includes a Cornish slate memorial to the Carhew Family, squires of Larkham since 1500 . . .' He looked down at the uneven flagstones, wondering how many Carhew corpses lay beneath. A door opened and closed. Two women entered bearing flowers in cheap metal vases. He sank into the nearest pew and bowed his head as if in prayer. They didn't notice him and carried on their conversation about a Mrs Somebody or other whose daughter was no better than she should be.

"Well she's not the first round here. *That* we do know. Won't be the last while they American boys be yer neither I 'spect," said the woman wearing a straw hat with daisies, and a wrap-around apron.

"He's going to marry her, though. They came to see Hubert last week." The second matron in twinset and pearls, possibly the vicar's wife, placed her vase of Michaelmas daisies on the pulpit and tweaked at a few flower heads.

"Which is all very well and as it should be," daisy hat replied, "but having all these boys in their fancy uniforms is changing our community. Have you heard the music they play at the church hall of a Saturday? 'Jivin' about' they call it. You've never seen the like. Girls jiggling about with no shame." Daisy hat had got the bit between her teeth. "It's bad enough having the government tellin' us what to do with our land and how much food to eat, without dealing with strangers on every corner. My Bert says your land's not your own no more."

"It is for a very good reason, you know."

Daisy hat gave a heartfelt sigh and whisked a duster from her pinny. Wafting it along the back of a pew, she caught sight of Bob. "Beg pardon," she muttered and hastened to her companion.

The women finished their tasks and left in silence. Bob stayed where he was adding their titbits of local information to the Hentree jigsaw puzzle. What the women were discussing illustrated the closed nature of the Larkham community. He had been right to ask Laurie to stay in civvies, and right to think that asking questions about the Slattery family would need something of a sideways approach.

Except he wasn't going to find anyone to chat to, lingering here. The vicar wasn't around, and there was no sign of church registers to peruse, either. He dropped a threepenny bit in the 'voluntary contributions' tin by the pamphlets and opened the heavy door.

Outside, bright sunshine made him squint and he stayed in the porch until his eyes adjusted then took a stroll around the cemetery, looking for Slattery graves. Among the long, unkempt grass and hollyhocks there were numerous Pascoe tombstones edged with lichen, some leaning sideways, some polished smooth by the Atlantic rain – until the 1900s. Their names and dates consolidated what Laurie had told him. The only Slattery grave, however, was on the far side of churchyard – as if its occupant did not belong. A plain piece of granite was inscribed with the words 'Adelina Slattery (1835 – 1875) Wife of Joseph and mother to Josiah'.

Bob shook his head at the implicit sadness then tried to do a bit of mental arithmetic. Assuming Josiah was now in his seventies, he might still have been a child when his mother died, and if, as the contents of the Ridgeway drawing room suggested, his father, Joseph, had come to North Devon from elsewhere, the widower very likely had no one to turn to in his grief. But where had the patriarch Joseph Slattery been buried if not with his wife? And where was his grandson, also named Joseph, who had died in a tractor accident? Why wasn't he here either?

Leaving the churchyard behind him, Bob chose a street at random, peering at shop windows to see which was the grocer's. Apart from locating the shop, he also needed shaving lather and new underwear or he'd have to go back to Cready for more clothes.

'Evans and Hook', turned out to be the General Store. The doorbell tinkled and Bob returned to an ecclesiastical gloom. Waiting once more for his eyes to adjust, he slowly took in shelves of paint and peas, soap boxes and tubes of talcum powder, babies' bottles and hot water bottles. Lined up beneath one counter was a row of gumboots and galoshes. On the other counter he was pleased to see a display of socks and vests, women's aprons and men's overalls. As he crossed the wooden floorboards to select his socks, an elderly man in a Fair Isle jerkin appeared out of the back room.

"Afternoon, sir."

"Good afternoon. I need some socks if you've got my size." Bob fished in his jacket pocket for his clothing coupons.

"Cotton or wool, sir?"

Bob explained what he needed, deciding to let the shopkeeper assume he was a holidaymaker who was staying longer than planned before he revealed his real reason for being there.

"If you'm in need of more things, sir, we got a second-hand department here now. My daughter set it up, what with all these coupons and not being able to get what we want in Bideford and the like. Very old town, Bideford. Lot of history in these parts."

"There is. I was in your church –"

"Prettiest church in Devonshire. Old as the Bible itself."

Bob warmed to the old man and let him ramble on about the area, about what had happened to the Carhew family in Queen Victoria's time, and what was going on at a place called Daneman Court, where there were 'arty folk and vurriners'.

"Your family has been here for generations, I can see." Bob tried to lead the chatter to local families but was curtailed as the old man led him into a back room full of clothing. Men's jackets and suits hung from one rail; women's frocks and blouses from another. Behind them was a table crowded with shoes and boots. It smelled like a jumble sale but Bob revised his opinion immediately as the old man selected a navy serge suit and held it out to him. "Mr Hennessey brought this in. Says he can't get into half his clothes no more and we best have them so others get the benefit." Bob tried to respond but the salesman had found his pitch. "Mr Hennessey plays the organ for our weddings and funerals. He was a proper musician in London. In a proper *hor-ce-stra*," he added with emphasis. "Got all sorts of fine things in his new bungalow. I've been there. Very nice. Very modern. If you like that kind of thing. We don't get much call for being modern down yer as a rule."

Listening with half an ear, Bob slipped off his rumpled jacket and tried on the serge suit jacket.

"Could have been made for you, sir."

"Is there somewhere I can try on the trousers?"

"I'll shut the door into the shop. Nobody'll come in from the kitchen."

Bob had one leg out of his own trousers when the latch to a door leading from the kitchen was lifted and a toddler wearing nothing but a red woolly sweater and a pair of tiny gumboots trotted through to the shop door. He struggled for a moment with the latch to that, then raced into the shop.

"Catch him, Dad," yelled a woman running after him. "Quick or he'll piddle in they wellingtons again."

Bob got his leg back into his trousers but not before nearly toppling over and sending the men's clothing rail to the floor.

There was a muffled silence as the woman wearing a headscarf as a turban pulled the rail upright. "Lord almighty," she gasped, "there's a man yer."

"Course there is, you daft woman! He's trying on Mr Hennessey's suit." The shopkeeper poked his head around the shop door, "So sorry, sir. I'll put you to rights dreckly. We just got to catch Eddie first."

"Too late," the woman cried. "Edward, stop that now. You hear me!"

Bob tried not to smile and sat on a chair beside the shoe table to collect his breath.

The woman reappeared with a giggling Edward bundled under her left arm. "Sorry about this, sir. We're s'posed to be looking after him for my daughter Joyce, but he's such a handful and I'm not as quick as I was. Runs me ragged, he does." She gave a heartfelt sigh and returned to the kitchen, shutting the door firmly behind her.

Bob decided the trousers were a bit long in the leg but were worth having if he got a pair of decent braces. He then selected a couple of good shirts. As he put the clothing on the counter, he checked the maker's label in the jacket: Savile Row. More than pleased, he paid what the old man asked then re-initiated the conversation about the local area, but this time explained why he was asking and showed the old man his police identity card. The shopkeeper went quiet so Bob said, “Three generations then, in this shop. That’s something you don’t see often.”

“Four if you count young Edward,” the shopkeeper responded proudly. “I don’t ’spect to live to see it, but he’ll have it one day.”

“Are you Mr Evans or Mr Hook?”

“Evans, sir. Mervyn Evans. There’s been no Mr Hook since 1910. You’ll not be writing down what I say, will you, sir?”

“No need for that, but anything you can tell me about Hentree and Ridgeway Farm will be useful.”

“Ah, well, it’s true then?” Mr Evans relaxed. “I did hear about that business down at Hentree in the Star and Anchor last night. Young Greville, they said. Bad lot that boy, but . . . Well, not for me to say.”

“Actually, sir, I’d be very grateful if you would.”

Mervyn Evans grimaced, “Yes, well, if I must. . . Jack Lee says the Pascoe land is up for sale, but I can’t believe that. Josiah Slattery selling Hentree? I don’t believe it. It b’ain’t his to sell. It’s Pascoe land, see.” He began folding a shirt, ready to wrap in brown paper. “Josiah’s got no son to pass it on to now, though, and Quentin’s long gone, so if he needs cash . . .”

“Quentin?” Bob snapped to attention.

“Josiah Slattery’s daughter’s boy. Ada – the daughter – left him with her mother – ooh, it’s a good while ago now. Water under the bridge. Her husband got killed in France in the trenches, and . . .” He tutted and shook his head. “Sad business. I can’t say what happened ’zactly, but she left her boy with her mother, bit like my granddaughter Joyce is doing with her

Edward, 'cept she's doing it because of the war and comes home of an evening to put to him to bed."

"And Ada Slattery didn't return for her son?"

"That she did not, sir. Proper ol' scandal it was. And him growing up a tearaway." Mervyn Evans shook his head as if the abandoned child had belonged to his own family.

"And Josiah Slattery was married to . . .?" Bob prompted, going back a generation.

"Martha Pascoe. Too good for him by half. They'll all tell you that."

"Martha Pascoe?"

"She who married Josiah – Lor' knows why. Martha's a kind, good person. Help anyone, Martha would. Kind and thoughtful. Was a time I thought of courting her myself back in those days, but Josiah would have wrung my neck and I was never one for a ruckus. Can't be easy for her now, poor maid, being bedridden and having to rely on him for everything."

Bob nodded, not ready to mention just yet that Mrs Slattery was more than just bedridden. "When did you last see him? Mr Slattery that is."

"Oooh, two, three weeks ago now. That Greville gets their sugar and cooking fats, and his broken biscuits. I knock them down a lower price see, the broken ones. A nice young lady came in last week for soap, though, now I come to think of it. Land Army. Working at Ridgeway. That'll be a help for him I says, more like a hindrance, she said. She was laughing but it can't be easy, Josiah Slattery doesn't want nobody in his house. They're a private lot, the Slatterys, his father was the same, I remember."

"What about Mrs Slattery's rations?" Bob interrupted.

"I don't follow, sir? She can't get about. Someone has to get them for her."

"Ah, yes," Bob nodded and waited for Mr Evans to continue what he was about to say.

The elderly shopkeeper had lost his thread but soon began again with, "I wonder what'll they'll do now Greville's gone. Oh, that's a *very* strange business."

"Could there have been ill-feeling between Greville and the Land Army girls, do you think?"

"No! The one who came here was a proper young lady. Very polite. Who'd come and shoot Greville, anyway? Must a been a haccident. Poachers after rabbits. Some was saying last night as how he could have shot hisself, him being so handy with a shotgun. Or – now here's a thought – could it have been they G.I. fellows out practising and Greville got in the way? Not that they should a been on Hentree land but they'm all Yankees, they don't know diffen-rence between a field of teddies and the great Prairies, they don't."

Bob considered the possibility Greville might have upset someone from the army camp. "Did Greville socialise with the Americans, go for a drink with them perhaps, do you know?"

"I couldn't say, sir."

"Greville was Mr Slattery's nephew, wasn't he? He'd come to help out?"

"Greville's not a Slattery, no, he's Davy Beere's sister's boy, far as I know. Davy Beere was the one got hisself killed by Germans in France. From Barnstaple, he was. Courted Ada Slattery when he came to do some carpentry work here in Larkham back in '14. His family are all Barnstaple folk, but he got on all right yer."

"And Davy Beere married Ada?"

"During the war, yes. Quiet do, in Bideford – the Slattery family not being Church, nor the Beeres neither. Non-conformists, they were. But proper. They lived at Hentree after that. Davy's father was a policeman. There was a boat accident a few years ago. I remember reading about it and thinking that was Davy Beere's dad. Killed the week before retirement he was, trying to save some daft bloody holidaymakers from drownin'."

"Shame." Bob waited to see if there was anything more about the Beeres of Barnstaple. There wasn't, so he helped the old man wrap his new clothes into a parcel.

As the shopkeeper handed it to him, he said, "Josiah and me was at school together. Sixty year ago, now. We'm long past retiring, I s'pose. Josiah's been managing on his own for years, since Young Joe died. Terrible sad that was, but not like this business with that Greville boy." He suddenly went to the linking door and shouted, "Peggy! That Greville's a Beere boy as well, isn't he?"

Peggy appeared with her grandson squirming in her arms. She looked weary. Not surprising Bob thought, caring for her father and her grandson, and probably housing and feeding her daughter as well. There was a family story here too.

"That's right. Davy Beere's sister's boy," she said. "His mother's Sheila Beere: Sheila Healey she is now. Davy Beere married Martha Pascoe's girl, the one who went to London, remember?" Peggy settled her grandson on the edge of the counter and turned to Bob, "She's had a hard life, Martha has. I know what it's like now, looking after a little one and trying to manage everything else. Poor woman stuck up there on her own, no visitors, no friends. Josiah Slattery's seen to that. That's the trouble with folk who b'ain't neither Church nor Chapel, they don't have social occasions like we do, and he won't let none of us help. We can't even send an apple pie."

"You don't happen to know where Greville's family live do you?"

Peggy looked at her father who muttered as an explanation, "Police matter. He's a police detective."

The woman's eyes widened. "I can't say 'zactly. I think they're in Exeter. Sheila Beere, as she was, went for a housemaid in a big house in Exeter. The boy's ration book said St Thomas, Exeter, so that's where they'll be livin' now I should think. Is it true then, that Greville's been shot with a gun?" She smoothed the child's curls and smiled at him as if to protect him from what the adults were discussing. "I can't hardly believe it, such a thing happening down yer."

"This gentleman says Hentree's up for sale, like they said," her father informed her. Bob didn't recall saying anything of the sort but let it go.

"That's no surprise," Peggy responded. "Old Josiah can't manage up there on his own. Quentin was no use and now this Greville boy gone . . . difficult days for us all." She huffed as if the weight of the world and responsibility for its housekeeping were on her shoulders then gathered the boy up again. "Time I was feeding Edward his tea, Dad. You close up, will you?"

Bob wanted to ask about Quentin but took it as a dismissal, paid for his new wardrobe and left, intending to return as soon as possible. He wandered down the street lost in thought: word had got around that Greville had been killed, but not a word had been said about the possibility Josiah was involved. Then he cursed himself for not asking more about Quentin being a tearaway when it was mentioned.

Was it possible? Was the Quentin he had overheard at Peony Villas a Slattery?

Was Jessamyn Flowers, who had once been Pearl Pascoe in ribbons, the girl who'd run off to London leaving a baby boy behind? What had caused such a drastic action: had she been following her dream, as Laurie put it, or was there something more sinister behind it all? Something that might later cause her son to become a 'tearaway'? That's if the Ken who visited Ridgeway Farm turned out to be the Quentin Mr Evans had described. He somehow knew it would be, but on a very personal level, desperately hoped it wouldn't. Either way, he needed to find Mrs Flowers for a private chat.

Laurie was waiting on the front terrace when Bob got back to Peony Villas.

"Not here," Bob said before the boy could say anything. "Come up to my room."

As they went into Rose, Laurie let out a quiet whistle of appreciation, "Nice room, Sarge."

"Better than your Honeysuckle, yes," Bob replied, setting his parcel on top of his chest of drawers.

"I've no complaints about Honeysuckle," Laurie said, "heaps better than a school dorm."

"I should hope so. Right, tell me about Mr and Mrs Lee."

Laurie sat on the end of the double bed, flipped open his notebook and began, "Mr John William Lee, aged 53, born in Gloucester, son of . . ."

Bob gave Laurie time to recite Lee's biography, waiting to see if he'd asked the one key question that needed answering. He had.

"Mr and Mrs Lee have a regular stall at the Barnstaple pannier market on a Friday. Last Friday was their wedding anniversary and they stayed there for their midday meal. They've got a twelve-year-old evacuee from Birmingham called Ronnie – he was with them because he's still on school holiday. He recited what each of them had to eat and told me they didn't get back to the smallholding until late in the afternoon. They spent the rest of evening doing a jigsaw and listening to the wireless."

Bob gave a paternal grin of satisfaction, "And this is important because Mr Lee . . .?"

"Was sacked by Josiah Slattery for criticising his animal husbandry. He could have had a grudge. He does in fact hold a grudge, but mostly because he says the man's inherently cruel."

"'Inherently cruel' – his words or yours?"

Laurie grimaced, "Mine. Sorry."

"That's all right. Put it in a report for me, but use his words. Handwritten will do. I'll put it in our folder down at the station. That'll show them."

"Show them what, Sarge?"

"That we're not a couple of Cornish clodhoppers," Bob huffed. "Have the Lees seen anything of our missing farmer?"

"No, and they say he hasn't got any family in the area, either."

"What about Greville Healey? Anything?"

"No, they've never had any contact with Greville. Like Mrs Lee told us before, not even a 'good morning'. And they both think Mrs Slattery is bedridden and living at Ridgeway."

Bob pushed a hand through his bristly white hair, wondering if the boy had missed anything. Finding nothing to add, he crossed the room and extended his hand.

Laurie got to his feet. "What, Sarge?"

"Nothing, you've done very well. I wanted to shake your hand, that's all."

"Oh, oh, that's all right, then!" Laurie responded with such gusto Bob had to pull his hand away. "So, there's nothing else, Sarge?"

"Not that I can think of."

"Can I have tomorrow night off then, please?"

"'Course you can. Got a date, have you?"

"Hope so."

***

# Chapter 18

**Tuesday**

Of late, and due to living in the limited environment of what she considered a country-bumpkin town, Estelle Dobson, the esteemed contralto currently reduced to performing with the Wayward Players theatrical troupe, had restricted herself to pilfering only small *objets d'art*. Small *objets d'art* were essential for what she thought of as the next stage (pun intended) in her life: Exquisite Antiques. It was to be a charming little emporium in one of the more accessible side streets of a better sort of day-tripper location. Winchester, or Leamington Spa, or Dorchester; she was very fond of Thomas Hardy's novels. Somewhere she could join the county set and Horace could sing in the choir, which would keep him busy, *if* she allowed him to come with her. The decision was pending, not that he knew it.

The final stage of her plan would be reached when she really knew her trade and had acquired the wherewithal to specialise – majolica perhaps, or Meissen shepherdesses, or Regency hairbrushes. Or something equally charming that would establish her name and justify the final move. To Kensington. With a darling little apartment over the shop, which would smell of lavender and beeswax and vanilla sachets. And not a whiff of a man: no pipe tobacco, no shoe polish, no sheep-dip tweed jackets. Kensington was no place for a man.

This long-term plan being constantly on her mind meant that Estelle met what happened when the famous Dame Selena Candle and a drab young man named Mr Porter visited Number One with mixed feelings. On the one hand, it offered a glorious opportunity to extend her collection (Daneman Court was teeming with delightful antiques); on the other, it could handicap or halt her ambitions altogether.

While the Waywards were seated around the table in the dining room for their weekly repertoire meeting, Jessamyn knocked at the door and in her most irritating Lady Bountiful manner announced, "Dear friends, I have here two visitors whom I am certain you will wish to meet. Dame Selena Candle," all the men in the room got to their feet, "and Mr Porter of the Ministry of Information. They are here to ask for your help." She beamed again before adding, "I'll leave you to it then, I'm needed at a meeting myself to discuss billeting American officers. Still, if you are all going to be moving anyway . . ." She stopped and gave a coy, theatrical peek at Dame Selena, "Oops, not another word, darling. *You* have the room."

Estelle controlled a grimace and focused on the popular character actress, Dame Selena, who was looking her age, then at the man from the Ministry, who flushed scarlet under her scrutiny. Wendell Garamond proffered his chair to the great Dame, Mr Porter found a spare at the end of the table, and Estelle sat up straight to listen.

Dame Selena, whose various chins wobbled not far above the table top, engaged each of them with a momentary eye contact then said, "Shall we begin?"

Wendell, leaning in his most nonchalant manner against the striped wallpaper, stretched forward a hand and inclined his head, "We are yours to obey, ma'am."

Dame Selena ignored him. “Mr Porter is from the Ministry of Information, who I’m sure you know are responsible for producing informative, cinematic shorts. I expect you’ve seen them. Well, the Minister came to me a couple of weeks ago at a soirée in Pimlico – what’s left of it – with something of a proposition, but we need just the right sort of people because, as I’m sure you also know, most of our lesser known actors and actresses are involved in war work or in the Forces, and all the best people are working on these new full-length Anglo-American productions, which I for one wholly applaud because goodness me it’s raising the bar.”

Despite herself Estelle wanted to clap; Dame Selena’s breath-control was nigh perfect.

“Which is why, when I called to enlist sweet Jessamyn,” Dame Selena continued, “and heard she had a group of semi-professionals under her roof I hurried down. A wonderful coincidence, because it means we can shoot at Daneman Court. Over which I have complete control.”

Estelle’s indignation at being classified with ‘semi-professionals’ lost out to the prospect of being in a film *and* going to Daneman Court. She had visited Daneman Court many years ago, when she had been a respected light opera contralto – a proper professional, with no end of offers in London. The whole place was full of exquisite artefacts and curios, some very ancient, all of them valuable. Unfortunately, they were so ancient and valuable the owners would miss them immediately, but there would be odd knick-knacks, small items she could stuff up a sleeve or two. Deciding she was also in no position to oppose what they were being offered, because West End light operas were as much a thing of the past as her professional career, Estelle listened more closely to what the grand lady then the drab young man had to say.

"I thought Daneman Court was being used to house refugees?" Reg Dwyer said, lighting one of his filthy cigarettes. "They were talking about it in The Ring o' Bells a few nights ago."

"It is," Dame Selena answered, "and many of them have very useful talents: musicians, writers, a stage hand who has worked with Brecht, and even a set designer. We also have two opera singers from Vienna in residence, although unfortunately I haven't found anything for them yet."

Unimpressed by the reference to Brecht and the Vienna Opera Company, the Waywards were individually wondering if Ministry 'shorts' paid well, or if they paid at all. Wendell, as their leader, spoke up. Directing his attention at the man from the ministry, he said, "Your brief then is to provide informative, meaningful but enjoyable entertainment for the general public. Meaning the film will play in picture houses throughout the kingdom alongside the news. Before the main feature? It sounds like a spiffing opportunity, but exactly what will be expected of us?"

Estelle cast a sideways glance at Wendell: there was something about his diction off stage that made her more than a little suspicious about his origins. Nobody over the age of twelve said 'spiffing' in normal conversation. Perhaps it was deliberate.

"Does this mean we're going to become film stars?" Suky Stefano gasped. "Oh, that is lovely. I have two new songs and a dance that I could use."

"Heavens child," Dame Selena retorted, "it's not a musical! The title is *Careless Words*, and it has a very serious message. This is *not* for a seaside pier."

"But that's what we do best, Estelle, Horace and I," Suky bleated.

Appalled, Estelle opened her mouth to protest but Dame Selena got there first. "I'm sure you do," she said. "But if you are going to work for Mr Porter you won't be singing for a week or two. He might let you hum, perhaps. In an appropriate moment."

Estelle wasn't sure if this was sarcasm and began wondering if she had enough stashed in her hat boxes and portmanteaux to make a start on her commercial enterprise sooner rather than later. She was shaken back to the present by the sound of Mr Porter's surprisingly cultured voice.

"As Dame Selena says, 'Careless talk costs lives' is our theme. At present, we have a rough script with a married couple whose son, a naval rating, returns on leave and reveals rather too much about where his ship is going next and why. Mrs Bailey, the wife and mother, mentions this in the grocery shop. The grocer tells his wife, who tells her neighbour, who is a Nazi sympathizer and transmits it to Berlin."

Estelle gazed around the table. No one present could play the son, but she could do Mrs Bailey a treat. Looking up, she said, "Horace and I can do the couple. Suky can be in the grocery shop. Wendell can be the Nazi."

"I most certainly cannot!" Wendell's voice boomed across the room as if it were Covent Garden.

"But you speak German, Wendell, you'd be so convincing," Suky insisted.

"I do not speak German!"

"But I've heard you," the girl persisted. She really was very naïve. "On the telephone. More than once."

"On the telephone? I do not think so."

"Oh, gosh, I didn't know you were a refugee, sorry."

Out of the mouths of babes, Estelle thought, and turned to see how Wendell would react.

"It was Dutch, you ninny. I am *not* a refugee," he said and sat down heavily in an empty chair.

"Sorry, sorry," Suky squeaked.

Dame Selena brought the table to order. "No need to allot parts yet. Mr Porter and his colleague will adjust their script with a cast in mind. For now, dear people, do just tell us whether or not you would like to take part."

To Estelle's amazement there was considerable dissent. Mr Porter got to his feet looking thoroughly embarrassed and not a little annoyed. Wendell took it upon himself to show their visitors to the front door, promising to let them know by telephone which of the players would like to be involved. When he returned, he said, "I have to call them tonight at Daneman Court. Now, who is *not* in favour, and for heaven's sake tell us why?"

The meeting descended into a shouting match. Billy and Reg saying they'd be out of pocket unless they could be guaranteed work on the set; Suky saying she liked singing and dancing and there was no role for her except in a grocery shop. Then Estelle remembered that Dame Selena had contacted Jessamyn Flowers first, presumably to be Mrs Bailey the chatty wife. Well, if push came to shove and they paid her enough she'd be the grocer's wife.

Horace silenced everyone with his professional actor's voice: "It is a fine opportunity, and if I never have to wear Tudor hose again I for one will be most relieved. It could lead to other contracts and give us a chance to branch out, *and* escape any more dreadful village halls."

"But where do Billy and me fit in?" demanded Reg Dwyer.

There was more argy-bargy until Billy Bryant called a halt to it, slapping the table with a nicotine-stained paw. "I say we each write down what we think is right for us on a piece of paper then discuss each option and vote."

Heads nodded around the table. Happy a mutiny was being averted, Wendell said quickly, "Get some paper from Jessamyn's office, will you, Estelle, you're nearest the door. And see if she's got any spare pencils – I've only got this," he indicated his fountain pen and note pad. "It'll take ages using what's left of my precious ink making a list of what each of you prefers."

Estelle left the room, grateful for a moment of peace, and went to Jessamyn's tiny office under the stairs. It was exceptionally neat, the guest register set precisely in the centre of the table she used as a reception desk, but there was no kind of notepad or correspondence paper to be seen. Feeling uncomfortable about what she was about to do, Estelle edged her broad hips around the table to see if the bureau behind was unlocked. It was, but she hesitated. It was one thing to scoop up a tasty ornament, a silver hatpin or a valuable miniature into the ample pockets beneath her costume farthingale, quite another to poke around in someone's bureau. She inched open the door just sufficient to see a stack of opened envelopes. Scruples gave way to curiosity. Some letters were addressed to Mrs Arthur Puddicombe, some to Mrs A. Puddicombe. "That's why he calls you Puddi," Estelle murmured, referring to Wendell's pet name for Jessamyn.

She poked a finger to the back of the stack to see what was on a much longer, more expensive envelope of the type favoured by solicitors. Embossed in the top left-hand corner were the names Didcot, Lissman, Lester and Hook. It was addressed to a J. Slattery Esq. Behind it was a much older, yellowed envelope of a similar kind for a Mrs Ada Beere.

"Ada," Estelle muttered to herself, "really?" Tempted to pull it out and open it, she turned to check whether the coast was clear and was met by the imposing poplin bosom of Mrs Baxter-Salmon.

"You were looking for something?" the woman hissed.

"Paper and pencils. Wendell's conducting a vote and we need to write things down. You don't happen to know where Jessamyn keeps her notepads do you?"

Mrs Baxter-Salmon gave her a searching look. "Something has amused you."

Estelle gave in to a smug grin, "Our Jessamyn Flowers is really called Ada: Ada Beere, a.k.a. Puddicombe."

"And *you* are Edna Smollett," Mrs Baxter-Salmon replied flatly.

Estelle gasped. How on earth did she know that? She was tempted to ask if she knew the real identity of Wendell Garamond – which as pseudonyms went was as false as Jessamyn Flowers – instead she gave a small shrug, "We all have our little secrets. In my case, however, it was my agent – when I was to be *top of the bill* in an Ivor Novello – who *insisted* on Estelle. I was to be his star, he said."

That night in bed, after Estelle had created a new plot for *Careless Talk* with roles for each of the players, and Horace had wondered whether Reg and Billy would be offered work after all, she said, "How does that Baxter-Salmon woman know my name was Edna Smollett?"

"Maybe you were at school together."

"You are joking! She's decades older than me."

"Decades?"

"Well, considerably older."

"If you say so." Horace shifted onto his side.

"She's very close to Jessamyn. Too close, if you know what I mean? Oh, and that reminds me, Jessamyn Flowers is not only Mrs Puddicombe – Puddi as Wendell calls her – she's also Mrs Ada Beere. What do you make of that?"

Horace made nothing of it, he was asleep. Estelle sighed and tugged at the blankets, trying to get comfortable, but her mind was whirling with real-identity biographies for the inhabitants of Peony Villas. She stopped at Mr Robbins, though, realising he had the characteristics of a film studio police detective. Perhaps he was a police detective. The young man with him could easily pass as a police constable.

The thought set her back to wondering whether she had enough to make her break for freedom and Exquisite Antiques. She could say she needed to go up to London to see somebody – a specialist perhaps. Hushed feminine implications would serve. There was bound to be an air-raid while she was there, and Estelle Dobson could disappear. Except she'd have to sign a name to a shop lease. Did she really want to go back to being Edna Smollett, the stuck-up madam from Mafeking Terrace? More to the point, did she want to miss the fun and possibilities of filming at Daneman Court? No, not really.

***

# Chapter 19

That evening Wendell sat down at the table by his blacked-out window to finish abridging the rustics' scene from *A Midsummer Night's Dream*, but his mind kept drifting back to the film offer. It hadn't taken long to persuade Billy and Reg to stay with the company and at least give the film-makers the chance to employ them, although now he wasn't so sure doing the film was such a good idea after all. It meant leaving Peony Villas, and he still hadn't persuaded Jessamyn to marry him – and marry he must, and very soon. The refugees at Daneman Court would weasel out his true identity within hours. He might even know some of them if they were from Vienna – being an Austrian, and not Dutch.

*Where had Suky overheard him*? It could only have been the telephone here at Number One, and that meant others could have overheard him as well. The calls were all to Zurich in Switzerland, Jessamyn knew that, but she had never bothered to question him about it. Not even in their closest moments had she asked where he'd come from. Why? Lack of interest, or because she respected his private life, or because she didn't want to be obliged to share her own secrets.

His call to Dame Selena that evening, of course, had been entirely public and they'd enjoyed something of a celebration at supper with one of Arthur Puddicombe's last bottles of burgundy. Not that he was ever going to miss it. Would that man never die! Was there ever such an ailing, useless being that held so tenaciously to life?

Wendell replaced the cap on his pen and began to pace the room. To be at Daneman Court, or not to be?

They weren't to move for at least a week, but he had a lot in his room to organise. Pulling down the smaller of his two leather cases from the top of his wardrobe, he staggered somewhat and dropped it clumsily on the bed.

"Not getting any younger," he said to himself, and not for the first time in the past few weeks wondered how much longer he could go on moving from town to town, never staying long enough to have a chair at a fireside or be part of a community. Not that he dared risk befriending anyone too closely. And there it was again, his new fear: how soon before the more worldly people of Daneman Court, refugees who'd crossed Europe, realised his nationality? It was one thing to be an Austrian refugee who'd escaped persecution with a yellow badge and a bundle tied with string; quite another to be Austrian with fine leather luggage and no visible reason to be in England. Would they jump to conclusions he was the dreaded Nazi sympathiser like in the film, or feel sorry for him and mix him up with all the other refugees?

He couldn't bear the thought of either.

Added to which, if Jessamyn got wind that he had no income other than from the touring performances, which brought in a pittance – that he owned nothing and would inherit nothing now his parents' home had been seized . . . The unfinished thought made him sit down heavily beside the case . . . The minute she got wind of that all his wooing would serve for nought. As things stood, there was a mild romance and a prospect of more to come as soon as hubby shuffled off his mortal coil, but now . . .

Feeling as if his head was going to explode, Wendell unlocked the case and checked the documents tucked into the bottom lining: his Viennese identity papers were in the kid-leather portfolio his parents had given him on his twenty-first birthday. He stared at his home address. Would his aged parents ever see their home again? Were they still safe in their rented rooms in Zurich?

He lifted out a thick envelope containing the various residence and employment cards he'd acquired while he was in Geneva, then Nice. His Austrian passport had presented no difficulty when he'd entered the port of Southampton in 1936, but where could Wenzl Goldstein go now with such damning evidence?

He looked at the dates on the various permits: he had been on the move for nine years almost to the week. Nine years since the day he returned to his university teaching post to start the autumn term, to be told they no longer required his services. His father's family was Jewish: he was an embarrassment, they said, a liability and risk. "But my mother's family are all Roman Catholic," he'd pleaded. The Dean had shown some compassion but students had complained, their parents had made their views known. It was a polite dismissal, considering how some fared.

He experienced again the sense of being hollow, insubstantial, as if the world was turning without him. This, he had come to learn, was what powerlessness felt like.

He couldn't go through it all again. Ever. His plan had been to reach the United States, but Hitler had put paid to that as well. There had to be a way to stay in England now. Had to be. And Jessamyn was his only hope.

***

# Chapter 20

Suky and Laurie met for their first date after supper on Tuesday evening. As they wandered down to the quiet end of Bideford quay, Suky related all that had happened at the Waywards' weekly meeting and her mixed feelings about moving into 'informative shorts'.

"I suppose it is where fate is leading me," she sighed, tucking her small hand into Laurie's and giving him a moment of unexpected contentment.

He gave her hand a gentle squeeze and guided her to a wooden bench on the riverbank. As they gazed at the harvest moon she leaned in against his body. They stayed like that for a while then Laurie experimented with a gentle kiss and Suky reacted just as he'd hoped and they stayed on the bench until Suky said, "Come on, it's getting chilly and we ought to get back, I don't have a key, do you?"

"No," Laurie replied, "but I know how to get in through the kitchen door, and I've learned a quicker way to get back to the house than going up the High Street."

"Up Gunstone Alley, yes I know, but it's haunted."

"Haunted," Laurie scoffed. "A town this old and historic, I bet there's dozens of haunted houses."

"Are you making fun of me?" Suky slipped away from him and started walking towards the town centre.

Dutifully, Laurie followed. Catching her hand in his again, he said, “How do you know about the haunting?”

“From Hester. Hester tells me all the local gossip. Her father’s a policeman. We’re the same age, born on the same day, isn’t that a coincidence? Two coincidences.”

“If you say so.” Laurie heard Bob Robbins in his reply and felt embarrassed by his gruffness.

Suky must have detected it, for she said, “All right, we’ll go up your way, but don’t blame me if we have to come back down again.”

Rows of workmen’s cottages with occasional alleyways flanked the steep, narrow street. Painted white, they gave the place an other-worldly effect in the rosy moonlight.

“Think of it as your last private adventure before becoming a famous film star,” Laurie said.

Suky tutted, but he could tell she wasn’t annoyed and she made no attempt to contradict him. “It’s only a small film,” she said, picking up on her previous thoughts, “but it will lead to greater things I’m sure. Wendell says he wants us to do it and maybe even start our own film company, except I don’t think he actually wants to go to Daneman Court very much. He doesn’t want to leave Peony Villas, which is silly because we’ve performed in just about every village hall for miles around so we’ll have to move on up to Somerset or down further west anyway in a week or two. Hester says it’s because he’s in love with Mrs Flowers, but I can’t believe that. They’re much too old for that sort of thing.”

“Not sure age matters much. My boss has a soft spot for her as well. You should see the way he watches her.”

“Ah, that’s nice.”

Conversation became more limited now, for the street was very steep.

"Which house is haunted?" Laurie asked as they passed an alley resembling a black hole to nowhere.

"I'm not sure, but it's got a poltergeist that throws things and turns over the table and . . ." Suky paused and bent over to catch her breath. As she did so there was hissing sound from behind her. She screamed and grabbed Laurie's sleeve, "See! I told you."

"It's a cat, Suky. Only a cat. Look."

A large ginger tom cat, its hair standing on end like a porcupine, hissed at them from a ledge. Suky gaped at it, horrified. "Beelzebub," she gasped. "Come on, run!"

Laughing, but not a little unsettled as well, Laurie allowed himself to be tugged uphill. They didn't speak again until they reached level ground, crossed a broader street and passed alongside the high wall of the cider-maker's yard. A cloud swamped the moon, turning the unlit street completely dark.

As the moon re-emerged, a thin ray of feeble white light illuminated a squat monster, making Laurie jump sideways. An oblong figure with frog's eyes dashed across their path, carrying something that glinted in one hand and a sack of some sort in the other.

"It's got a knife," Laurie gulped and pulled Suky to him. "Stand still. Don't move. Wait until it's gone."

"It? What?" she asked. "I didn't see anything, only that funny man. He looked like Mr Pots with his motorcycle goggles on. He wears them sometimes. Hasn't got a bike, though."

"The chap who works in the kitchen?" Laurie whispered staring hard at what the scurrying figure was carrying in his right hand. Either a torch the size of a cosh or a knife the size of a machete. A torch, he hoped, and crossed his fingers.

"He's called Mr Pots," Suky continued. "Hester says he's completely loopy. Potty in fact!"

Suky started to walk on but Laurie held her back. Speaking in a low voice, he said, "Wait, stay here until I'm certain he's gone. Suppose he's got a knife?"

"As long as it isn't one of his guns."

"Guns!"

"He's got lots. Keeps them in cardboard boxes. Some are in Hester's broom cupboard."

"You are joking? Hester's pulling your leg."

"Don't see why. It's all right, he keeps the ammunition separate. That's with some other weird stuff in his garden shed."

"*Weird stuff*? What d'you mean, weird stuff?"

Suky gave an apologetic shrug. "I'm only repeating what Hester tells me. I'm sure Mr Pots is perfectly harmless."

"Harmless, with a kitchen full of carving knives and a cupboard full of guns and a shed full of bullets!" Laurie held her hand tight and started pulling ahead. "I've changed my mind. We need to get off these dark streets as fast as possible."

By the time they reached Peony Villas they were both out of breath. Laurie fumbled with the gate latch and they both burst out laughing. When he could speak again, Laurie said, "There, I told you it would be an adventure."

"I'll never forget this night," Suky said dramatically, then reached up to kiss him. He kissed her back. Afterwards, she said, "I hope you won't, either."

Later, as Laurie lowered his long frame onto Honeysuckle's narrow bed, he realised the absurdity of wanting to get off the streets to be in a house full of knives and guns, with a madman in the kitchen. The thought reminded him of a Conan Doyle story, Holmes saying the vilest streets of London do not 'present a more dreadful record of sin' than the countryside.

***

# Chapter 21

## Wednesday

Maud Puddicombe was preparing her brother's special soggy porridge in the kitchen when she heard her front door close. Quentin leaving – she hoped. He had come in late that evening, treating her home as his own as usual; making no excuses, giving no explanation other than he had to talk to his mother – which he may or may not have done. He had gone up to his room and she had gone to hers and put the door on its chain and not come downstairs until her usual half past six.

There had been another person walking around in the house later, though. She had heard footsteps and they hadn't been Jessamyn's – her high heels made a distinct tap-tapping sound – and she only ever came in to see Arthur after Nurse Williams had finished his morning bed-bath. Maud had opened the door on its chain and listened, wondering who it was but not daring to ask in case it was actually Quentin and he flew into one of his rages.

Now, as she stirred the porridge to cool it, she wondered if she had imagined it all. But her house was normally so quiet, so still compared to Number One. Any unfamiliar sound came as an intrusion, with Quentin all too often the intruder of late. Maud checked her watch: ten minutes to seven. He was probably due back at base by nine. If there was one good thing about this dreadful war it was that he had to obey orders: hopefully he would be posted abroad soon and she wouldn't have to deal with his unwelcome presence any longer. She listened again. The clock in the hall passage ticked. The tap over the sink dripped. Her house was blessedly quiet again.

Maud stirred Arthur's restorative honey into the milky oatmeal so he could swallow it, then set the bowl on his tray with his special invalid's cup and went upstairs. The door to his room was closed. She never closed his door in case he called out – in case he got his voice back and called out to her, or movement returned to his limbs and he fell out of bed. It might happen. Two doctors had said it *could* happen.

She pushed the door handle down with a bony elbow and went in, her heart already racing because something was wrong. Arthur lay on his back as always, but his head was twisted sideways, his grey face beneath what remained of his grey hair pushed sideways into the pillow. He hadn't moved his head like this on his own since his stroke.

Maud stared until she heard the cup rattle against the porridge bowl and remembered she was carrying a laden tray. She put it down on the chest of drawers then adjusted her spectacles as if to see better and went to the bed. She didn't need to place her fingers on the pulse point in her brother's neck, he was dead. Gone. The last of her family. They had all died in this house, in her care. She swallowed hard, picked up the tray and returned to the kitchen.

It took a while to scrape the porridge into the basin she used for food scraps, to wash and dry the bowl and cup, to put away the tray. After that, she sat down at the kitchen table placed her long-fingered hands on the green-chequered cloth and took a deep breath. Who should she inform first? The doctor for a death certificate, or Jessamyn, Arthur's beloved, unsuitable wife? Should she let Jessamyn call the doctor?

Maud sat absolutely still for at least five minutes, then she went into the downstairs kitchen at Number One. Mr Gormley was there. Harold Gormley had been Arthur's best friend at school: she had known him since she was twelve years old. As a girl – once upon time – she'd hoped Harold might ask her to . . . But then the Great War came and he went away. And the person who returned to Bideford was no longer the Harold she knew.

"Maud," he said now, "what you doin' here this time of the morning?" Then he answered his own question: "Arthur's gone, hasn't he?"

Maud nodded, grateful that the first person to know about her brother was Harold. He was the only one who'd ever been loyal to Arthur, apart from her, of course.

In the end, Harold fetched Jessamyn, saying it was her place to call the doctor and do what was needed, although Maud knew for sure she would end up doing it all anyway. At least Jessamyn had the decency to look sad, to appear genuinely upset. Jessamyn was an accomplished actress, fêted on the London stage, or so Arthur had boasted. He had loved her above everything else – a woman so false she wouldn't even admit to her own name. But Maud knew who she was, and where she came from. She had spent years waiting for shame to fall on her brother when the local community connected the smartly dressed, attractive wife of Alderman Puddicombe to a Larkham tart who had run away to London. That was why the awful Quentin was the way he was; because Ada had abandoned him as a babe. A tiny babe and she'd left him in her mother's arms and run away to sing and dance in scanty clothing.

Jessamyn was calm, but so cold she started to shiver. As soon as the door closed on the doctor, she handed the death certificate to Maud then said, "Could we have a cup of tea before we start what has to be done?"

Maud sniffed the way Jessamyn knew she would but led the way to her dismal kitchen and filled the kettle. Jessamyn sat at the table tracing patterns on the cloth until Maud stopped what she was doing and announced, "Quentin killed him."

Jessamyn looked up, frowning. "Quentin?"

"Your son. Killed his step-father, who never did anything against him, though God knows he should have done. He came in with an accomplice last night and killed Arthur in cold blood. I heard them."

Jessamyn's frown deepened. "What on earth makes you think that?"

"Arthur's door was closed. His door is never closed."

"A gust of wind could do that."

"There is no wind in this house!" Maud retorted sharply.

Jessamyn put a hand to her chest. Would Quentin do such a thing? It wasn't impossible, but – "But he was with me until late. He's been posted out East, he thinks. They won't know until their ship has left harbour. Why on earth would he do such a thing? And nobody was with him. He came on his own."

"I heard two men in my house last night."

"Together?"

The question gave her grim sister-in-law pause. "One after the other."

"You mean you heard Quentin come along the passage here in his uniform boots and then someone else. In boots as well?"

Maud had the decency to think beyond her wild accusation. "No, not in army boots. I heard the stairs creak twice though. The fourth and fifth steps: the runners are loose. I've asked Quentin to tighten them and he never has. I definitely heard them. Quentin's door opened and closed . . ."

"Could Mr Pots have popped up to check on Arthur? He does come and sit with him. I know that for a fact."

Maud bit her lips. "It was very late."

"Late for you, Maud? After nine or after midnight?"

Maud sniffed again more loudly and began pouring milk into a jug. The kettle rattled on the hob.

When it was quiet again, Maud said, "It could have been Harold. But he doesn't come in after supper. Usually. No, it wasn't him, I know Harold's tread. Why do you call him Mr Pots anyway? He has his own name. Why must you drag everyone into your stupid make-believe world? We have names. Good names. The Puddicombe name is respected in this town. My father was a benefactor – the rowing club, the clock on the cricket pavilion, the benches in the park . . ." Maud gave way to great sobs and plonked herself down at the table. "We are a respectable family and you have . . ."

Jessamyn took a deep breath, stretched out her hand, but Maud would accept no comfort so she stood up and said, "I'm going upstairs now. To say my last goodbye." At the door she paused, very quietly she said, "Everything you say is only partly true, Maud. What you don't know is that Arthur took me on out of charity. He was *my* benefactor. He saved me from failure and loneliness – and I have always loved him, in my own way. And Quentin had no need to kill him. No need whatsoever. I signed a cheque for him last night that will pay his bills for months to come. He will also get my mother's farm and land after she has gone. Quentin had no need to bring an early end to Arthur's suffering."

"You haven't asked *how*," Maud hissed. "You haven't asked because you know!"

Jessamyn turned and stared at her gaunt sister-in-law. "*How* what?"

"He was smothered with his pillow. Then it was pushed back under his head." Her words came out with accusatory force. Jessamyn stepped backwards. Maud took this as signal of complicity. "You *knew*."

Jessamyn was so astonished she could barely utter a word. "How wrong you are, Maud," was all she could muster.

Lost in unwelcome thoughts, Jessamyn climbed the stairs again slowly. The door to Arthur's room was open and she could hear the district nurse humming as she packed away the various items she left in his room. Jessamyn stood in the open doorway, gazing at the figure in the bed. Arthur had only been able to move his eyes and mouth since Easter Sunday. Nurse Williams had come in every second day since his return from hospital and she had never once said there was any change. Mr Pots came up now and then to sit with him, telling him whatever was in his poor broken mind – she'd heard him more than once. For all she supposedly adored her older brother, Maud rarely actually sat with him.

Five lonely months trapped in a bed: she would mourn his loss, Jessamyn thought, but she could not say she was sorry his suffering was ended. Unless . . . No, Quentin could not have done that. Why would he?

Nurse Williams looked up, "Mrs Puddicombe, I didn't hear you come up. I'll be off in a few minutes – unless you'd like a few moments now. I could do with a cup of that funny bottle coffee if you'd like me to go downstairs. I'm not due with old Mr Briggs for an hour yet."

The kind woman rattled on some more but Jessamyn wasn't listening. "Nurse," she said suddenly, "do you think – that is – did you find Mr Puddicombe in a different position to usual when you came in? Could he have moved in the night? Called for help?"

Nurse Williams shook her head. "Miss Puddicombe asked me the same thing, twice. She's got a bit of bee in her bonnet about it. Which is normal. Quite normal. Someone dies in the night and the husband, wife – sister – feels guilty she or he didn't hear anything. Didn't notice. It's sad but perfectly normal. I wouldn't fret yourself, m'dear. We've all done what we can for your poor husband. It's possible another attack jolted his body a bit. Not common perhaps, but the doctor's been and said nothing about it to me."

Tears ran unchecked down Jessamyn's cheeks. "Thank you. Thank you, Nurse."

Nurse Williams nodded and closed her bag. Jessamyn crossed the room, and kissed the cold face of her once warm husband. He had been a gentle, kind man; she would miss him more than anyone could guess.

"Time to move on," she said to herself as she followed Nurse Williams down the stairs and shut the front door behind her. "Time to escape the little world of North Devon once and for all. Back to life, Jessie." She passed along the dark hallway of Number Two and nipped down the steps to the basement, not bothering to say anything to Maud.

"You all right, maid?" Mr Pots asked as she walked into his kitchen.

"More kittens!" Jessamyn laughed, seeing him cradling a tiny, furry bundle to his bristly chin, then noting the mewing coming from a basket under his work table. "I thought we agreed you wouldn't bring any more home."

"Life and death, maid. Life and death," he said, following her gaze.

Jessamyn smiled and touched the tiny creature's head. "How many this time?"

"Seven."

"Where are the puppies?" she asked. "Did you find somewhere for them, as I asked?"

"I did, maid. They'm all gone. Like you said."

"That's all right then. Mr Pots . . ." she was on the point of asking him what he would like to do when she handed Number One over to the Americans and went away, then stopped. There was no need to worry or upset him now. Her deed of gift would secure his future. Maud might even take him in willingly. Although she might not care for his pets.

***

# Chapter 22

There was a hearse parked outside Peony Villas while Bob was getting into his second-hand new suit in readiness for the inquest on Greville Healey. It took a while to adjust the braces so the trousers covered his paunch and didn't trail on the ground, but when he went down to the front door the hearse was still there. He paused on the top step then backed into the porch of Number One. Mrs Flowers and the grey-haired woman from Number Two were standing on the terrace next door watching the undertaker's men manoeuvre a body on an unsteady trolley out of the tradesmen's entrance. It was an undignified exit, whoever the deceased might be.

Bob lingered in the porch. His first reaction was 'not another one', then he heard Joan warn him about flippancy in the face of tragedy and stopped himself just in time. Joan was right: it was a bad habit. Still, it was unfortunate timing under the circumstances. He had tried and failed to get Jessamyn Flowers on her own yesterday; now, by the looks of her neighbourly concern, he might have to wait another entire day. There were urgent matters to clarify, and the lovely Jessamyn was possibly the only person with the answers he was seeking. DC Charlie West had said none of them at Bideford police station had much local knowledge, but the desk sergeant had given him the address of Peony Villas when he'd reported what happened at Hentree Farm. Was that a coincidence? No. Because in his experience, coincidences were usually founded on solid connections. And in this case Mrs Flowers was – he was almost certain – a link in the chain of reasoning.

He rubbed his chin, which reminded him had forgotten to get shaving cream; an excellent excuse to return to Larkham General Store for another informative chat about Josiah Slattery's son-in-law's family, and whether old man Slattery was known to be violent. Mervyn Evans had said he hadn't wanted to get involved in a 'ruckus' with him when they were young men. Had that bad temper developed into domestic violence or abuse? There'd been no signs of aggression on the woman they believed to be the long-suffering, long-deceased wife, but there was a reason she had died at Hentree on her own.

Thinking about what they had found at Hentree made Bob try to observe Mrs Flowers more objectively, but as he stepped forward for a better view of what was happening at Number Two, Laurie roared up on his motorbike. Bob flinched at the noise and tried to wave a warning hand at him, but the boy had seen the hearse and switched off the engine. He waved at Bob to come down to him then began pushing the bike to its parking space alongside the garage wall.

Bob stayed where he was until Laurie bounced up the steps saying, "Sarge, we have to get down to the station before the inquest. There are developments."

"Such as?"

"Healey's parents have been in asking questions and someone has to take them up to Ridgeway to get his stuff. Do you want to talk to them before they see their son or after?"

Bob huffed, annoyed at the fact that he'd got to hurry so couldn't ask about the death next door. He then felt guilty because Laurie had posed a sensible question and he hadn't been paying proper attention.

Noting his boss's somewhat muddled expression, Laurie added, "Do you think they – the Healeys – will be more forthcoming about their son if you talk to them before or after seeing the body?"

"Hmm, not sure. Wait a minute, I need to go up to my room." He had forgotten his wallet, but he wasn't going to tell Laurie that.

While he was there, Bob took a moment at his bedroom window to watch Mrs Flowers standing by the hearse. She was speaking to the older of the funeral director's men. About the deceased, presumably. Why was she doing that, not the woman next door?

Distracted, he tried to remember why he'd come up to his room then had a moment of panic: was he losing his faculties? Forgetting his keys, his cap and now his wallet; thinking he'd seen a solicitor's document then discovering there wasn't one. He wanted to retire again, that was certain, but not be let go because he'd muffed a murder inquiry. Or did he want to muff it? "Oh, sod it all," he muttered, grabbed his wallet from the chest of drawers and stomped down to the front door.

"In and out like a fiddler's elbow, I am," he grunted at Laurie. "Come on, get in the car."

"We can walk, it's only down on the quay."

"And walk back up again! My knees'll never stand it. Bad enough all the stairs in this ruddy tower."

Laurie started to chuckle then saw his boss's expression and wiped the smile off his face.

A briefing or meeting had recently come to an end as Bob and Laurie entered the police station near the bridge; plain clothes and uniformed men and women emerged from a large room chatting briskly. Bob and Laurie waited like concerned members of the public at the desk until the duty officer could separate himself from his colleagues. It took a while and Bob had the decided feeling they were being ignored on purpose. Eventually the first desk officer he'd met lifted the flap and inserted himself into his bar.

Bob leaned across the polished wood and said in a low voice, "Sergeant . . . sorry, I never did get your name."

"Edson – Gerald Edson," the man replied affably, making a fuss about looking in one of his ledgers.

"Sergeant Edson, then, I'd like to see Mr and Mrs Healey before the inquest, if possible. Have you got an address for them?" Bob watched the desk sergeant's expression to see how he would take the comment. "Which reminds me, it was you who gave me the address for Peony Villas. Very grateful. Lovely place. You know Mrs Flowers personally, do you?"

Sergeant Edson's fingers closed around a pencil. "Never met her."

"Ah, perhaps you knew her first husband. At least, I think he was her husband. He was a Barnstaple boy. David Beale, was it? Davy Beere? You'd be of an age, I'd think. Unless you worked with his father, PC Beere, before he retired."

The sergeant's expression changed and he nodded in response to something going on behind their backs. Bob turned to see DC Charlie West signalling from the stairs leading up to the offices.

"Detective Inspector Drury will see you now," Edson said.

DI Drury, back from helping out in Ilfracombe, was in his office waiting for them at his desk. Another Barnstaple man in his late fifties, he was slight of build and fair-faced. He had the look, Bob thought, of someone who embezzled company funds or did something stupid for a floozie and got caught. West ushered them in, then followed and went to a desk with a typewriter, where he rolled in a fresh sheet of paper without saying anything.

Was West was going to type down the conversation about to take place? Bob opened his mouth to complain then decided to wait and see what was going on. DI Drury had not got to his feet as they entered and Bob revised his first impression, the man looked weak and culpable, he also had a mean streak.

"Sit down, Sergeant Robbins. PC Oliver, take that chair over there." Drury indicated the chair in front of West without the least attempt to introduce himself or open with the usual civilities.

Bob gave free rein to dislike while DI Drury spent a full minute shuffling papers: a delaying tactic or a sign of rudeness not unlike the desk sergeant's? Finally, he located a medical report, but instead of handing it to Bob, kept it under his hand. Clearing his throat, he announced, "Firstly, I would like to thank you for stepping in and helping us in a crisis. We're very short-handed here, what with all our extra war duties: black-out regulations, fire-watching teams, rationing and so on and so forth."

"Same in Cready, sir," Bob replied blandly. "I was on a spot of much-needed leave but I'm happy to do what I can. PC Oliver came up on my request. He's been indispensable: we've had a lot of miles to cover one way and another, but we're getting to the nub of the problem. Once the inquest is over this morning and I can talk to the parents we can really start to move on this. Looks like a family feud over a potentially lucrative inheritance."

"Does it? Ah, well, good job, good job. But we can take over from here. I'm back full-time now and we've got help coming in from Barnstaple so – so what I'm saying is – we'd like you to give a full report and do your bit at the inquest as a witness to the Hentree Farm incident, and we'll take over the murder inquiry from hereon. DC West and a diver have been out to the cliff path and made a thorough search of the shore area you missed out. You can leave the rest to us professionals now."

*Professionals!* Bob grabbed the sides of his chair. He opened then closed his mouth, knowing he could only make a bad situation worse. DI Drury took his silence for acquiescence and continued, "We'd like you to stay a couple more days, though, to find the missing farmer you think you saw lying injured."

"I didn't *think* I saw him: I saw him."

"But no one in the past week has reported him missing, or found him lying injured on his farm. He hasn't gone over the cliff, either."

"I said he hadn't. He was injured or unconscious. Where I saw him, it was too far from the edge of the cliff for him to have dragged himself there – not in the time it took me to get into my car and drive up the lane, anyway."

DI Drury stared at him. "Are you sure? Think about it."

"I have done, sir. I have also retraced my steps and examined the area closely. I haven't missed out an inch."

"Except the cliff itself."

"No, we looked down there as well."

"Well it's all a bit odd."

"It is a bit odd. Decidedly odd. And why your men didn't locate him after I reported the incident, when he might have still been alive, defeats me. Your men were up there, trampling boots into every scrap of possible evidence and no one saw a ruddy thing." Bob tried and failed to keep the sarcasm out of his voice. "Did anyone try to find a bullet near the boy's body for example? I don't even know if it's still in him, just that it was from a pistol."

"Still in him. Weren't you told? Well, you don't need to worry about the boy now anyway, just do what you can to locate the farmer." Drury re-arranged some papers and keeping his eyes averted, continued, "The fact is, my men quite rightly chose to prioritise a missing toddler, not a miserable old man who's never done anything but cause others pain."

Bob's head and shoulders snapped to attention. "You know him?" Drury's eyes narrowed. "The 'miserable old man who's . . .'" Bob quoted.

"Ah, no. Hearsay only. Small country town – word gets about."

Bob heard Laurie shift in his chair at the word 'hearsay' and turned to catch his expression. The boy's face was a studied blank, but he'd heard what Drury had said and would no doubt comment on it later.

Mentally filing Drury's reluctance to pass on insider information, Bob turned back to the detective inspector and gave a mild shrug. "A policeman's lot if ever there was one. What happened to the little girl? Not good news I suppose if it's taken so long to find her."

"No, not good news. We have found her, though, in the river."

"No – oh, poor little soul." Bob felt involuntary tears prick behind his eyes and hastily added, "So, you want PC Oliver and me to go back up to Hentree and give it a final once over, then I can get back to my holiday and he can get back to earning his promotion, correct?"

"Correct."

"Suits me. Is that the doctor's report on the body in the bed at Hentree, by the way?" Bob waved a podgy finger in the direction of the typed sheet under Drury's pale hand. "Or are you waiting for the coroner's permission to act on that as well?"

Drury lifted the typed sheet and gazed at it uncertainly, obviously reluctant to pass it to Bob, but not entirely sure how to proceed. Then, as if on a whim, he placed it in his in-tray. "Natural causes, from the preliminary examination. No obvious signs of violence or toxicity, although we won't know that until the coroner orders a full autopsy."

"But she's been dead – one, five, ten years?"

Drury looked back at the typed sheet, "Between three to five years . . . in an advanced stage of decay . . . dry remains. No soft tissue, no fluids."

"Age? Any way of knowing if it was the missing man's wife?"

"Well over sixty, doctor thinks."

"So, she's almost certainly Mrs Slattery, who died of neglect. Or who died and was placed in a bed in an empty house, not the grave she deserved." Bob tapped the wire frame of the tray. "Shouldn't I attach this to my report?"

"No need, West can do it. He can locate her birth certificate and so on."

"So, you only need us to *find* the missing man, is that right?" Bob wanted it spelled out loud and clear so when the case came to court, or became even more tangled – and it was rapidly going that way – he'd got a solid reason as to why he didn't do more.

Drury leaned back in his chair and giving no indication of understanding or caring about Bob's situation, said, "DC West tells me we've got everything you've done so far in a folder, apart from your witness statement at the inquest. If anything comes to mind about the woman's body tell him and he'll deal with it."

*You can't get us out of the way fast enough, can you*? Bob thought, but said mildly, "Right you are." Standing up, he dragged his chair noisily across the room to Charlie West, then turned back to Drury, "About the old lady, do you want this raised at the inquest on the Healey boy or does she get her own later in the week?"

"Have you got a date fixed for her, West?" Drury barked.

"All in hand, sir. You'll be called on Friday for that, Sergeant Robbins. Eleven o'clock." DC West looked at his superior for approval.

Drury nodded then added flatly, "If, while you are searching for Mr Slattery you do find anything that will lead to a prosecution regarding the woman we'd be grateful, obviously."

Bob kept his thoughts on that to himself and watched DC West pull the sheet of paper from his typewriter and replace it with another blank sheet. Bob raised an eyebrow, but West avoided his gaze. While Bob waited, he reviewed the advantages and disadvantages of divulging what he'd learned about Mr Slattery's son-in-law, and the fact that his father had been a police hero. But revealing he knew about the internal police connection to the hero of Barnstaple and thus their interest in Slattery wasn't going to make these men like him any better. It would all be out in the open within the hour anyway, once the inquest had confirmed Greville Healey's identity. But damn it all, they were being bloody-minded treating him like some kind of amateur private investigator.

Out of sheer cussedness, Bob turned to DI Drury and in a voice he hoped would carry out of the door, said, "Not sure how valuable this is, but if it's extra information you're after for a conviction, I do know there's a connection in the boy's murder to Barnstaple police," and had the satisfaction of seeing Drury grimace.

"According to my informants," Bob went on, "Mr Slattery's daughter married a carpenter called Davy Beere, who was the son of a popular Barnstaple copper, PC Beere. Not sure how this Davy came to be at Hentree or Ridgeway Farm, but my guess is that he was working in Larkham and courting Miss Slattery, then married her and moved into Hentree Farm, making him someone who might inherit Hentree through his wife. Now, as you've just mentioned, sir, the girl's father, Josiah Slattery, was a miserable devil: he could have named his son-in-law – Davy Beere – as being in a protected occupation, farm work, but he didn't. He let him get called up and sent off to the trenches. The boy was killed – as was to be expected. PC Beere and his family and colleagues in Barnstaple must have been angry about that."

"And your point is?" DI Drury asked coldly.

"No particular point, coincidence, that's all. Curious, if you like, that this boy Greville Healey is the late PC Beere's grandson." Bob gave a shrug of dismissal. "Funny old world. Only you'd think the victim would have been the old man, not the boy who might, with a bit of legal soliciting, have got the farm. Of course, if we locate the old man you could be dealing with a double murder."

"We are aware of this, Sergeant," Drury said, getting to his feet and heading for the door. To chat with his old buddy the desk sergeant, Bob thought with an inward grin. And then he was genuinely glad, relieved he was off the case – near enough.

***

# Chapter 23

Bob's sense of relief was short lived thanks to Laurie's astute comments as they made their way to the inquest in the municipal building. The boy, in his typical 'verbal reasoning' manner, was thinking aloud.

"Are they trying to get rid of us, Sarge?"

"Oh, yes."

"But not because they want to close the murder inquiry faster, or cover it up?"

"No, not exactly."

"They don't want us to see their methods, though. They want to find the Healey boy's killer and –"

"Keep the rest from prying eyes. Cops look after their own – when it suits them."

"*Them*, Sarge? Not *us*?"

"I was at the wrong end of an internal inquiry once, Laurie, you know that. No bugger stepped forward to save *me*."

"But they still want us to find the old man," Laurie continued.

"Two days they said. Two days we'll give them. Then it's back to Cready for you and up to Exmoor for me."

"I don't mind staying on longer," Laurie said, "if I'm needed."

"By Suky Stefano. I thought they were moving on to this Daneman Court place."

"To make a film, yes. Suky says I could be in it. What with –"

"You being six foot and pretty to look at."

"It's not like that, Sarge."

"If you say so."

Bob pushed open the door into the small courtroom and glanced around at who was seated in what he always thought of as the 'spectators' gallery', except this was all on one level. "They're the parents, then," he commented, assessing a smartly turned out couple sitting bolt upright on hard wooden chairs. "Hmm," he murmured as he moved in their direction, intending to find a way to make personal contact with them before the proceedings, in order to lessen the intensity of the private questions on the Slattery family he was hoping they'd answer for him afterwards.

"What's up, Sarge?" Laurie whispered.

"Not sure, but there's more than one story here, lad, and the second one's to do with the proceeds from that Hoblin's Holiday Camp palaver or I'll eat my cap."

In the end, Bob had no chance to speak to the Healeys before the inquest began into the death of their son because the coroner was pushing through his schedule as quickly as he could. Bob was called to give his account of the incident at Hentree and the doctor confirmed that cause of death was due to a single shot from a nine-millimetre pistol. After that there were no further witnesses and the coroner ordered a full autopsy. Bob moved to wait at the back of the courtroom, signalling to Laurie to stay at his side. Then, before the parents could leave with the press at their heels, he pushed his way along to where they were sitting and pulled a chair around for himself to speak to them in as unthreatening a manner as possible.

Mr and Mrs Healey, dressed as a matching pair in his and hers summer black, moved in their seats to face Bob sideways on, reminding him somewhat of Victorian book-ends. The difference being that Mrs Healey's mouth was pinched tight like a miser's purse and Mr Healey's was slightly agape as if ready to supply a word, if only he could remember it. They both had greying hair and probably needed spectacles, for they both peered at him as he spoke as if trying to get him into focus.

Bob opened by introducing himself and checked to make sure Laurie was within hearing distance, he wanted a second opinion on their reactions to his questions. Starting with the appropriate condolences, he waited for a natural reaction but Mrs Healey's lips only pursed tighter; her husband's gaze wandered with embarrassment. Taking this as a signal neither would break down in tears – which he was pretty sure he would if he were in their place – he pushed on.

"Do you mind if I ask you a few questions about your son?" Two heads shook in unison. "That's very kind of you. Can you tell me, when did Greville move to Ridgeway Farm, or was it Hentree?"

On the last word the couple exchanged a rapid glance, but only Mrs Healey responded. "April. When he was turned down for the Forces because of his asthma."

"Asthma? Sorry to hear that. A delicate child, was he? Very disturbing asthma attacks, I've seen it. Poor mites gasping for breath."

"We had to rock him in our arms next to a steaming kettle right up to he was five or six. He got stronger after that, though."

Mrs Healey looked at her husband and he added, "Stronger, yes."

"But it meant he wasn't going to go into uniform, I understand. Mixed blessing. I've got a son about the same age out in an aircraft carrier. Worries me no end." Bob's voice was gentle, the words genuine. The response wasn't instant but it came through in the rest of his inquiry. "Brave of your boy to take on farm life with his condition, though. All that hay and straw."

The Healeys' eyes met again and Mrs Healey said curtly, "We all have to play our part in the war effort." Bob nodded and waited for her to continue. "It wasn't exactly what he wanted, but he was restless you see, embarrassed about not being able to join up, and our neighbours in the street . . . They weren't kind about it."

Bob shook his head in commiseration, "No, I can imagine. But Mr Slattery must have been delighted to get his help. I bet your boy had some funny tales to tell, what with him being a townie and going up to that old farm – still living in the olden days a bit out there at Larkham Cross, they are. Ah, forgive me, you're family, aren't you?"

"In a manner of speaking. Not blood relatives, but my brother was married to Mr Slattery's daughter." Mrs Healey began to fiddle with the clasp of the black handbag on her lap.

"Ah, yes, I see," Bob smiled. "And your brother and his wife had no children to help on the farm?"

"No." Mrs Healey's response was short and final. Staring Bob in the eyes for the first time she said, "No," again. And again, the word came too fast and too definite. Her husband gave her an admonishing look and she added reluctantly, "Well, there was a boy, Quentin, but he went off up country somewhere soon as he was old enough. My brother died, you see, during the Great War."

"His widow didn't marry again locally?"

"Ada!" Mrs Healey's look of disapproval would have shrivelled fresh paint. Bob responded with a questioning tilt of the head. "That flibberty-gibbet!" The woman sniffed as if at something deeply unpleasant then continued, "Ran off the moment the telegram arrived. Left her baby boy in his grandmother's arms and disappeared to London."

Bob struggled to combine disapproval with sympathy and pushed on to confirm his interpretation of the family history,

"So it was left to your son Greville to fulfil the role of the eldest son – although Mr Slattery did have a son, didn't he? Did I hear he was injured in an accident?"

"Tractor. Overturned on a hill. Trapped under it, he was. Mangled like a sheet, they said. I told Greville he wasn't to go anywhere near a tractor no matter how much that evil old . . . Mr Slattery insisted."

"Understandable. He'd have had his work cut out, though." Bob switched his attention to the husband, "Farm labour's not exactly light industry, is it? You have to like the outdoor life, manage all manner of equipment, even shoot vermin."

The husband nodded and taking his cue to speak, said, "He could have come into the gentlemen's outfitters where I work, but he wasn't interested. Likes mechanical things, Greville. Anything with switches and fiddly bits. He'd have been good in the Army."

The man swallowed hard in distress, and Bob smiled in response but carried on regardless, there were things he had to know. "All on his own, though, up at the farm. No one of his own age to be friends with. Quentin didn't come back for visits?"

"Greville never mentioned it."

"No. So, who do you think might have been on the farm, when the shooting happened. Assuming it was an accident. Who else was up there, do you know?"

The couple shook their heads in unison then Mrs Healey said, "That's not what you said at the hearing. You said the shot couldn't have been accidental."

That wasn't precisely what he'd said, but her attitude served his purpose. "Well, someone took a shot and Greville got in the way. Or – we have to face the fact that possibly someone wasn't too keen on Greville being there at all. The farm – Hentree – was Greville going to inherit it? Given that Quentin showed no interest in the family farms?" Mr Healey cleared his throat. Mrs

Healey opened and closed the clasp of her handbag. Neither spoke. "Mr Slattery didn't have anyone else to leave it to, did he?" Bob asked.

The couple exchanged glances then Mrs Healey said, "We did hope. I mean, nothing wrong in that. Greville gave up a good job at a garage to go all the way up there to help out. It's only right he should have been rewarded."

"An ancient property, land and woods. I expect your boy could have really made something of it. In the Pascoe family for years, I heard. Mrs Slattery's family that is. Might it come to you as her daughter's sister-in-law? Bit complicated these family trees."

Mrs Healey prevaricated and her husband looked away. Eventually she said, "Everything is owned and managed by Mr Slattery. He controls everything. Which is as it should be. Husbands know best. Why isn't he here? He should be here. He was supposed to be looking after Greville – my boy's not twenty-one yet."

Bob frowned. "No, well, as I said just now at the hearing, we don't actually know where Mr Slattery has got to."

Mr and Mrs Healey gaped at him. Bob could almost see the acquisitive cogs faltering in the woman's brain. It had been her idea to send Greville to work for old man Slattery, a boy with asthma and a good job at a local garage: would her husband blame her; would he forgive her? Bob looked up at Laurie stationed a yard or so to his left, leaning against the wood-panelled wall. Then, choosing his words and tone carefully, he went on, "From what I saw, I think it's possible Mr Slattery had some sort of attack, a stroke perhaps. We do need to locate him as quickly as we can. If . . . if the worst has come to the worst, that is, *when* Mr Slattery dies, what do think will happen to the two farms?"

Mrs Healey gave a prim sniff. "There's no one else to get the property now, except Quentin, wherever he is. Or Ada." The realisation that she had overlooked a significant person in her scheming suddenly crossed her face. "Oh," she said, "someone will have to tell Ada."

"Do you have any idea where she is?"

Mrs Healey sniffed again. "London, I expect. London . . ."

"No, Sheila, you saw her picture in the newspaper, remember? Opening the regatta last year."

Mrs Healey's eyes flashed fury at her husband. "I only said it *looked like* her. Heavens, we haven't seen her since 1916, how on earth am I expected to know if the woman in the photograph was Ada?"

"Local regatta, was it?" Bob asked innocently.

Mr Healey looked warily at his wife. "I might have been mistaken, sorry." He looked away, clearly troubled, then said, "It's that we heard she was back in North Devon, you see? Greville said . . ." He bit his lip, cast a glance at his wife and looked away again. "No, nothing."

Bob sighed, the sooner he confronted Jessamyn Flowers the better. He also needed to find Quentin, a.k.a. Ken Beere, and pull him in for questioning. Then he remembered it wasn't his case anymore. Even so, whoever had shot Greville could have disposed of the old man as well.

Had Greville's murderer got the old man out of the way in that short space of time? Dragged him into a vehicle and driven away? But why would Quentin do that if he needed a death certificate for his grandfather? Assuming he wanted to set in motion his inheritance claim and the subsequent sale of Hentree. There was a piece missing. Could it be Ada? Could Ada be working *with* Quentin – even reluctantly? Or could Ada be sheltering her father somewhere, trying to protect him?

Bob gave himself a mental shake and turned his attention back to the Healeys. Ending their informal interview with the usual thank yous and 'if you think of anything' comments, he then surprised himself by offering to take them up to Ridgeway to collect Greville's belongings. He was delighted when they refused. Then wondered why.

***

# Chapter 24

Bob and Laurie walked out of the sombre courtroom into bright sunshine, but as they turned the corner onto the quay the day darkened as a huge camouflage-covered, open-backed lorry crawled past, followed by three others, each full of American troops. Before they got much further, the convoy halted and a soldier with a map jumped down to consult a local. Arms pointed this way and that while exhaust fumes choked the air. Bob put a handkerchief to his face and Laurie stepped back into the lee of a building, where half a dozen others were waiting.

Eventually the lorries lumbered away, great alien beasts in a quiet estuary town. An educated male voice cut through the remaining smog: "War comes to Bideford. Not for the first time. God help us, may it be the last." There was a chorus of 'amen to that' then an elderly woman with a shopping basket said, "What I don't understand is why all these young men are travelling all the way from America to protect us here, when our own boys could stay at home to defend us instead of being sent to the far corners of the Earth the way they are. My grandson is in India. It isn't logical."

There was a general murmuring and Bob distinctly heard the educated male say to a colleague, "Not for our defence in this case, happily."

Bob looked up at Laurie, "Time for a quick pint and a sandwich, if we can get one," he said and set off briskly down the street to the nearest hostelry.

As they walked, Laurie said, "Now what?"

"First a pint and some grub, then you get on your bike and take a ride to Ridgeway. Chat up either or both of the girls. I need to know Slattery's daily routine and anything else – *anything* at all – they can tell you. Then," he skirted around the woman with the basket who was now stationed in the middle of the pavement talking to two other women in identical costume, "then you come back and tell me all the gossip. That's what I want you to do. Gossip. Get the girls chatting then get what you can out of your sweet Suky."

"Suky? What on earth has she got to do with it?"

"Ah – erm . . ." Bob waited until they were at the pub door and lowered his voice. "I think Mrs Flowers might be a local woman: you heard what Mr Healey said about the regatta. Spend some time with the weird players, see what they know about her background."

"Crikey," Laurie muttered.

"Small old world," Bob replied, and pushed open the heavy, nail-studded door of an Elizabethan tavern.

Laurie lowered his head and, staying bent over to avoid ancient black beams, followed his boss to the bar. Bob ordered two pints and asked about sandwiches. Beer was limited to halves, they were told, sandwiches a thing of the past.

As he watched the barman fill his mug with froth, Bob huffed, "You could put a collar and tie on the neck on that."

"You'm lucky to get a half, sir. Them that come later won't, not with all these Yanks here."

Bob huffed again, paid and led the way to a small table. Picking up where he'd left off, he said, "We need to know as much as any of them can tell you about Josiah Slattery's daughter called Ada, who could be our charming Mrs Flowers." Laurie lowered his glass, wide-eyed. Bob repeated what he'd learned about the young widow who had run off to London, and why he had a suspicion she was now called Jessamyn Flowers.

"You can't think she's involved?" Laurie said.

"Oh, I can. Unfortunately. She's an actress to the quick beneath her painted fingernails – and my fingers itch the moment they touch her front door. My itchy fingers also tell me that if we find Ada Slattery, we might just find her pa."

As soon as they got back to Peony Villas, Laurie leaped up the stairs for his motorcycle gear and Bob went hunting for Jessamyn Flowers. He was still curious to know who had died next door, but more curious to confirm inklings that led back to Jessamyn's birth certificate, and his growing suspicions regarding a short-tempered man named Quentin. Not that it was his case any longer, but it could very well lead to the whereabouts of the missing farmer, or so he reasoned.

At the sound of cutlery being set on tables he peeked around the dining room door and was pleased to find Hester the maid of all work laying up for the evening meal.

"Need a hand, Hester?" he said in a hushed voice. The girl was so surprised knives and forks clattered to the floor. "Sorry, love, didn't mean to startle you." Bob went to the table and stooped to retrieve the dropped items.

It was while he was in this undignified position with his ample backside above his shoulders that Mrs Flowers' light tones carried across the room. "Were you looking for me, Mr Robbins? I'm here."

Bob jerked up, bumping his head soundly on dark oak. "Bugger," he grunted, making Hester smile. Jessamyn Flowers smiled as well, but her expression was one of laughing with him not at him and Bob laughed out loud despite the lump on his skull. “I was, Mrs Flowers. Looking for you. But not under the table.”

He handed Hester an errant fork and went to join his landlady, who led off towards her cubicle office.

“You want to tell me something,” she said. It was a statement not a question.

“Yes, I did . . . I do, yes. It’s that we’ll be leaving – should be leaving – in three days’ time, PC Oliver and me, so we may only be here for another two nights. Thought I better let you know.”

“Thank you.” Mrs Flowers’ smile was now one of dismissal, but Bob had some pressing items on his personal agenda. This wasn’t the time or place, but he’d got her undivided attention so he said, “Your neighbour’s family have had a bereavement. Her husband?”

“Brother.”

“Oh, dear, sorry to hear that. Must be upsetting for you, living so close, the houses being joined like they are. I expect you know them well.”

“Yes.” Jessamyn turned to her bureau, locked it with a small key and placed the key in her pocket. When she turned back Bob was exactly where she’d last seen him. “Oh,” she said, “still here. I’m sorry you’ll have excuse me, I’ve got a busy day,” and headed for the service stairs.

“Sad,” Bob said vaguely into the hallway, cross that he’d allowed himself to be dismissed, but unsure how to react. “I’ll be going upstairs now. Need a wash and change, it’s a busy old day for me, too. Inquest this morning: young man killed out on a farm towards Larkham Cross. I was there myself, unfortunately.”

“At the farm?” Mrs Flowers took a sharp breath then said in an even tone, “Larkham will be pretty at this time of year. The leaves are starting to turn already.”

Taken off guard, Bob suddenly remembered what he'd planned to say, "I was in the church and got chatting with some locals. Mr – erm, and his daughter – at the General Store as well." Jessamyn Flowers pushed open the service door. "Local history," Bob plugged on. "I was reading about the church – from a pamphlet – then they were telling me which families are still in the area after all these generations."

"Rural communities, Mr Robbins, not many move away – unless they have to. You are based in Cornwall, aren't you? You should know that."

"Some have to move on down there," he replied. "Miners certainly do, all the way to South Africa; farmers who can't make ends meet emigrate. A few of them come back when they've made their money, though."

"Do they? Yes, I expect they do, if their family ties are strong. If they still have a home to come back to. You must excuse me, I need to finish some chores. I'll make up your bill ready for you later. We have a few other bills to make up. The Wayward Players are moving to Daneman Court to make a film. Isn't that exciting? Now I really must speak to Mr Pots," she said and disappeared down the wooden stairway.

Seeing he had been neatly outmanoeuvred, Bob tapped the banister with his pudgy knuckles and started up the dreaded carpeted staircase, then halted. Checking to see Jessamyn wasn't returning, he tapped his pockets like a bad actor and said, "Think I must have dropped my wallet under that table."

Hester was folding starched napkins. "Ah, Hester, you're still here," he said, entering the dining room a second time, "very sad about the neighbours. Mrs Flowers looks quite upset." It wasn't entirely a lie, she *was* ruffled. "Not one of her family, I hope. A brother?"

Hester stared at him. "Brother? No, it was Miss Puddicombe's brother. Mr Arthur Puddicombe. He's – was –

Mrs Flowers' husband." The girl stopped and flushed puce. "I don't think I'm supposed to tell you that."

"No, not to worry," Bob was all reassurance. "Our little secret. I never asked and you never said. Mum's the word. Careless talk and all that, like the posters say, eh." He placed a forefinger to his lips. "I'll let you get on, sweetheart. Just looking for my wallet, don't you mind me." He made a dumb show of hunting the wallet then slipped out of the dining room and struggled up the stairs, trying to fit this new piece of information into the unfinished puzzle of Quentin/Ken's conversation with – his mother. A woman who went away and left him in his grandmother's care. A young man who wasn't 'after the money' but stood to inherit a valuable property – as long as his supposed grandfather didn't sign it over to an interloper first.

Not that it was his business any more.

Jessamyn closed the service door firmly behind her, fearing Detective Sergeant Robbins would find an excuse to follow her, and raced down the wooden steps to the kitchen. A she-cat was nursing a mixed bundle of kittens in a new basket under the table. She sighed with exasperation: Mr Pots had promised no more kittens. The back door was open so she went out to the yard to see if he was with his aviary on the paved area. He wasn't, but there was a new guest there as well, a blackbird with a broken wing. The sound of scratching beneath its perch made her look down into a mess of straw and twigs: three tiny mottled quail were making a nest. "That's more like it, quails' eggs," she muttered then turned to identify a much louder noise; the sound of hammer blows.

Up the garden steps, on what remained of a patch of lawn, Mr Pots was assembling a hutch-like structure with a chicken wire run.

"Have you got some rabbits now as well?" Jessamyn asked brightly, trying to keep displeasure from her voice and not surprise him. Mr Pots had a history of violent reactions to being surprised from behind.

"Only two," he mumbled, not taking his eyes from the hammer in his right hand. "In that box."

Jessamyn prised open the flaps of a cardboard box expecting to see two plain domestic rabbits. One of them was black and very sleek with long, floppy ears. Someone's spoilt bunny. Looking round at her cook and late husband's war-damaged friend, she said as kindly as she could, "I don't think we are allowed to keep pets any more, you know. We have talked about this." Getting no response, she said more loudly, "Will they eat our left-over greens or do they have a special diet?"

"Greens."

"That's all right, then." Jessamyn wanted him to stand up and make conversation, she wanted to ask him – casually – if he'd gone up to Arthur's room the night before, but not so as to upset him. Mr Pots' emotions could be hard to handle and she was in no state to deal with hysterics, or worse, a grown man sobbing his heart out. Seeing another cardboard box with holes punched in it, she asked, "What's in that one?"

"Guinea pigs."

"Guinea pigs! Where on earth did you get them from?" Silly question. Jessamyn closed her eyes in despair. But where was the harm in keeping a few rabbits and guinea pigs for company? "Can they all go in the same hutch?" she asked.

"Yes."

"That's good." Jessamyn watched Mr Pots stretch a length of chicken wire over the frame. He was very good with his hands – or he had done this before. "Arthur told me once that during the war you managed to escape and then they caught you again."

There was a slight nod of the head bent over the new hutch. Taking it as assent, Jessamyn asked, “Where did you go?”

Harold Gormley, also known as Mr Pots, sat back on his haunches and stared into the runner bean canes further up the garden. After a moment he said, “I got into France. Lived in the woods. An old lady, Miss Virginie, found me and took me in.”

“Ah,” Jessamyn was taken aback. It was possibly the most she had ever heard him say at one time.

Then, voluntarily, he added. “I looked after her animals. A billy goat and two females, four sheep, some rabbits. Not the geese. She did those. It was peaceful. I liked it there.”

“Why didn’t you stay?”

“Walter came.” He pronounced the name with a ‘V’.

“A German?”

“Deserter.”

“Heavens, what did you do?”

“I cut his throat.”

Jessamyn put a hand to her mouth, the rest she knew: he was captured again and not released until after the end of the war. “Mr Pots,” she began quietly, “have you been out to Barley Cliff or Larkham lately?”

“No.”

“Ah, well, that’s all right then.” She looked back at the box containing the guinea pigs, “Do they breed like rabbits, guinea-pigs?”

“Hope so.”

End of conversation.

Jessamyn wandered around what remained of her garden, noting how Mr Pots had still got runner beans and carrots growing together, and how their salad lettuces had been protected by sheets of broken glass. Reaching the shed, she caught a whiff of the compost heap and turned back. Passing her cook, still kneeling on the lawn, she said, “Welsh rarebit with your special herby-cheesy sauce tonight, then. As we agreed."

There was no response so she returned to the house. Trying to keep Mr Robbins' words and Maud's accusation out of her mind, she wandered into the Peony Villas joint basement refuge room. It was cold. She pulled her pastel green cardigan off her shoulders, pushed her arms into the sleeves and slumped down onto the nearest mattress. Rolling into a ball, hugging her knees to her chin, Ada Puddicombe cried dry tears for the husk of the man they had taken to the chapel of rest.

"Oh, Arthur," she sighed, "you thought you were doing the right thing bringing me here, but it's all gone wrong, and it isn't going to get right again, ever. I'm going to have to leave – go back to London."

She wanted to stay where she was for now, though, to weep for Arthur, but Quentin kept intruding. She had been a bad mother and now she was paying for it through guilt and fear. She was afraid of her son, and glad – yes, glad – he was being sent abroad. The further and the sooner the better.

Maud's words – words that had been rattling around her head since the moment they were spoken – would not be silenced. Had Quentin brought Arthur's life to a quicker end? Very possibly, yes. But why?

"Because he could," whispered her mother's soft voice. "Because he is your father's grandson in every way."

***

# Chapter 25

Forgetting Laurie would have to get out, Bob parked his Morris alongside a thick hedgerow a few yards past the only pub at Larkham Cross, then climbed out and had to wait for the lanky lad to negotiate the handbrake and gear stick. As Laurie emerged into the sweet-smelling country lane, he closed his eyes and took a deep breath, "Honeysuckle," he announced. "There I lie. No, it's 'Where the bee sucks, there suck I. In a cowslip's bell I lie.' La-la-laaa-la-la . . . something, something 'merrily.'"

"Bit early to start singing, we're not inside the pub yet," Bob grunted, locking the car doors: a pub was a pub wherever it was located.

"Shakespeare, Sarge."

"Gawd n'bennet, not you as well."

"You did say to make myself pally with the players."

Bob's head shot up. "I did. What have you got?"

Laurie beamed, his eyes a brim with delight. "They want me to accompany Suky at the Littlehamholt performance tomorrow afternoon." Then, seeing Bob's face, he added, "On the piano."

"Play the piano, do you?"

"Also: violin, not so well, chess, rugby football and I'm a pretty fast fast-bowler."

"Talk about Renaissance man."

"Is that a compliment, Sarge?"

"If you want it to be."

"I didn't think you'd know about Renaissance man."

"I'm not entirely ignorant." Bob headed for the entrance to an inviting, white-washed hostelry named the Star and Anchor.

"Oh, no, I meant – that is, I didn't mean . . ."

"Save your grovelling, we've got work to do."

"Right-ho."

As Bob opened the pub door he said, "If asked, you're my nephew, we're on holiday and –" he waved a paw in the air, "leave the rest to ruddy Shakespeare."

A brass plaque over the lintel said 'Duck or grouse'. Bob passed under it without comprehending, Laurie bent down from the waist and entered unharmed. Bob turned to see him straightening up and grinning. "What?" he demanded.

"Nothing, Sar – nothing, Uncle Bob," Laurie coughed and followed his grumpy new relative through a jumble of pint-wielding elbows to an arched bar decorated with horse-brasses and government issue respirators. Bob put a hand out and lifted a gas mask, the round nozzle end reminded him of a pig's snout. He dropped it back into place with a shudder: people had become blasé about the possibility of a deadly gas attack, but this particular tremor of disgust had not been for phosgene or mustard gas.

Turning to Laurie he hissed, "Where have this lot all come from? It's jam-packed in here and not even a bicycle outside."

The burly inn-keeper must have heard him. Leaning over the polished oak bar he said, "Star and Anchor's known for miles hereabouts."

"In that case two pints of your best ale, landlord, if you will," Bob replied.

"No beer here, I'm afraid," landlord replied. "Can't get it for love nor money out this way. Lorries empty in Bideford, see? Even Bude's gone dry, and that's a proper town."

Bob gaped. “No beer. What’s this crowd here for then?”

“Cider. Local brew.” As he spoke the landlord pulled two half-pints of a clear, golden concoction.

“Halves?” Bob grunted.

“House rules. Grockels get two halves, maximum – if they can manage it.”

“Don’t tell me apple juice is rationed now as well.”

An ironic, knowing expression crawled around the landlord’s craggy features. “That’ll be one and fourpence. Enjoy your apple juice, sir.”

Bob scrabbled for change in his pocket, paid up then handed a half-pint mug to Laurie. Laurie took a long draught immediately, but Bob edged his way over to some vacant bentwood chairs in a far corner. Annoyed, because he’d come all the way out to Larkham Cross in the hope of picking up some local gossip and the crush meant he wasn’t going to achieve anything, he sat down and took a doubtful sip of the cool liquid. It was sharp, dry and to his surprise delicious. He took a longer drink then settled the thick glass mug on a low, round table. The mug swivelled around and started to slide off. Laurie just saved it at the edge. Bob gaped at him as if it had been some sort of magic trick.

“The bottom’s wet,” Laurie said.

“What?” Bob leaned forward trying to hear over the loud Devonshire burr around them.

“Your bottom’s wet!” Laurie shouted.

“My bottom’s wet?” Bob shouted back.

The pub went silent.

Bob gave an exaggerated sigh: “It’s my glass! My glass – not me!” He waved a finger at the table before him, “See, the table’s been polished and the surface is . . . oh, never mind . . .”

A kindly eye winked. A gnarled hand patted his shoulder. Then an aged rustic gaffer in a cap that looked as if it had grown into his wizened forehead settled himself on the third chair. "I reckons as how Gwyneth do it on purpose," he said as an explanation. "You'm laughin' at us b'ain't you, old maid," he shouted in the direction of the bar. "I knows your tricks!" Catching sight of Bob's expression, the old gaffer said, "Gwyneth's Mervyn's mother. My cousin by second marriage."

"Ah," Bob nodded, "and Mervyn is the landlord?"

"S'right. His pa was a Jack but his grandpa and great grandpa afore him they were Mervyns. Like me. Only four Mervyns left now in my generation in Larkham Cross. You met one of 'em already. At the store. 'Spect we'll be died out soon." He shook his head as if the world were about to end and turned his cider mug upside down in the air.

Bob took the hint. "Can I get you another one of those?"

"Kindly spoken, kindly received," said the old man, and handed his mug across the table to Laurie, who took the hint and went to the bar. As he did so, the old man leaned over the arm of his chair towards Bob and said, "You'm that police fella been sniffing round Hentree."

Taken by surprise again, Bob gulped, "Erm – yes, I am. How do you know that?"

The old man tapped his purple-mottled nose and leaned forward again. "Where is he then, eh? Where's the old bugger got to? He owes my granddaughter's husband for two months' meat, not to mention all the extras that boy Greville's been adding to the bill."

"Ah," Bob responded but before he could continue the old man was off again.

"I seen they maids going into Mervyn's shop for their knick-knacks as well. Buxom one of them is. Haw yes! If I were her age, haw, I'd have her in the haystack, I would."

Aware he was being taken for a soft touch, tapped for a free drink by an old man nobody else would listen to, Bob rubbed his chin and decided to take advantage of the situation himself. Latching onto the comment about the general store, he started there, saying what a comprehensive emporium it was for a small village and progressed to groceries. The granddaughter's husband's butcher's shop turned out to be next door but one to the general store. It didn't take long to find out how much food was being consumed at Ridgeway Farm, and who was actually living there, and that nothing for human consumption went to Hentree. Feeling pleased with the way things were going, Bob smiled as Laurie returned with a fresh pint of cider and set it in on the tricky table. Before the boy could resume his seat, though, Bob cocked his head in the opposite direction and Laurie wandered away to join a crowd at the dartboard.

"Know him well, do you, Josiah Slattery?" Bob asked the old man over the rim of his half-pint mug.

"Well as any bugger yer-abouts."

"Not one for a drink here, I take it."

"Too mean to use the shoe leather to get yer."

Old gaffer Mervyn got stuck into his cider and the next thing Bob heard was laughter and voices saying, "Drink up boy, improve your aim no end."

"Down in one."

"Thatta boy!"

Bob turned to see what was going on but his elbow slipped off the arm of his chair, nearly pitching him into the fireplace.

"It do that to you, Star 'n Anchor cider do. Knees 'n elbows every time. You're not used to it, see." Old Mervyn laughed till he choked and had to drain his brew to get his breath back.

Over at the dartboard, Laurie was standing legs apart, right arm extended in the act of aiming a dart. He looked every inch the Greek athlete but the locals were rapidly forming a semi-circle well behind him.

The dart shot from Laurie's hand and a voice squawked, "What you bloody doin', boy? Nearly pursed my yerlobe, that did."

Laurie coloured up puce to his own earlobes and everyone started laughing. Bob grinned and returned to his conversation with Gaffer Mervyn. "Mr Slattery hasn't had much of a success with Hentree Farm by the looks of it."

"'Bandoned, it is," Old Mervyn nodded. "Terrible shame. In the Pascoe family for generations – sheep mainly – and they did well out of 'em. Good folk, the Pascoes were. My missis was a Pascoe second removed. Dead now she is. Wimin's complaint. Not that she ever complained, bless her dear 'eart."

Bob nodded in consolation. The same had happened to his wife Joan, but he wasn't going to mention it. "Only pigs and hens there now, from what I've seen," he said, referring to Hentree Farm.

Old Mervyn gave a twisted, wry look. "You want to be careful with they pigs. Don't get fed very often from what I yer tell."

There was another roar of laughter from the dartboard area and Laurie lurched back to Bob's table bearing an empty pint glass.

"Oh, they haven't? Don't tell me you fell for it."

"Fell – I'm falling, falling, falling from apple juice heaven," Laurie slurred and slumped into a chair.

Old gaffer Mervyn chuckled and tapped the boy's arm. "You've broke our law young Mr Policeman. Only halves allowed to grockels, that's the rule."

Noting how Laurie's face was turning yellow, Bob lurched out of his seat and pulled the mug from the boy's clenched fist. "Come on, PC Oliver, time for some fresh air."

Getting Laurie out of the pub with any semblance of dignity proved impossible. Being considerably taller and longer in the limb, Bob had no choice but to drape the boy's right arm around his neck then drag him under the low beams and out of the door. Once outside, he pulled Laurie around the corner of the building then shoved him up against the wall and watched him slither down to a sitting position.

Bob rested against the whitewashed wall, closed his eyes and drank in the fresh air, which set his own head spinning. "What do they put in it?" he mumbled.

"Pure al-col-hol," Laurie stated. "Hundred per-cent proof. Not for grockels like you, Sarge. Too strong, see."

"What are these bloody grockels I keep hearing about?"

"Up country buggers," Laurie supplied.

"And they are . . .?"

"Grockels, tourists, day trippers. It's what they're called in the West Country."

"'Up country bugger': I've heard that before. Is that what Mallet calls me?" Bob asked, referring to the bumptious desk sergeant at Cready Police Station.

"Think sho," Laurie slurred.

"Hmm," Bob swatted at a squadron of gnats hovering above his head. "Persistent species of biters they've got down here. Probably breed them to harass their ruddy grockels." He halted in the act of swiping at his chin, "Breeds, species, family – up country buggers. I keep hearing about the Pascoes, 'gentry folk' they were. Nobody mentions the Slattery clan, and they were gentry if their drawing room is anything to go by."

"That's because they were newcomers, outsiders, according to Mrs Lee, although that was before her time. Out-*ciders*," Laurie giggled.

"Is that why nobody cares what happens at Ridgeway?" Bob mused. "Must be. If Mr Slattery senior was another 'up country bugger' . . . who bought a farm, and . . . and didn't know how to farm it. Wait here."

"Where else?" mumbled Laurie, watching his boss hasten back into the pub.

"Mervyn, Mervyn," Bob regained his seat next to the old man, "Mr Slattery's family, they weren't local, were they?"

"Not they, no. His father came from up country. Bought Ridgeway . . . ooh back in the 'sixties that would be. Three hundred acre and a fine house. I remember Faither talking about it, sayin' as how Mr Slattery was a townie and didn't know first thing about farming. Not a blazin' clue. Farm went downhill moment they walked in, Faither said. The wife played the organ at church. Pretty as a picture she was, 'pparently. He never went, though. Nor Josiah. Adelina, she was called. Lovely name. And refined. They both was. Educated man Mr Slattery 'ccording to Faither. I think. Memory might be playing tricks with my ol' brain, but I do believe as how Josiah was sent away to school. But then he came back and started at the elementary with the Mervyns and me."

"But he didn't fit in."

The old man gave his twisted, wry grin. "Never did. Private people, the Slatterys. Not proper country folk. His pa taught him boxin', though. To protect hisself from us. Kiddies are cruel little beasts."

"So that's why there aren't any of his family hereabouts?"

"That's why. There b'ain't none."

"But his mother played the organ at church – so they weren't chapel folk?"

"Ah, no, no. His *faither* was agistic, acrostic – agnosthick – one of they what don't believe in Jesus Christ nor nothin' else."

Old Mervyn turned his mug upside down again meaningfully, but Bob was lost in thought. "Do you think Mr Slattery senior might have gone bankrupt? You said he wasn't much of a farmer."

Old Mervyn sniffed and examined the interior of his mug then leaned forward, "Some say as that's why Josiah married Martha Pascoe so young. Mervyn Evans at the General Store was sweet on her but Josiah's family were a cut above, if you know what I mean? Least that's what the Pascoes might have thought. Poor Martha, miserable life she's had."

The old man stopped, lifted the peak of his cap and scratched his forehead. The skin under the cap was baby pink. "Families, eh?" he muttered sadly.

"Families – yes, I know. Right, that was very helpful Mr . . .?"

"Hook. You'll find me yer of an evenin' if you need anything. You should speak to my boy, George Hook. Done very well for hisself in Bideford. Solicitor is George."

Bob nodded and took the empty mug to the bar. "Got what you came for?" the landlord enquired.

Bob ignored the probe and placed two shillings and eightpence on the bar. "That's for Mr Hook, a pint tonight and another tomorrow. Thank you very much. Good night." As he left, Bob felt a score of eyes on his back but didn't turn around.

***

# Chapter 26

Pleased to be back in the fresh air, Bob was relieved to find Laurie where he'd left him. "Rain's stopped. Can we go now?" the boy said.

"It hasn't been raining," Bob replied. "Light's going, though. Nights are drawing in. Let's see if we can get back before it's completely dark." He waited while Laurie rolled onto his knees then unravelled himself to stand with a hand against the wall for support. "Can you make it to the car, or shall I send for a taxi?"

"Sorry, Sarge," Laurie said, hanging his head. "I shouldn't have moved. Think I'm going to be –"

Bob pushed the boy away from the wall in the direction of the road, "Bring it all up, lad. I'll back the car round."

It took Bob a while to extricate himself from the hawthorn and honeysuckle hedge, which was probably just as well because it gave Laurie time to empty the contents of his stomach.

For the first mile back to Bideford neither of them spoke. Eventually, Bob said, "First thing tomorrow, you go up to Hentree on your bike and search the place like Sherlock Holmes with a ruddy magnifying glass. Pick up anything, *anything* that isn't rooted in Devonshire soil."

"Right-ho, Sarge,"

"I'll drive up and walk the lanes between the two farms. Which reminds me, you still haven't told me what the Land Army girls said."

"Oh, Bunty told me about seeing a well-dressed woman walking back towards a parked car in the lane on Friday afternoon. She thought it was someone from the council or the evacuee organisers. Wearing a plain hat, tall for a woman and well-built. Not young."

"Tall for a woman," Bob repeated. So not Jessamyn.

"Cilla said she thought, only thought, Ken, her army friend, had a row with Josiah Slattery then went off with Greville to Hentree last week. And they both said Mrs Lee is as likely to make up a story to keep us happy as tell the truth. And . . . and I've got the rest in my notebook."

"So, nothing new except that Ken or Quentin – if it is Quentin – and Greville knew each other. Did you ask about Mrs Slattery?"

"They didn't know there was a Mrs Slattery. Leastways they assumed she was dead. Cilla said it stood to reason that there had been a Mrs, but no one ever mentioned her."

"Poor woman," Bob muttered. "Right, no more talking, sun's gone down and we've still got a mile of pitch-dark lanes to get through. If Hitler knew how many civilians get killed by cars without headlights, he'd slap his leather shorts with glee."

After a few minutes, Laurie said, "Supposing Slattery didn't want to sell Hentree . . . supposing he was refusing to sell and someone who stands to benefit wanted him out of the way."

"Like the grandson or Greville Healey – possibly on Ma Healey's instructions. Yes. Go on."

"But then who shot the boy? A rival claimant, next in line to the farm?" Laurie queried.

"Or to prevent it being sold at all. According to the land agent there's been muttering and discontent in the local community.

Locals aren't too keen on having grimy city kids spoiling their landscape. Which," Bob huffed, "widens the suspect list very nicely. Not that we need to worry about that, of course."

"No, but it might help us find Farmer Slattery."

"Exactly."

As they turned a corner, Bob slammed on the footbrake, sending Laurie's fair head smack into windscreen. A figure stood momentarily in the middle of the road, then dashed to the other side and disappeared into the hedge. "Stupid bugger!" Bob yelled. Winding down the window, he shouted into the darkness, "Wear something white at night! Do as you're bloody told you daft, inbred yokel."

"Mr Pots," Laurie said, rubbing his forehead. "On his nightly jaunt. Got his sack and the knife?"

Amazed, Bob squinted at his passenger, "You still drunk?"

"Squiffy. Def-nite-ly. But that was Mr Pots. He'd got his goggles on."

Bob shook his head in wonder, "What on earth . . .?"

"No idea, Sarge. But we've seen him before. Out foraging, Suky reckons."

"Well I won't ask what for, if you promise not to tell me, all right?"

Laurie gave a feeble salute and slumped back into his seat. "It's only a knife, not one of his guns or weird stuff."

"*Weird stuff*?"

"That's what Suky says. He's got guns and ammunition and 'weird stuff' in his garden shed. And Hester's broom cupboard."

"In a broom cupboard! What, pistols in with the polish?"

"Suppose so. I didn't ask."

"Why ever not?"

Laurie blinked and grinned, "I had other things on my mind at the time."

"I bet you did, but I'm not interested in that. Tell me about this Mr Pots and his armoury."

"Apparently, when he's not cooking, or breeding stray cats or out on one of these nocturnal foraging trips, he's shut up in his garden shed."

"Poor bugger. If he really was a prisoner of war he might find being up there, all closed in, comforting. One way of avoiding those blasted thespians' anyway. 'Wayward Players' – wayward in the head, if you ask me."

"Suky is perfectly sane," Laurie enunciated carefully. "And very talented."

"'Course, she is. And proving a useful pair of ears and eyes, I hope. What has she said about Mrs Flowers?"

Laurie shook his head. "Haven't had chance to talk to her about that yet."

"Never mind. What else does she say about the cook?"

"Not much. Only that they all think Mr Pots is potty."

Bob rolled his eyes and returned to peering over the steering wheel into the darkness, lit only by his specially shaded, dipped headlights. "Is that true, do you think, that he's got boxes of guns? We ought to check. Sure as hell he hasn't got a licence."

"They'll be war relics, won't they?" Laurie replied, sitting up. "Doubt if he's got any live bullets or anything like that. Might have a grenade or two, though."

"*A grenade or two!* And he's harmless?" Bob scoffed, crashing through his gears. "Stark blooming bonkers they are in that house. The lot of them."

***

# Chapter 27

## Thursday

Jessamyn put down her cup and lay back into her feather pillow, reluctant to start the day. There was too much to be done, too much to be decided. Arthur's funeral was scheduled for Monday afternoon at the parish church, it would draw a large crowd for, as Maud constantly reminded her, the Puddicombe family were local benefactors and Arthur had been a well-respected member of Bideford District Council.

She started to make a mental list: funeral tea to be organised at the Tudor Rose Tea Rooms (too many people for Peony Villas); tell Lavinia about the Americans moving in at the beginning of October (should she ask her to deal with it now?); tell Lavinia she was going up to London (say she was grieving and needed to get away on her own, which was almost true). Next: arrange for Hester's cousin Ruth to come in and give all the rooms an extra cleaning when the Waywards left; make sure their bills were up to date; make sure Wendell didn't leave anything behind as an excuse to return (he was promising – threatening – never to leave her); ask Maud for her petrol ration and fill up the car. Then there were private things only she could do, starting with Quentin's room (make sure there was nothing incriminating there, no stash of NAAFI goods, or worse); tell

Maud she was leaving Bideford as soon as the funeral was over, but pretend she was only going away for a short break.

The thought of what she was going to tell Lavinia made Jessamyn sit up. Running her fingers through her thick chestnut hair and trying to clear her head, she remembered she had her weekly appointment this morning as well. But first, before anything else, she needed to get back to Ridgeway and find out why the police were up there: what on earth had her father done? Attacked someone? Heaven knows he'd threatened enough people. Not one of those Land Army girls, surely? Or was it Hentree Mr Robbins had been referring to? Quentin had been up at Hentree, she was sure of it.

Or not go to either? What she didn't know, she couldn't worry about.

Hairdresser, tea rooms, confirm order of service at vicarage . . . Jessamyn swung her legs out of bed. Time to get a move on: the running order would slot into place somehow during the day. Then another nagging, guilt-laden thought sneaked in: should she make more of an effort to see her mother? Refuse to leave the property unless she spoke to her.

Why, oh why, hadn't she done this before?

Was it worth asking for forgiveness this late in the day, though, when she was planning to run away again immediately? Her father had said she was too ill to be disturbed, but her mother would want to see her, surely?

Why was her father still so set against her after all these years?

Had Lavinia been up there, trying to be an intermediary? That could have made things worse. Or had Quentin riled him? "What a mess," Jessamyn sighed.

There was a sharp rat-tat and Lavinia put her head around the door. "Jessie, you'd better see this," she said. Crossing the room quickly, Lavinia dropped a copy of the *Western Morning*

*News* on the counterpane. It was folded open at a small entry on the third page.

> **Bideford Tragedy**
> Young farmer found shot dead.
> Greville Bradley Healey, only son of Stanley and Sheila Healey of 14, New Station Crescent, St David's, Exeter, was found shot dead at Hentree Farm, Barley Cliff, near Bideford on Friday last by Detective Sergeant Edgar Robbins, who is holidaying in the district. Miss Helena Angela Bazeley (Women's Land Army), who is currently working on an adjacent farm, declared that the victim was often at Hentree Farm shooting vermin and rabbits. The owner of the two farms, septuagenarian Mr Josiah Eli Slattery has not been located. The jury heard that Mr Healey had been shot by a pistol by a person unknown. North Devon Coroner Dr. Amos Parsons said at the inquest in Bideford on Wednesday that there was little doubt the death was intentional. A verdict of unlawful killing was returned.

Jessamyn looked up at Lavinia, "Why would he shoot Greville?"

"Who, your pa? Nothing to say that he did. All it says is that he can't be located. He's gone missing."

"How can that be? Unless . . ." Jessamyn's face went white. "Oh my God, do you think he shot his grandfather as well?"

"Grandfather?"

"Oh my God, no. Please say it isn't true."

Lavinia stared at Jessamyn. "Who? You don't think – you can't – you can't think Quentin did a thing like that?"

Jessamyn bit her lower lip and slowly nodded her head. "He wanted to be sure he was in Josiah's will, made me go up there to talk to him. But Father wouldn't speak to me except to say I was never to set foot on his land again, as if I were some sort of poacher. But . . . Quentin went on and on about it so I went back. He wasn't there, but a car like Mr Robbins' was in the yard. I thought I'd try and talk to Father while he'd got visitors, so at least they could see I was *trying* to get back to my family. I know what they say . . ." She paused and bit her lip.

"What happened?" Lavinia asked quietly.

"Nobody heard me knock so I used my old key . . ." she took a deep breath. "I walked into the house – like a thief. I thought they'd be in the yard so I went to his office and looked for his will. I've been asking and asking George Hook about it and he won't tell me anything and Quentin's nagged and nagged."

"Did you find it?"

Jessamyn nodded. "I found a letter from the solicitors from years ago. It was about including Greville Healey – my nephew – in the will. The letter says Quentin's name had been erased and replaced with Greville's. He was to get Hentree, which isn't even Slattery property. My mother owns it. I'd been cut out – obviously – but Quentin lived there when he was little, you see. Except he got away as soon as he could as well. I told you about this years ago."

"But that was this week – when you got the letter?"

"Yes."

"Why didn't you tell me?" There was a moment's silence, then Lavinia whispered, "I've been up to Ridgeway Farm as well. I thought I could persuade your father to soften to you. Did you know?"

Jessamyn cocked her head to one side. "Say that again. To persuade my father to 'soften'? Is that what you said?"

Lavinia, nodded. "I was trying to help."

"Me or Quentin? He's been at you as well, hasn't he! 'Soften' that was his word exactly."

"Don't get angry with me, please don't get angry with me."

Jessamyn sighed heavily, "I'm trying not to." She looked up at her old friend, "Did you see my mother?"

"No, I'm sorry. I should have gone to her first, shouldn't I? I'm such a fool without you, Jessie."

"That's nonsense, don't be silly," Jessamyn shook her head, tears welling in her eyes.

Lavinia retrieved the newspaper and stared at it for extra information. "This Greville Healey, he's a nephew?"

"My nephew, I suppose, by marriage. He's not connected to the Pascoe family."

"But was Josiah leaving Hentree to him as well as Ridgeway?"

"Looks like it. Technically, my father can't leave Hentree to anyone. It belongs to my mother's family. It's always been entailed in the Pascoe family line. It should, by rights, come to me. I promised Quentin he could live there. I don't want to, for heaven's sake. But when I spoke to George Hook about it, he said entailment has been abolished, so property can be inherited by anyone outside the family now."

"So, if this Greville has been shot, might Quentin inherit something now – or are you the only surviving relative?"

"I really don't know." Jessamyn paused, "Vinny, what did Quentin ask you to do?"

"What I just said, speak to your father, try to get him to let bygones be bygones."

"He didn't say anything about Greville Healey?"

"Um – well, not in so many words. He just wanted to know what was happening on the farms."

"So, Quentin has been going up there?"

"Yes."

Jessamyn swallowed hard then she said coldly, "Vinny, where were you on Friday afternoon?"

Lavinia's round, brown eyes closed tight shut. She scrunched her hands into her skirt like a naughty child and Jessamyn wanted to slap her very hard.

“Where?” she demanded.

“I thought I was helping,” Lavinia gulped.

“What have you been doing?” Fear iced Jessamyn’s tone.

Lavinia took a couple of paces backwards. “I was only trying to help – you and Quentin. For both your benefit.”

Jessamyn’s mind rushed through the events of Friday. She had been to Daneman Court in the morning to see Selena Candle. She had come back and tried to catch up on her accounts for the summer months. Lavinia had taken the car and left without saying anything. Had she taken Quentin up to Larkham? Or had she been on her own?

“You’d better go now,” she said.

Lavinia moved towards the door then looked back and said, “You should have gone and made your peace when you first came back to Bideford. Arthur wanted you to. You should have asked forgiveness and –”

“Forgiveness! After what my father did to Davy? Never!”

Lavinia lingered by the door, a plump white hand on the white porcelain handle. “Talk to Quentin,” she said quietly. “Let him tell you what he’s been doing. Trying to do. Give him a chance to explain his side.”

“That’ll be difficult. He called last night, he’s on a troop ship leaving from Plymouth this morning. They’ll have a hard job finding him, let alone getting him back – if – if anyone suspects him. Pass me that robe, will you.

“Like that Mr Robbins, you mean?” Lavinia lifted a rose-tinted satin robe from the hook on the door and handed it to her. “Why don’t we take a drive out to Larkham? I’ll come with you. Your mother will need someone if –”

“No!” Jessamyn’s response was adamant. “I am never setting foot in Larkham again. Ever. I’ll be getting the first train up to London on Tuesday, after the funeral.” She pulled on her robe and tied it tightly at her waist.

"I'll start packing," Lavinia said.

"No, Vinny, I'm going alone this time. I need to make a complete break. And after this . . . things have changed between us. Besides, I need you here to look after the house for me."

Lavinia stood very still. "You're going away with that Wendell creature."

"Don't be silly, why would I do that?"

"I know what's been going on. He comes to your room at night. I've seen it with my own eyes."

"Perhaps you have. But you are making entirely the wrong assumption. Wendell's idea of intimacy goes as far as stroking the back of my hand. We sit on my chairs," Jessamyn indicated two white-tasselled easy chairs in front of her grate, "and he tells me about growing up in Zurich and holidaying on the Côte D'Azur and the night life in Nice, and all sorts of exotic places, and I tell him whatever nonsense comes into my head. That's all. Wendell has no interest in women."

"If you are trying to tell me he's one of those theatrical types who prefer his own sex, you are wasting your time."

"What? Like you, Vinny?"

"I don't know what you mean."

"Really? I've watched you watching me for the past twenty odd years. Well, I'm sorry, but you'll have to look elsewhere as of next week."

"You can be very cruel, *Ada*."

Jessamyn let the barb pass. "I learned it from the cradle. But I have never knowingly been cruel to you."

She went up to her old friend, the woman who had become her dresser when she was a rising star and had stayed at her side out of loyalty, tied to a secret that only they understood for nearly half a lifetime. "Tell me you're not involved with anything it says in the paper."

"I'm not, I promise."

Jessamyn stared Lavinia in the eye then, gently touching the older woman's round face, she said, "We have always looked after each other, you and I. Could you stay here and look after Peony Villas for me now? As soon as the Waywards leave some American Army officers will be moving in. Maud won't be able to cope, and we can't have Mr Pots left on his own." Smiling kindly at her friend, Jessamyn moved to her dressing table. "I'm a bit worried about how he'll react to foreign uniforms around him, to be honest."

Lavinia put a hand to her mouth, "You don't think what's happened out at Hentree could be *his* doing? I saw Quentin with him last week – when? I don't remember but they were out at the aviary and Quentin was talking to him – telling him to do something, I think. Like he did with me. He stopped the moment he saw me. Mr Pots has got all those old guns, remember."

The two women exchanged glances in in the dressing table mirror in silence, then, turning, Jessamyn said, "I hid a box of bullets, but Quentin could have brought him some more from the camp. Oh, Lord, Vinny, get that bloody box of guns. Wait until nobody's around and bring it up here. Don't let anyone see you. And don't mention this to anyone, either. It could all be an awful coincidence and neither Quentin nor Mr Pots are involved."

"Jessie, you're not thinking clearly. Suppose someone finds out *you've* got access to a pistol, *and* you've that other box of ammunition we found up in the attic – suppose they start to think it was *you* who went out to Hentree and . . ."

"Why would anyone even make the connection? Nobody knows about my family except you and George Hook, and he's proved himself to be a proper limpet – with me anyway."

"Maud knows."

"Maud barely goes out of her front door. And I can't see her boasting about her famous sister-in-law to anyone in her precious Bideford, can you?"

"No, but think about it, Jessie. Your photo has been in the newspapers, opening the regatta, and at the cricket club dances. Someone will connect you sooner or later."

Jessamyn knew she was right. That someone already had. Quentin had been pestering Hester again, she was certain of it. He could have let slip where they came from in his sweet-talking; and Hester could have overheard all manner of details over the past few years. She could easily have said enough at home for her policeman father to make a connection. "Ah," she said aloud, "that's why."

"Why what?"

"The car I saw parked at Ridgeway the last time I was there – it looked like the one Mr Robbins drove. It *was* his car."

"And he's still a policeman, not retired?"

"A detective sergeant, brought out of retirement for the duration and now poking his nose into my family affairs. That's why he's here. I knew there was something fishy."

"Jessie," Lavinia interrupted her thoughts, "you mustn't leave after the funeral. It will look like you're running away. Stay here with me. We'll see this through together, like we did before. I'll stand by you: you know I will."

Jessamyn shook her head, "I can't. I have to get away and be on my own. And this confirms it." She picked up the newspaper, "If I don't disappear, I'm going to have to stand up in court . . . and then . . . and then all our dirty washing will be aired in public. Arthur doesn't deserve that."

***

# Chapter 28

Lavinia closed the door with the jasmine plaque behind her slowly, but her heart was racing at a far different rate: Jessie was leaving without her. After all they had been through together. After what had happened back in '22. Their secret bond. Consumed by a sense of betrayal, she slunk down the stairs and returned to the morning room to finish her breakfast out of habit.

Mr Robbins was sitting at his little table. He took one look at her face, jumped to his feet and said, "Whatever's the matter, you look like you've seen a ghost?"

"I have. My husband, lying at the bottom of the stairs," Lavinia gasped then burst into tears.

Bob settled Mrs Baxter-Salmon in the chair opposite him and poured her a cup of tea. "Tell me about it," he said quietly, and knowing he was inviting the dreaded unpleasant confidence or a request to investigate, he sat down to listen.

"Roland – my husband – was affected, badly affected by the last war. He was quite a heavy drinker before he was called up, but afterwards he just drank and drank. If I said anything, he shouted at me. Screamed at me. Said if I'd seen what he'd seen, I'd drink. He lost three fingers of his right hand. People said he'd done it on purpose. What they called a 'blighty' – shooting yourself to get an injury and sent home. He hadn't but . . . but it made it difficult to get a job and – gradually, quite quickly really

– we ran out of money. My parents helped but I was ashamed to ask. So, we took in a lodger. She was a sort of dancer called Pearl Pascoe. It was her stage name in those days. I met her at the bus stop one afternoon when she fainted. I took her home because it was just across the road – then she moved in. But Roland wouldn't leave her alone. And he was getting worse. And dangerous. He threw knives at me in the kitchen if his food wasn't right . . . Then, when Jessie wouldn't let him into her room . . . It was awful. For both of us."

For a moment there was silence. Mrs Baxter-Salmon stared at the table, seeing nothing but a vivid memory.

"Go on," Bob encouraged gently.

The woman's vast bosom heaved with the weight of her sorrow, "Jessie – Ada as she was then, she became Jessamyn after that, when we moved to London and I became her dresser and sort of manager – well, Jessie had a good idea how to stop it . . ." She blinked rapidly and gave him an apologetic smile.

Bob looked out of the window and waited, then said quietly, "And Roland?"

"Marbles. On the stairs. She invited next door's children to come in and play a special game of marbles on the stairs. So, when he came home . . . it looked like a silly, horrible accident. That we'd forgotten to pick them all up." She stopped, then started again. "I thought he would just be injured, you see. That he would break a leg and have to be in bed, and so he'd stop drinking. But Jessie had it planned that way from beginning. She was glad he was dead."

Bob lifted his lukewarm tea and took a sip. "Clever," he said to himself. "Very clever."

Realising what she had just revealed, the woman put a hand on her ample chest and inhaled deeply. "Will you arrest us?" she asked.

Bob shook his head. "Over twenty years ago, wasn't it? Nothing to do with me."

Except it was, because it was another link in the chain he'd been making. And, unfortunately, it demonstrated a cold, very calculating streak in the adorable Jessamyn Flowers.

***

# Chapter 29

Wendell opened his bedroom door just as Jessamyn crossed the landing. Her face was white, her hair a mess. He'd never seen her looking so dishevelled. "Morning, Puddi," he started to say then stopped. This was not the moment. And definitely not the right name. Soundlessly, he closed his door and turned the key. After the funeral, when she joined them at Daneman Court to play her role in the film, that would be a good time. He'd ask her to marry him, suggest a glorious future in film, a move to Hollywood when the war was over, he had contacts there – which was true. Then, once they were married, he'd say he'd lost his passport and use their marriage certificate to get a new one as Wendell Garamond.

Later, though. He could wait another week or two, a month even. It wouldn't do to rush her too fast and risk frightening her away. Jessie would learn his Austrian name, of course, and where he'd really come from, but at least she wouldn't make the connection between her widowhood and their marriage.

Sitting at his small table, he ran his hands through his mane of hair. His fingers told him it was thinning – rapidly. Hardly surprising considering the life he was leading. Wendell closed his eyes and imagined himself back in the blissful silence of his father's study in Vienna. Was anything left there now? Had all the books been taken and burnt? Tears pricked his eyes, he took a handkerchief from his pocket and tried to bring himself under control.

Lying back in the chair he tried to disconnect: to float free of all the stress that surrounded him. After a while he got up, straightened his shoulders and mentally donned the mantel of Wendell Garamond, actor-manager, once more. Time to face the day, and another dreaded performance in another dreadful village hall. *Smile, Wendell, it'll soon be over.*

The day, which had begun with unseasonable heat, turned into a heavy, humid afternoon. The Wayward Players arrived early enough for their last afternoon show to change into costumes in the kitchen area of the Littlehamholt church hall without undue hurry. The vicar and his wife were there to greet them with home-made barley water.

None of the players felt much like being sociable, however, and the refreshing drink was taken in virtual silence, then each went about their preparations for the show. The vicar's wife went to set up the table for the entrance fee. The vicar went into the hall to help supervise arrangements for the audience with Billy Bryant. Members of the local Boy Scout troop were setting out folding chairs, leaving an aisle down the middle of the hall for easier access. The vicar said there would be a full house.

Reg Dwyer began organising their few props. Wendell and Estelle went up onto the rickety boards of the un-curtained stage. It didn't look as if it would support a ballerina, let alone a contralto of Estelle's proportions plus supporting cast.

Wendell's real intimations of disaster began while watching Estelle manoeuvre her framed farthingale into place, judging where to stand for her Good Queen Bess rendition of *There'll Always Be an England.*

"You'll have to move nearer the front," Wendell said, "we've got to get behind you for the chorus." He jumped off the stage and walked backwards up the aisle to get an idea of how they would look.

Estelle moved a step forward and began her vocal warm up, causing the scouts to halt whatever they were doing and gawp at her. She sang the first few lines of a song Wendell didn't recognise and the boys burst out clapping. Estelle finished the verse, smiled and gave a gracious curtsey, and Wendell could have sworn she was three stones lighter. "Stage presence," he said to himself, wishing he had it. But he was a humble Literature professor, not a true thespian in any way.

"Good acoustics, actually," Estelle said, looking up to check the lighting. "No proper lights, though."

"There never are, Estelle. It's still broad daylight outside and look – no curtains on the windows either."

"They were black," said one of the scouts. "Vicar said we could use them for blackouts at home."

Wendell forced a smile of acknowledgement while repeating to himself his new mantra: 'The end is nigh; the end is nigh.'

The hall was stifling hot, and within minutes full to bursting. Latecomers jockeyed for position around the walls. Children were chivvied out of chairs to sit cross-legged down the centre aisle. Wendell suddenly felt much happier. This would be his last performance in what he secretly thought of as amateur dramatics. That it was in a village with a name he could barely pronounce for people who would be horrified to hear where he came from made it all the more bitter-sweet. He made his way backstage, checked his Macbeth costume, dabbed on the silly moustache, then waited beside the stage, where he could see but not be seen by very many.

At five-thirty precisely, Horace stomped onto the stage in Malvolio's yellow hose and crossed-garters and proclaimed: "*An Afternoon with Shakespeare* from the London Troupe of The Wayward Players, with songs from the famous Estelle

Dobson, contralto, and sweet Suky Stefano, soubrette. Mr Laurence Oliver accompanying."

There was barely a titter at the boy's name, which was a mixed blessing, Wendell thought. Those who'd never heard of Laurence Olivier wouldn't be expecting a West End performance.

The door at the back of the hall opened and Jessamyn and the Baxter-Salmon woman sidled in. The vicar, seated on the back row gave up his seat, pushing the sexton off his in the process. It had taken a lot of persuasion to get Jessamyn to come. He regretted it now: she had never looked so sad.

The door opened again and the dumpy Mr Robbins entered. He was left standing by the vicar, which was as it should be: Robbins had been too friendly by half with Jessamyn. Robbins, he had just learned, was a police detective. How fortunate the Waywards were moving to Daneman Court.

The single light bulb hanging over the stage was briefly extinguished and Suky came on as Olivia in *Twelfth Night*. They'd simplified the cross-garter scene with Malvolio using puttees for humour, but now for the first time Wendell saw it was basically meaningless. Horace roused the first laugh of the night nevertheless, and they were off.

Suky was back on again, with her new young man at the tuneless piano to close the first half with a touching rendering of *Hey Ho the Wind and the Rain*, but before she was through the first verse, two matrons in pinafores pushed their way down the centre aisle, climbed up onto the stage and exited stage right to put on the various outsize kettles in the kitchen area for the intermission tea. None of the audience batted an eyelid and Suky sang on like a trooper, but it was the final straw for Wendell.

This was it! Enough!

No more silly acting for village yokels: no more wandering around the country at all. Jessamyn *must* see sense and provide him with some security, tonight he would tell her the truth and beg for her assistance.

But there was worse to come.

It happened during his scene as Macbeth with Banquo's ghost. Reg Dwyer, as the ghost, had forgotten to take off his shoes. Squeak-creak, squeak-creak – his cracked leather shoes squeaked in distress and the floorboards creaked at every step. The audience howled with laughter.

"This is not funny!" Wendell shouted at them; his pronunciation wholly Teutonic. "This is a *tragedy*!"

The audience laughed louder.

Completely unaware of his diction, Wendell pitched his voice over the mayhem: "I am a great leader here."

The audience howled.

"The humour comes later, you Philistines!" Wendell hissed under his breath and started to shake.

Reg adjusted his spectacles through the eyeholes in his sheet. "You all right, mate?" he asked, bringing tears to half a hundred pairs of eyes.

"No, I am not all right!" Wendell retorted; his Austrian intonation stronger than ever. Grown men and women rocked in their folding seats. One chair collapsed altogether, snapping its victim like a crocodile and sending everyone around into bladder-threatening paroxysms.

Sweating, shaking, unable to control his tears, Wendell crept off stage left. He was having a nervous breakdown. And no surprise after what he'd been through in the past five years.

But all was not lost. Jessamyn raced to the stage, crossed it as fast as she could and pulled him into her arms.

Wendell opened an eye, then another, then gave the smallest sigh of satisfaction: Robbins had followed her and was watching every moment.

For a heartbeat Wendell felt guilty: Jessamyn was too good for him, she didn't deserve a flawed husband, but immediately succumbed to self-interest. "Oh, Jessie, Jessie," he whispered, milking the moment for every drop of melodrama – and loud enough for all to hear, "take me home. Take me home."

***

# Chapter 30

Bob didn't linger to see any more. Pushing through the shambles, he quickly made his way out to fresh air, and sanity. If he'd been a smoker this was the ideal time to lean against a nearby oak and inhale nicotine. Instead, he slouched against the tree and closed his eyes, inhaling the sultry air. For the space of ten seconds there was absolute silence. Then a blackbird sang out. A stonechat chat-chatted on the low wall. He opened his eyes to see it bob up and down, and smiled. Then he noticed a woman in a voluminous Elizabethan gown coming around the side of the imposing vicarage opposite the hall. It was Estelle of The Second Bathroom. Who else would be wandering about in a farthingale on a late summer afternoon in 1942? Perhaps she had been using the house for its sanitation facilities. Bob watched her cross the road, lifting her weighted skirts, then duck down so she wouldn't be seen from a side window by anyone in the audience and disappear around the back of the hall.

Were they going to finish the performance? Should he go back in? Deciding he didn't want to see anything more, and that Laurie could make his way back with Suky, Bob climbed into his Morris, wound down his window and set off down the road. Otherwise lost, he soon found himself at a junction that he recognised from his trips to Barley Cliff and Larkham Cross. He took the Barley Cliff turning.

Leaving his car exactly where it had been on the afternoon of the shooting, Bob got out, pulled off his linen jacket, then tugged off his tie, rolled up his shirt sleeves and wandered down to the stile that led onto the cliff path. Cursing that he didn't have his binoculars with him, he decided to retrace his steps anyway, footprint for footprint – except for the area of the pigsty. That, he didn't need to revisit.

As a sickly ochre sun slowly descended into Barnstaple Bay, a fishing trawler crossed the bar, the distant chug-chug of its engine lending depth and a sense of reality to the timeless scene. Despite the cloying heat, Bob strolled at ease along the path until he came to the spot where he had stopped previously. The grass was slightly damp but he sat down anyway, then with a satisfied sigh, lay back and closed his eyes. Bees droned among the red clover and mauve-veined sea campion; a beetle strayed from a weed onto his bare arm, he flicked it off and drifted into a contented doze.

The crashing 'bang!' that woke him this time was not that of a shotgun or a pistol, it was mortar fire from across the bay. Bob sat up, disorientated, then gathering his wits and shielding his eyes from the bright sunlight, tried to see what was going on. There were three more almighty bangs then silence. In the far distance, barely visible among the sand-dunes, troops were practising with landing craft. Bob gave a small nod of acknowledgement: this must be what all the fuss and hush-hush business was about. Military personnel were trying out new weapons – or possibly – could it be? – rehearsing invasion tactics. Whatever, he could use the unexpected noise for his own purposes and start his replay again.

He got up and walked up the unploughed, un-grazed field to the gateway where he had spoken to the boy he now knew as Greville Healey. The old man had been on his back, unconscious. Yes, he had been unconscious, definitely.

Meaning he had had a seizure or stroke or simply fainted, or that Healey had shot him, by accident or otherwise with a Springfield single cartridge rifle. Twice.

So many questions still unanswered. Had Josiah Slattery really been coming down to tell him to get off his land? If so, he had had his back to Healey and Healey had shot him – by accident or on purpose. Two shots in immediate succession from a typical farmer's shotgun. Or two shotguns? Was that a possibility? And was it possible that the wound or wounds inflicted could have caused instant internal damage, but no visible (from the front) bleeding?

Easing his open collar away from his neck, Bob went back to his place under the tree and flopped down. The heat was unbearable, and not a breath of air. "Thunderstorm later," he said to himself. "Come on, Robbins, this could be your last time here. Get on with it."

He checked his watch, made a mental note of the time, scrambled to his feet and set off back along the cliff path. Stumbling now and again, Bob searched his memory: was there something, some little detail he'd overlooked or failed to notice? Had he simply forgotten something? He was getting forgetful, that could not be denied. But he had noticed the movement in the trees. He stopped and stared at the woodland area. Not a leaf moved.

Somebody could easily have been hiding among the trees and waiting until he was out of the way. Somebody who liked guns. Mad Mr Pots, for instance. Was he a likely murderer? Bob let out a loud sigh. Everything kept switching back to Peony Villas; to Quentin/Ken and – he was almost certain – Ada Slattery, a.k.a. Pearl Pascoe, a.k.a. Jessamyn Flowers, a.k.a. Mrs Puddicombe.

But where was the old man? Six days had passed and nobody had been able to find him. Had Ada Slattery been here? Farm-girl Ada would have learned to shoot. A pistol, though, where would she get a pistol from? Ah, Mr Pots' box of mortal tricks. Or her son, an Army corporal. It wouldn't be impossible for him to get hold of an officer's pistol.

Or, had farm-girl Ada with a past to be ashamed of and a previous un-proved homicide to her name, been out here with her protector, dear Mr Pots? Had *he* shot Josiah Slattery? Had she then removed her father's body – hidden it somewhere she would know about on this very land? But why on earth would she do that? It was in her interest to have Josiah certified dead; surely that was what dear Quentin wanted. . . Quentin, who had access to guns and a motive to kill both Slattery and Healey. But again, he'd need the old man's death certificate to claim his inheritance.

The regular tugga-tugga-tugga of another engine broke into his thoughts, growing louder and louder. A two-seater plane banked up from a low flight across the bay, appearing over the cliff edge like a Hollywood monster. Bob ducked down automatically then felt foolish and waved at the pilot like a schoolboy. The plane lifted higher, cleared the ancient trees bordering the eastern side of the farm and headed inland. Bob watched it go, suddenly afraid it was a spy plane and he ought to do something about it. This was his current default mode: the sensation that there was something horribly wrong and he should do be doing something to prevent another tragedy.

"What is it?" he demanded of himself. "There's tragedy here all right, but the answers aren't only here. They're in that bloody bed and breakfast set up," he sighed again, angry and frustrated that something – a little 'something' – was nagging at him and he couldn't grasp it.

He resumed his purposeful walk back to the stile then over it and into the lane. "Where are you, Josiah Slattery?" Bob asked aloud as he opened his car door then checked his watch. Nine minutes. Allow another two or so to get in and start the engine: ten-eleven minutes – deduct a minute for the plane, barely . . . round up to ten minutes, he hadn't been in a hurry.

He made a three-point turn for the third time and drove back to the farm. This time, he had to get out and open the gate, but he parked beside the old tractor as before. Switching off the Morris's engine, his fingers stayed on the steering wheel, twiddling up and down of their own accord. The Healey boy had shot Josiah Slattery, intending to make it look like an accident. He could say he'd been shooting rabbits from the farm gate and he hadn't seen Mr Slattery on the steep slope below. He could then call the police and ambulance and explain it had all been a terrible accident. Bit like marbles on a staircase. Except in *that* case there had been a man's body to bury if not mourn.

One clear point to be taken from this: Greville Healey had thought he'd been alone. That's why he was so angry when a ruddy tourist appeared on the scene.

The dog had been over there, chained up yet silent. At no time had Bob heard the dog bark. Because it was too weak? Because the poor beast was starving? Meaning young Mr Healey didn't give a toss about animals, and that the two Land Army girls were telling the truth when they said they didn't come here. Even Cilla would have fed the poor thing.

Who fed the pigs, though? Greville. That's how Greville knew about Hoblins, the holiday camp business. He'd been here when their representative wandered in. He knew all about the offer. An added bonus. Wouldn't his mother be pleased?

But they'd need to be in the old man's will, and they'd need his death certificate.

Bob looked to his left, observing the house, its late secret occupant giving it a posthumous sense of evil. Giving way to a very unprofessional sense of disquiet, he walked into the barn then turned to stare down at the place he'd found the boy. But had the boy been coming in or going out? Had he fallen where he'd been shot or moved into the shadow behind the big door?

Bob paced backwards inside the barn. This was where the shooter must have been. Not outside, but inside the barn. He knew the place. Had Healey known his killer?

But why was the boy in the barn? They'd combed its floor and found nothing. Had Healey dragged the old man into the barn, meaning to leave him there, and the old man had recovered and . . .? Unlikely. If the shotgun pellets in his back had produced internal bleeding, the old man wouldn't have recovered sufficiently to turn a pistol on the boy.

Bob closed his eyes, trying to recreate the scene in his head, but nothing else came to him. He looked through the murky atmosphere at the door leading out to the pigsty area. It was slightly ajar. He forced himself through the dusty, dark nave of the barn and edged through the gap. Waiting for his eyes to adjust to daylight, he listened hard for grunts and snuffles. There were sounds that could have been made by pigs, but none of the beasts emerged from under the broken roof to challenge him. Exhaling with considerable relief, he re-entered the barn. Daylight streaming in illuminated something – some things – hanging from the roof beams. "Agh!"

A row of dead crows, rooks and blackbirds were strung by their claws from a rope tied between two major crossbeams. The birds hung, wings outstretched, for all the world like the fairground bunting to celebrate Armageddon.

Why hadn't he noticed them before? Why hadn't Laurie or any of the Bideford coppers mentioned it? Because they had all been focused on the ground and the ruddy cliffs. Their eyes, his included, had been looking down, not up. Was that their mistake, had Old Man Slattery got himself up somewhere and not been able to get down?

Approaching the loft ladder, Bob had to give himself a serious talking to: "No, you are not too old for this. Wherever Josiah is, you can get there too, because – let's face it – he's a damned sight older than you."

He went up, but there was nothing to be found in the loft this time either. Nor anything new visible from the open window. Taking great care with the wobbly rungs of the ladder, Bob returned to ground level.

Laurie had done another thorough search of the house, and his eyesight was good, but was it worth another round? Reluctantly, Bob went back in through the kitchen door. This time, however, he stopped his search for the old man and started searching for clues to the Pascoe and Slattery family, specifically to a runaway daughter and the child she left behind.

Now, he started to notice things. The child and its mother had lived here once. Decoration was more feminine with none of the genteel poverty of Ridgeway Farm. Faded curtains had been floral cotton, light and airy. A small bedroom contained a child-sized bed and an old tea-chest still contained stuffed toys and bits of wooden tractors and trains. A larger bedroom had been occupied by an older boy. On top of a sturdy chest of drawers was a wooden box containing a dozen lead soldiers with model tanks and artillery. Had the boy run away to become a soldier, as his mother had run away to become an actress? He still had no concrete proof of that.

And that was what had to be remedied right now. Leaving everything exactly as it was, Bob headed back to Peony Villas. He had put off talking to her as long as he could – because he didn't want to know the truth. Because he didn't want her to be Ada Slattery. But Mrs Flowers' time was up.

Where had she been on Friday afternoon last? With a bit of luck, darling Wendell would give her an alibi. Mrs Baxter-

Salmon might offer the same, but he wouldn't believe either of them.

When he got back to Peony Villas, Bob raced up the stairs to his room faster than he could have dreamed possible. He grabbed the double photo of mother and child and raced back down to confront the lovely Jessamyn with her past.

Except she wasn't in. Nobody was in the house at all apart from Mr Pots in his basement kitchen. He was laying a shroud of pastry over an oven dish containing who knew what.

***

# Chapter 31

"That looks tasty. Chicken pie for supper, is it?" Bob asked.

No reply.

"Is Mrs Flowers outside, do you know?"

"No."

"Any idea where she might be?"

"With the German."

"German? I didn't know there were refugees here."

"There aren't."

Bob blinked, wondering who, and then twigged. "Mr Garamond?"

"That's him."

Bob sat down on the nearest empty chair. "Tell me about Mr Garamond," he said.

"Nothing to tell. Came yer and started the malarkey going round village halls."

"And you think he's a German?"

"I was there. I yerred it in his voice. Knew dreckly where 'e'd come from."

"Does Jess – Mrs Flowers know this?"

"Not my place to ask."

"No – but," Bob grimaced, "the thing is, I'm a police detective so it's my job to know quite a few things that don't concern me dreckly – directly."

Mr Pots sniffed and lifted the heavy oven dish. Holding it up on his left palm he began slicing off the excess pastry with an evil-looking blade. His arm muscles bulged. Transfixed, Bob said casually, "You've known Mrs Flowers a long time."

"Puddicombe's her name. Mrs Arthur Puddicombe."

"You knew her before she was married to Mr Puddicombe, though?"

"Only by yersay."

"Hearsay?"

"Local gossip. Arthur told me the truth of it."

"But you can't tell me?"

"No, he can't," came a sharp female voice from behind them, "but I can and will, Detective Robbins. What do you want to know?"

It was the woman from Number Two. Dressed now from head to foot in black she strode into the room and placed herself in front of him. Bob kept his seat: she was much taller than him.

"Ooh, nothing formal, I was just enquiring about Mrs Flowers. Puddicombe," Bob stuttered out.

"Puddicombe is her married name. I am Maud Puddicombe, her sister-in-law."

Bob laid open the double photograph frame on the floury table top. "Perhaps you recognise this," he said.

Maud Puddicombe glanced at it then looked him in the eye, "Where would you like me to start? Before or after she ran away?"

"Before," Bob said quietly, and pushed out a chair.

Much of what he learned matched what he'd pieced together from conversations in Larkham and from what he'd seen in the two houses. Maud was less informative about Josiah Slattery's background but he soon learned what he'd suspected, that he was a disappointed failure of a man, both as a father and farmer; that he had an evil temper and was given to cruelty. "That,"

Maud said, "has always been her excuse. How she managed to run away and leave behind her child – knowing – knowing! – the boy would be the victim of her father's disgust with her, that I have never understood. Is it any surprise Quentin turned out the way he has? He has his grandfather's temperament, made worse, in my belief, by treatment he must have received once his mother had left."

Bob frowned, "She didn't try to get him back, when he was a baby?"

"Oh, she says she did. She told Arthur her father wouldn't let her on the farm, let alone speak to the child. You can believe that or not."

"Your brother believed it?"

"He was besotted with her."

"I see. Tell me how they met."

Mr Pots banged shut the oven door. "Going up to my shed," he said, winding the mechanism of an ancient alarm clock then stuffing it in a trouser pocket. It took a while and broke the confidential atmosphere. Eventually, he picked up a heavy cardboard box from under the table and left without another word.

Bob waited until the back door shut behind him. Maud began gathering bits of unused pastry from the oil cloth covering the kitchen table. Rolling them into a grey lump, she said, "I don't know how they met exactly. He went up to London on council business and attended a play and came back a different sort of person. He went up to London on four more occasions and on the fifth returned with a wife. They had married in a registry office. I wasn't invited. I wasn't even told."

"So, this house, Number One, belonged to your brother?"

"Yes. He let her invite all manner of unsuitable people to stay, though. Then, when she heard about the Blitz, she invited them to actually live here."

"She has never tried to go back to her father's farm?"

Maud squashed the lump of pastry with her right palm. "To be fair, she did. She has always been anxious about her mother. That I do know, and that I believe to be true. But it's all based on guilt."

"Would you say she hated her father?" Against his will, Bob examined the woman's words for a motive. How much did Ada Slattery hate her father? Or was it revenge?

"Hated him?" Maud Puddicombe said, as if also examining the words for an ulterior meaning. She shook her head. "No. She feared him. Hated him for sending her first husband away, yes, but do you know . . ." she paused, "I sometimes wonder if Mr Slattery didn't do that for a good reason. This is speculation, but we all know Josiah Slattery couldn't run his father's farm, his father had run it into the ground and Josiah wasn't able to make a go of it either. I do wonder if he didn't send Mr Beere off to join the Forces back in '15 to *help* him. Not dissimilar to how Quentin now has a chance to make a new life in the Army. Safest place for him, in my opinion. Proper discipline."

"Except there is a war on," Bob muttered, thinking about his own son.

Continuing in speculative mode, Maud said, "I've often wondered why Slattery hasn't just sold up. Perhaps Ridgeway is entailed as well. His wife's farm was tied up in all sorts of legal knots, from what Arthur told me. Hearsay of course."

Hearsay, hearsay! Bob was sick of it. The only person who could tell him what he needed to know was Jessamyn. Did Ada Slattery hate her father enough to arrange his death and possibly arrange or kill the boy Healey to provide her son with his inheritance? It was an awful thought. "Thank you," he said, abruptly. "Thank you, Miss Puddicombe, that has been most helpful." He got up to leave, picked up the photographs and with the briefest smile of acknowledgment headed for the steps up to the ground floor.

"Aren't you going to ask me about what has happened at Hentree?" Maud demanded.

'No,' he wanted to say, but instead turned and said, "Tell me anything that you know *for a fact.*" Maud scowled, squinting her eyes like a malevolent witch in a children's story. If looks could kill, he thought. "Facts, Miss Puddicombe."

"Well if it's facts you are after, I can tell you one thing that should inform your entire investigation: Ada Slattery is false to her fingernails."

"I know." Bob nodded, remembering his own words. He started back up the steps.

"And don't forget that Baxter-Salmon woman," Maud called after him. "She'd do *anything* her little Jessie asked. Start by asking her where *she* was on Monday night!"

"Monday?"

"She's strong enough. One push of a pillow and what chance did he have?" Her voice rising into a hysterical squeak, Maud screamed, "Find out if it was her or that lizard Garamond. Ask them! Ask them. Which of them killed my brother? You're a detective. Find out!"

Bloody Norah, Bob thought, as he climbed the steps, the place is full of clowns and hysterical females, not to mention the loopy cook . . . Seeing Jessamyn going into the dining room stopped him in his tracks.

***

# Chapter 32

After listening to Maud Puddicombe's version of life at Peony Villas, Bob wasn't expecting to see Jessamyn quite so soon and was caught wrong-footed as she crossed the hallway in front of him.

"Miss – Mrs . . ." Knowing how to address her escaped him so he just followed her into the fortunately vacant dining room, where she began changing candles on the sideboard. "Can I talk to you for a few minutes?"

Jessamyn turned to him, closed her eyes and shook her head as if in despair. Oh, lummy, she's going to cry, Bob thought. But she didn't, she smiled at him bravely – it was definitely a 'brave smile' – then said, "Do you want to stay a few extra days?"

"No. That is, yes, I'd like to but, erm – I need to ask you about Hentree Farm."

"I have told Inspector Drury everything already. Yesterday."

'Yesterday': they've known all along, Bob thought. Those Barnstaple coppers – they've been using me for a stooge to get at her – or her father. Bob didn't know whether to laugh or be angry.

"He came here, did he, Inspector Drury? While I was out, running around on his case?"

"He wanted to talk to Quentin. I told him it would be difficult, and now he's probably, almost certainly, at sea somewhere. He called late last night, although he couldn't tell me where he was going, naturally, careless talk and all that."

"Ah, right." Bob shifted from one foot to the other, ran a hand through his hair, then said, "Look, can I just ask you about Hentree Farm, the place? I shan't bother you after that. Not if Drury's got it all tidied up." In some ways it was relief: it meant he didn't have to confront Jessamyn and deal with her expert lies. On the other hand, he did want to know what had been going on.

"All right," Jessamyn seemed marginally relieved and pulled out a dining chair. Indicating the one in front of her, she sat down. "What do you want to know?"

"Well, can we start with this?" Bob propped the double photo frame against the salt pot on the table.

Jessamyn's mouth formed a perfect 'o'. "Where did you get this?" she asked.

"Hentree Farm. It's you and Quentin, isn't it?"

Jessamyn traced a scarlet fingernail over the boy's tousled hair. "He was such a beautiful child – and I left him. I thought he'd be better off with my mother. I was such a mess, you see. After Davy died. Davy was my husband. He was killed in the trenches." She looked at Bob, "If you've got these photos you know all about that already, don't you? Inspector Drury was a young police officer with my late father-in-law in Barnstaple. He'll have told you."

"No," Bob said with a sigh, "he didn't." But it was exactly the connection he'd suspected: the two farms, the Barnstaple police and the landlady of Peony Villas. "What happened?" he heard himself say and gave a small gesture for Jessamyn to continue.

"I went away, and – oh, but you saw me, in my Pearl Pascoe days. I was lodging with Vinny – that's Mrs Baxter-Salmon – then. We all go back quite a long way here. Reggie worked at the Aldwych Theatre. Wendell was there too, later. Only a prompt but he was so good we got away with murder on more than one occasion. I think it was because his English is so very correct – he's a foreigner, you see."

"I did wonder. Where's he from?"

"Won't say. I've asked a few times in different ways but he won't tell. Probably one of those poor Jewish people who lost their homes when that nasty Mr Hitler got started. Not that I think he was poor. He's terribly well-educated, knows about philosophers and English literature and lots of clever things."

Bob gave an inward sigh, Jessamyn Flowers was very taken with clever Wendell. He didn't stand a chance. Not that he could even consider it under the circumstances . . . Considering the circumstances brought him back to his next task: to get Jessamyn back on track. "Long way from Bideford, your London life. Did you not come back to see your little one, or think of moving him up to London to be with you?"

"Oh, I did. I really did think about it a lot, but the time was never right. Lavinia even offered to have him at her house. Then I got my first season at the Aldwych thanks to dear Montfort Yardley, the impresario. He took me out of Pearl's ribbons and put me in proper pearls in some darling farces, and – well, he taught me rather a lot. Vinny did too, but that was on the domestic side. Really, I owe my West End success to Montfort." She tweaked a stray lock of chestnut hair from her forehead and added pensively, "We lived together for a couple of years, Monty and I, but in end he was rather more interested in my frocks than me. He only really needed me on his arm to keep the angels happy."

"Angels?" Bob frowned.

"The people who finance plays. Anyway, being with Montfort led to Noel Coward's *Hay Fever* in a roundabout way so no complaints. I did hope to be in *Private Lives*, but it wasn't to be." She gave Bob a brief *c'est la vie* smile then added, "Where was I? Ah, how the Waywards came to be here. Horace was with me for a season in a door-slamming farce after he left the D'Oyly Carte Opera Company. He was a wonderful Sir Joseph in *Pinafore*. You might enjoy Gilbert and Sullivan, I think."

"I do as it happens." Bob grinned, and began to hum: he could quite see Horace of the Second Bathroom singing 'When I was a lad I went to sea'.

Jessamyn's eyes sparkled. "Did you see him?"

"Not knowingly. Joan and I saw *Mikado* and *HMS Pinafore* and . . . and we're getting right off the topic again. Tell me about when you came back to Bideford."

"Do I have to? I'd really rather not."

Bob folded his arms and gave her an 'I'm waiting' look.

"Oh, if you insist. I let my husband – Arthur, my second husband – you know about him by now I suppose – I let him persuade me it would be all right. That they would want to see me and it wouldn't matter if people connected the London actress with the girl who lived out at Barley Cliff. That it was something to be proud of. Arthur was immensely proud of me, you see. He had this fixed notion I was going to be a local celebrity. He wanted me to open the new cricket pavilion and give out the cups at the summer regatta and all sorts of silly things.

"I did it for the first year, but then one of the *Gazette* writers started asking about where I came from and I panicked and said I was from London. Which is not untrue. I do own a little house near Kew. If it's still standing? Anyway, this young reporter started asking personal questions and it all got too embarrassing and awkward. By now Quentin had found me and I really, really didn't want our dirty washing aired in public so I said 'no more celebrity, thank you very much'.

"Arthur was so disappointed, but I couldn't face being seen as a rejected daughter and all those people out at Larkham knowing our family business and then getting myself on the front page of the *Gazette* as some sort of star . . . Well, I was. I mean, I did rather well as an actress. But that was all over."

Jessamyn halted and gave another brave, sad smile.

Bob said nothing and waited for her to start again, which she did with a delicate shrug of the shoulders.

"Well, Arthur was terribly disappointed. He wanted to show me off. That's why he pushed and pushed for me to rectify matters at Ridgeway and Hentree. I did try. But I never let him come with me. Perhaps I should have done. Perhaps my father would have been less . . ." she waved a hand in the air, "with a man there. Then Arthur had his first stroke, and then another one and everything here changed."

Bob rattled the fingers of his right hand on the tablecloth, making the cutlery jiggle: she was side-lining him again. Was it deliberate? If so, she was jolly skilful. "But you did go back to Ridgeway to make your peace?"

"Absolutely. I tried. I went on my own twice – to each farm. I managed to see Mother briefly on the first occasion at Ridgeway. She looked so very unwell I wanted to stay and help but she said it would only send him into a rage and she hadn't the strength for it. That was four years ago and I haven't seen her since."

Tears welled in Jessamyn's eyes, but Bob pressed on. "Did Quentin keep in touch with them?"

"He went back now and again. Not often, I don't think. Not in the last few years anyway because he joined up in '39 and was sent up north somewhere for basic training or whatever it is they do with recruits. He learned to use a bayonet and scale walls and then he was sent for officer training. At one time he thought he'd make it into 'special operations' but he failed the test. Both tests. 'Not officer material' they said. That's not what he told us, of course. I thought he'd get through, despite his poor education. The Slattery family are hardly yokels, the Pascoe side were landowners, gentlemen farmers. Perhaps that's why it's such a tragedy, seeing what the farms have come to."

"And Quentin was angry about being weeded out?"

Bob regretted his words the moment they were spoken. Jessamyn was lost in her own thoughts, though, and merely replied, "Oh yes, very cross. He said he wanted to transfer to the RAF, but that was a bit of a bluff and he was sent to join an artillery unit down here. Which was a mixed blessing to be honest."

Bob's fingers stilled of their own accord. In among all the blah-blah Mrs Flowers had just given him a gold nugget. Quentin had had access to weapons supplied to officers and had learnt how to use them. He was in an artillery unit now, and had either kept a weapon for himself or had sourced one. And being local, he could get in touch with land agents and be in the know about Hoblins Holiday Camps. The middle section of the Hentree jigsaw was beginning to come together.

Jessamyn started speaking again. Bob tuned back in. "Someone must have told Quentin about how I left – but never why – because he started coming here to Peony Villas as if he lived here. Arthur was very good about it but. . ." Jessamyn paused. "It was awkward. I wasn't surprised that Quentin was angry with me. He had every right. But I hadn't expected him to be quite so . . ." Fingers wafted in the air as if trying to catch a word, "aggressive."

"Aggressive? To you? Physically?"

"Not exactly physically, but there were some very menacing, unpleasant shouting scenes. Just like my father, really, he was a failed man. A failed farmer who had never wanted to be a farmer. *His* grandfather had been a notary in Birmingham and his father had been to Oxford. But my father's father wanted to escape city life and have a simpler life. He was a bit of a dreamer, I think. Different times, of course."

"Do think Quentin blamed you or his background for not being commissioned, for not being the sort of person they were looking for?" Bob was beginning to think there was something unbalanced about grandfather and grandson. Experienced officers on the training course would have picked it up straight away.

"Oh, I don't know. Do we inherit the sins of our fathers? If so, Quentin should be more like me or my first husband. Davy, Quentin's father, was a good, plain, kind, ordinary man. An absolute sweetheart to be honest."

"A policeman's son."

"Yes. You know about that, do you?"

Bob gave a lop-sided grin, "In a manner of speaking. Quentin came here, you say, threatening you for – for what?"

"Money, always money. He didn't want to be reconciled. All he wanted was money – until very recently, that is." She halted, looked away then cleared her throat and started again, "I think Arthur gave him quite a lot to stay away. But it didn't work. Then there was that awful scene and –" Jessamyn closed her eyes. "Arthur had a stroke. Maud blamed Quentin. She even thinks Quentin . . . but that's not relevant to Hentree, which is what you wanted to know about."

"I do, yes. When did you last see your mother? Can you remember?"

"As if it were yesterday. March 21$^{st}$, 1938. It was her birthday." Tears glistened in Jessamyn's blue eyes. "I should have gone to help her in secret. But she said he would get angry with her if he saw me. I should have found a way to see her, I know I should."

"So, you haven't seen your mother in four years?"

"No. Look, I've told Inspector Drury all this." Jessamyn smothered her mouth with a hand. Tears rolled down her cheeks. "She's dead, I know. And I caused her so much sorrow."

Bob got up and went to put his arm around her, to offer comfort, then stopped himself. He was Detective Sergeant Robbins. It wouldn't do.

She looked up and put a hand out to him, "Mr Robbins – Bob – do I have to attend the inquest tomorrow? Inspector Drury said I should."

"Not if you don't want to. No legal reason for you to be there."

"It'll start unnecessary talk, you see. Reporters will get hold of it and . . . I can't face it."

"Not to worry. As long as you've told DI Drury everything that he needs to know about you and Quentin . . ." Bob left the name hanging deliberately and sat down again.

Jessamyn ignored it and took a pretty, embroidered handkerchief from her dress pocket and dabbed her eyes. "What I find so sad – and unforgivable – in all this business at Hentree is that Quentin hadn't tried to see his grandmother either. After all she did for him. I can understand him being angry with me, but why ignore her – why?"

"Oh, love, I can't tell you that. I can't begin to imagine . . ." Bob checked himself. "About the inquest: did Inspector Drury tell you that it was me who found her?"

"Did you come here to spy on me?"

"No," Bob replied, taken by surprise. "But I may have been sent here for something similar without realising it. Someone down at the police station knew you were Ada Slattery, I'm afraid."

"Hester's father."

"Hester's father!"

"Hmm. He's a police sergeant. Not a very nice man I'm afraid. She often arrives in the morning very teary. Hester worked for Arthur; he wanted her to live in but her pa wouldn't allow it. I expect she tells them things at home and when this business of the holiday camp came to light – Inspector Drury says a lot of people are against it. I didn't know anything about that, of course."

Bob frowned: Hoblin's Holiday Camp on land that an old man wouldn't or couldn't sell. An old man two – three people counting the Healey boy – would be happy to be without. But each of them needed his death certificate. Where was he? Was Jessamyn leading him around the houses to avoid discussing that? "Did Inspector Drury ask you where your father has got to?" he said quietly.

"Yes. I told him I don't know."

"But where might he be? Who would he go to if he wasn't well, for example?"

Jessamyn shook her head. "Nobody. I can't think of anywhere he'd go." She got up, went to a flower vase and re-arranged a few rust-coloured chrysanthemum blooms. "Will I be asked questions at my mother's inquest, if I go?"

Bob hated the smell of chrysanthemums, they reminded him of funerals. "It won't be like a trial. The coroner's role is to determine the likely cause of death then he might order an autopsy to find out for sure. It's not for the coroner to say *who* did it or question people about events leading up to the death, although sometimes they do if it looks like a tragic accident, or an unlawful killing. *Why* it happened is for the police to investigate. That's why they wanted to talk to you about Hentree Farm."

"The press will be there, though. Nothing else for them in this horrible little town." For a moment Jessamyn stood perfectly still with her back to him, then she turned and said, "May I go now?"

Bob jumped to his feet, "Of course."

"Please tell everyone I do not feel well," the diva instructed him from the doorway. "I should not have gone to the show at Littlehamholt. It was only because it was their last performance and Wendell begged so. But I shouldn't have gone. My husband is not yet buried, and now . . . all this! It is too much. All too much . . ." She stopped and looked into Bob's eyes. "When?" she asked in a whisper. "When did she die? Not when Quentin was up there last week. Please say that's not true."

"Quentin was there last week?"

"He'd got embarkation leave. I told Inspector Drury all this yesterday."

"Did he see your father?"

"I suppose so." She stopped again. "Why has nobody told me about my mother, do you think?"

"Nobody knew. People in Larkham all think she's bedridden."

"There! You see. I was right. They've been talking about me for years, and not one of them knows the facts. Not one of them!"

Giving Bob no chance to say another word, Ada-Pearl-Jessamyn flung herself out of the room.

Bob slumped back down in his chair and put his head in hands. "She's played you like the proverbial fiddle," he muttered. Then, mixing his metaphors, added, "What a flaming pig's ear you made of that, Robbins."

Then he sat upright: the locals might not have known about Martha Slattery, but surely Quentin did. She had raised him, looked after him like a mother; how come he didn't want to see her when he visited his grandfather? A phrase Laurie had used about Josiah Slattery crept into his head: 'inherently cruel'.

Did the word 'inherent' come from inheritance? Was cruelty, the capacity to ignore or enjoy someone's suffering – human or animal – genetic? Could cruelty be inherited? If so, Josiah had handed it down through his daughter. The daughter on the other hand, despite abandoning her child, appeared to have a generous heart. Just like her mother, Martha, who was said to be ‘kindness itself’. Then he remembered what Lavinia Baxter-Salmon had told him about marbles on a staircase.

“Ah, well, maybe not,” he huffed and looked at his watch. Twenty minutes until supper: time enough to raid a broom cupboard for a nine-millimetre pistol while the cook was boiling the potatoes.

***

# Chapter 33

Getting back down the service stairs and into the scullery area unseen proved easier than Bob expected. Mr Pots had his back turned, moving saucepans from one gas hob to another. The broom cupboard was in the passage to the refuge room, easy to locate and easy to raid – he hoped. Using the feeble light from the high, barred window and his pocket torch, Bob identified an upright vacuum cleaner, two types of broom, a dustpan and hand-brush, a bag of dusters, a tin of furniture polish and a tin of silver polish. There was space enough for the legendary box of firearms, but if it had ever been there it had been removed. Where? Somewhere below stairs because Mr Pots never appeared in public. Then Bob remembered what he'd seen earlier while Maud Puddicombe was spilling her venomous accusations. Mr Pots had said he was going up to his shed; he'd picked up a heavy box from the floor. Not containing kittens this time, Bob suspected. The shed: that was where he needed to look. Up the garden path.

Passing Mr Pots to get out of the back door, however, could be difficult this time. Was there another way into the garden? Bob made his way along the passage leading to the indoor air-raid shelter then further until he came to the kitchen area of Number Two. That kitchen was empty and its back door led into a walled garden, but there was no connecting access to Number

One as he'd expected. He retraced his steps, pausing at a door he'd not noticed before. It wasn't locked.

It was a very small, airless, rather smelly room. More of a cubicle than a room, with barely space enough for a bed and a chair. Shoved in tight between the bed and the wall were various cardboard boxes. Checking behind him, Bob sidled in and shone his torch over them. They had all been closed by lapping flaps into each other. He lifted the flaps on one: it was empty. As were the others. Boxes awaiting recipients then, with air holes for living creatures. Bob panned the bed. It was being slept in. Presumably by the mad cook.

Bob edged back through the door, leaving it exactly as he'd found it, then returned to the kitchen to wait until the cook had his head in the oven. It took a while. Hester came and went with odds and ends then, finally, the cook bent down to open the oven door, emitting the delicious aroma of hot pastry.

Bob's stomach rumbled. Mr Pots turned fast as a trained assassin, brandishing a long knife not a wooden spoon in his right hand. "I can see 'e!" he declared.

"Me? Oh, yes, I was looking for Mrs Flowers again. Haven't seen her yet, I suppose?"

Mr Pots squinted at him suspiciously. "What you want with her all the time, eh?"

"Me? My bill. We're leaving soon, you see. That our supper? Smells wonderful." Bob gave a dramatic look at his watch. "Goodness, nearly that time already. No wonder your kitchen smells so good." Which it did, and with all the activity this day, Bob was starving hungry.

Before Mr Pots could utter another word, Bob was up the service stairs with a speed that surprised himself and sliding into his chair in the dining room. The room, like the cupboard below was half empty. Only Laurie and Suky, the Bathroom Duo, Reg Dwyer and Billy Bryant.

"Bit thin on the ground, aren't we?" Bob quipped.

Horace and Estelle turned to look at him in studied silence. Reg and Billy kept their gaze on their empty plates. Laurie and Suky had eyes only for each other.

Hester eventually appeared with the divine pie and a huge bowl of floury potatoes, and Bob gave a genuine sigh of relief, then said reluctantly, "Should we wait for Mrs Flowers and Mr Garamond?" Members of the Wayward players exchanged glances. "Is something wrong? Have I missed something?" Reg and Billy guffawed in unison. Bob looked from one to the other, "Oh, private, is it? I see, dining out together to celebrate."

"We do not have much to celebrate this evening," Horace's sonorous voice declaimed as he pushed the pie towards his wife. "Do start, my dear."

Bob pushed the bowl of potatoes towards Suky saying, "That's right, it was your last appearance as The Wayward Players this afternoon. How did it go?" Bob withheld the information that he'd been present and Laurie looked at him questioningly. Bob ignored him.

Reg and Billy chortled again in unison then Billy said, "A memorable performance. Wendell was tragedy personified. There wasn't a dry eye in the house."

"Crying they were," Reg Dwyer supplied. "Said they'd never seen anything like it. Not since Groucho Marx played Hamlet."

Suky giggled. "It was quite funny."

"Something special to remember, that's good," Bob responded blandly and served himself a generous helping of the pie, feeling slightly guilty because as everyone constantly reminded each other there was a war on and food was scarce.

The meal was eaten in relative silence until Hester appeared with a huge glass bowl of nutmeg-topped egg custard. Estelle played Mother and they finished dessert in short order. Bob waited for the Waywards to leave, but when Laurie got up to follow Suky he gave a meaningful cough. Taking the hint, Laurie pecked her on the cheek and resumed his seat.

Bob waited again, then checked there was nobody behind the door, shut it and said, “Night-time raid. Come to my room, midnight. Be ready, soft shoes, dark gear, torch in hand.”

Laurie’s eyes flew open with surprise. “What we raiding, Sarge?”

“Mr Pots’ shed. You’re going around the back via the garage first, to check the coast’s clear.”

Laurie gawped at him, “Crikey, this sounds serious.”

“Too bloody right, it is. He might be armed,” Bob replied. Laurie snorted as if he were joking. “Don’t know what you’re sniggering about, you’re the one who told me he kept a box of live hand grenades.”

“I didn’t say they were live, Sarge.”

“Blimey O’Reilly, do you think he spent his war years wandering around battle fields collecting used ones! How’s that possible? Eh – eh?”

“No – I suppose not. But grenades have to be adjusted or set in certain way, I think, for them to go off properly.”

“You think?”

“They showed us at school once. I wasn’t paying attention, sorry.”

“Head in a book, I suppose.”

“*Wuthering Heights*.”

“How apt.”

Laurie appeared at Bob’s door some minutes before midnight. He looked dishevelled, as if he’d fallen asleep in his clothes and woken with a start. Which was how Bob had reacted to the soft tap-tap at his door.

“Shall I get going?” he asked.

"Come in!" Bob hissed. Once the door was closed, he said in hushed tones, "Go out of the front door and do a quick rekky round the front of the house. Check outside and inside the garage, if its open. See if there's anything there. And be on the lookout for the cook and his meat cleaver."

"That's not funny, Sarge," Laurie responded.

"No, neither it is, so watch your back. If anyone sees you, let them think you're out on the razzle. Cider again: got me?" Laurie nodded. "Good lad. Meet up with me in the back garden: I'm not doing that shed on my own. But give me time to check cupboards downstairs and do a rekky of the basement yard area. If you hear my voice it'll be because someone's out there. I'll be taking a stroll – too hot, can't sleep."

"Um, Sarge," Laurie's hand hovered over the door handle. "Can I ask why you haven't asked Hester or Mr Pots directly about the box of guns? Hester's father's a policeman after all."

"I know, and that's why we're here. Using us to find out what they suspect without getting their fingers rapped if they're wrong."

Laurie shook his head, "Sorry, Sarge, I don't follow."

"Nah, nothing for you to worry about." Bob wasn't going to add that the real reason he hadn't approached the maid or the cook directly was because it hadn't occurred to him. He'd got so used to everything being difficult and devious, it simply hadn't crossed his mind. "It's better this way," he said. "Pots won't be able to fib when we've got what we're looking for."

If Laurie saw through this, he was good enough not to say anything and left the room as quietly as he'd entered.

Bob waited by his window for a few minutes to give Laurie time to get downstairs. Through his open window came the distant 'crump-crump' of a bombing raid. Some place was getting it, but where? He tried to think what town in this part of Devon was large enough to merit German bombs, and failed.

This stretch of coastline had no towns of any size except Barnstaple, twelve miles away. But that was a market town as well; there was no industry that he knew of. Unless they were after major road bridges. Maybe a small spy plane had crossed the channel that day with troop locations and information about specially designed new landing craft in Barnstaple Bay. In which case Bideford might get it later as well, on both counts. Thunder rumbled, underpinning the threat. Bob gave an involuntary shudder then gathered his two different sized torches and set off on a mission of his own making.

The house creaked and sighed as he moved, but at no time did he have the sense anyone was up and about. Not even Wendell in his silk dressing gown and cravat.

The kitchen was equally vacant. Clean and tidy as a hospital surgery. His rubber soled shoes squeaked on the washed tiles, reminding Bob of the debacle that afternoon and making him smile. The smile disappeared when he found the kitchen door open and checked to see if the door leading to the refuge room, Mr Pots' cubicle and into Number Two was also open, and found it was. Bob switched off his small torch and swapped it for the larger, heavier one from his trouser pocket, which could be used as a cosh if need be.

Outside, there was still no sign of Laurie so he crept, bent low, up the steps towards what had once been a lawn and was now a vegetable garden. Tall canes stood like tepees supporting the last of the summer beans. It was the only place that offered any kind of concealment so Bob edged himself between them, getting somewhat tangled in the process.

Within seconds Laurie was coming up the steps. Bob squeezed out from between the canes, making the whole row move in the moonlight. The boy froze to the top step.

"It's me," Bob hissed.

"Oh, thank heavens." Laurie had a hand on his heart. "You made me jump, Sarge."

"Well?" Bob demanded. "Anything?"

"Nothing."

"All right. Ready?"

The boy gave a thumbs up sign just as the first crash of lightning lit the sky. The roll of thunder that followed deafened anything either of them might say so Bob tugged the boy's sleeve and they headed up the narrow path towards the compost heap and Mr Pots' shed. There was a scurrying around them. A smelly fox jumped straight across their path and disappeared under the thick hedge. Bob waited until his own heartbeat returned to normal then tugged on Laurie's sleeve again.

They stood outside the door of the shed, just as Bob had planned – shoulder to shoulder – more or less. Bob pushed at the door with his foot. It didn't budge. Laurie opened the latch. As the door swung in a swarm of warm bodies surged out.

"Bloody Norah!" Bob heaved, swatting at his trouser legs as furred skins ruffled past him.

"Cats!" Laurie exclaimed.

"I could have told you that," Bob huffed, his stomach now located somewhere in the region of his loins. Gulping, he forced himself to move forward.

"Oh, yuk, what is that?" Laurie indicated a metal bucket lying on its side spewing fish entrails, then pulled out a fine lawn handkerchief and slapped it over his nose and mouth.

Bob did likewise with the palm of his left hand and panned the interior with the heavy torch in his right.

"There," Laurie pointed, "in that corner. The boxes."

Bob directed his torch beam over two sturdy boxes. Laurie hunkered down and cautiously opened the first. It contained about twenty hand grenades of the small pineapple variety. The second contained, at first reckoning, various pistols and an army revolver, plus the stock of an old rifle and sundry bayonets, including one with saw-like teeth.

"What now?" Laurie asked.

"We take them back to my room." As Bob spoke the town air-raid siren wailed into action; the sound of rising panic reaching a crescendo. "Oh, would you bloody believe it!" Bob huffed. "The one blasted night we need a bit of peace and quiet and Jerry has it in for Bideford of all places." He looked at Laurie, who was clearly waiting for instructions. "You take the grenades and I'll take the guns and let's hope the Luftwaffe doesn't catch us going down the garden path or we'll both be going sky high and taking Peony Villas with us."

Worse was to come. As they entered the kitchen area Jessamyn was ushering the Waywards into the refuge room. "This way, quickly," she said, pointing at the basement door. "Quickly, quickly."

"No! No, we can't," Bob replied. "We've got to – oh, hell's teeth!" It suddenly dawned on him they were almost certainly bringing live grenades into a house that could be bombed. Maybe Laurie was right, that they had to be adjusted or set in some way before the pin could be pulled for an explosion, but as neither of them had a clue he wasn't taking any chances. "Out! Out!" he yelled at Laurie, pushing him back the way they'd come and charging as fast as his short legs would permit out past the garage to the middle of the tarmac, then down the road towards the countryside – and on and on until he couldn't take another breath.

"Drop that box under that hedge," he gasped as Laurie stopped at his side.

"Oh, right! The grenades, of course."

Bob shook his head in despair and followed the boy to drop the box of guns alongside it.

Overhead, lightning cracked open the sky and German bombs dropped from planes on their illuminated targets.

Bob closed his eyes. “Armageddon,” he whispered. “I never thought it would be like this.”

“Erm, Sarge,” Laurie jolted his arm, “shouldn’t we try to get away from here – as fast as possible.”

“Yes, go. You run, run as fast as you can and get into that basement. I’ll follow. I shan’t keep up with you, but I’ll get there. Now go, make sure your Suky’s safe!”

Laurie legged it. Bob stayed exactly where he was, watching the mortal firework display. “Come and get me,” he whispered. “Come on – come and get me. I’ve had my time.”

Joan would be waiting. “Late as usual,” she’d moan, but she’d be there, waiting.

Slowly, slowly, arms extended, tempting the bombers, tempting fate, Bob stepped into the middle of the road and wandered back to Peony Villas.

***

# Chapter 34

**Friday**

Bob dragged himself awake at the sound of his portable alarm clock and sat on the side of the bed, waiting to see if there was a bone in his body that didn't ache. There wasn't, and there was a very full day ahead. Starting with getting Mr Pots' weaponry into Bideford police station before the inquest into Mrs Slattery's death scheduled for eleven-thirty.

Laurie was tucking into his toast and marmalade as if nothing had happened when Bob got downstairs. He dropped his car keys on their table. "Nip down to where we stashed the boxes, will you. Put them in the boot of the Morris then come back and finish your breakfast. If anyone sees you, say you're out for a morning stroll."

Laurie took a long slurp of tea and left without a word. Bob poured himself a spoon-bender then stared into the cup: no problem with rations here, the tea was strong, plenty of butter on the table, meat in the pies . . . Suddenly he was alert again, Mrs Flowers came into the morning room, wearing black for the first time. It didn't suit her.

Taking Laurie's vacant chair, she said, "I keep meaning to ask you a favour, Sergeant Robbins, and what with Arthur and the Americans and everything it keeps slipping my mind. Before you go, would you be an angel and investigate a problem we are having with some petty thefts? Actually, not so petty." She didn't give Bob time to respond. "Both Maud – Miss Puddicombe, next door – and I have had items taken from our houses. Chelsea figurines, in my case, eighteenth century and rather valuable, and Maud has lost two Spode trinket dishes, and some silver items. We've both questioned Hester, and it's absolutely not her. Besides, her father is a policeman. It's not Mr Pots, either. We did wonder if it was one of the Waywards, but that's silly because what would they want with Chelsea figurines? One can hardly sell antiques and *objets d'arte* nowadays. The Dobsons are well off, and Reggie and Billy . . ." her manicured hand waved away the very thought of their involvement.

"So that rules out all your suspects," Bob laughed.

"Yes, I suppose it does. More or less. I have wondered about Estelle, but then what would she want Spode trinket dishes for? She can afford to buy her own. They aren't even living in Horace's flat so where would she put it all? It is annoying, though; I do hate deception."

Bob blinked at the comment and muttered, "Don't we all."

Jessamyn cocked her head to one side questioningly, causing a lock of hair to fall across her face. Bob returned his hand to the table; it had strayed upwards of its own accord. There was a pause, then she said, "The inquest: I've forgotten what time Inspector Drury told me to be there."

"Eleven-thirty. I thought you didn't want to come."

"I don't. I haven't decided." Without another word, she got up and left the room.

Bob returned to his toast and lathered on a week's rations of butter and marmalade because he could. When Laurie returned, he told him about the thefts. He was still cross. "Chelsea figurines and Spode, as if I'm supposed to do a dawn raid on her guest rooms."

"She's probably doing it herself and doesn't know it. Or Estelle. They are the right age."

"Right age?"

"Mmm, like my Aunt Christina. She pinched mother's dressing table set and all her Wedgwood fairy plates when she came to stay while they were decorating her new house. Hormonal kleptomania, my pa said."

"Knows about that sort of thing, does he?"

"He's a consultant obstetrician, he knows all about women's problems. Obviously."

"Obviously. What happened to this aunt?"

"That was the tricky bit because she's one of the FitzAlans so mother didn't dare accuse her of anything because that would have caused all sorts of family upset, and if it had got out . . . You can imagine. It was all right in the end, though. We went on a visit to see Aunt Christina's new house and ma pinched it all back again. I carried the bag."

Bob leaned back in his chair. "Families. Who'd have 'em?"

"Don't you have a family, Sarge?"

Bob shook his head. "Not any more. My boy Jim's in an aircraft carrier somewhere out east as far as I know, and he won't be starting a family any time soon. Come on, we better get those boxes into DI Drury before the inquest. I want that little problem off my hands A.S.A.P."

DI Drury peered into the box of guns, then pulled back the flaps of the second box and jumped back a yard, knocking his chair sideways. Bob swallowed a smile and gave him an informative verbal report as to how and why they had been located.

"DC West," Drury called out across the room, "get up to Peony Villas and bring the cook in for questioning."

Bob gave a polite cough. "It might be wise to send backup with him. The cook – he might get a bit difficult. Spent three years in a German prisoner of war camp, and he's not altogether in the head. Clever with his knives, too."

"You think he'll get violent?"

"It's possible. He might go the other way and crumple on you. Either way, your officers will need to use a bit of psychology."

"You," Drury said, pointing at Laurie, "go with DC West and give him a hand."

Laurie gave Bob the briefest, questioning look and Bob had no option but to agree: Laurie wasn't needed at the inquest and that would take up the rest of the morning. "I'll need him this afternoon," Bob said to Drury.

The chamber in which Bideford inquests were held was virtually empty, but to Bob's surprise Jessamyn Flowers was there. The proceedings relating to the death of the woman believed to be Mrs Slattery were brief in the extreme. Dr Amos Parsons ordered a full autopsy and an enquiry into why the body had remained unburied, and it was all over.

Jessamyn sat in silence throughout, twisting a handkerchief in her hands but dry eyed. She was, nevertheless, deeply affected by what she heard. Bob had a brief word with DI Drury, who went back to his office, then went over to her.

Helping her to his feet he said, "It's a bit early, but you look as if you could do with a stiff sherry."

"Oh, I could," Jessamyn replied, "but can we stay until the local newshounds get fed up of wondering why I am here?"

Bob sat beside her, bursting to ask how she felt, if she'd learned anything that surprised her, if she'd suspected her father could have left his wife of forty-plus years to die alone in bed and remain unburied. He remained silent until a small demon at his shoulder prodded him into saying, "Has DI Drury said anything about why Mr Slattery isn't here?"

"DI Drury says he's still missing."

"Ah, that'll be it then."

"Didn't you know? You were up at his farm. I saw you." Jessamyn turned to look him in the eye.

Bob looked away, rubbing the fingers of his right hand on his leg. "Was it you who took a letter from his study?" he asked. "A solicitor's envelope with a copy of a document."

"Yes, but there was no document, only a letter."

"Why?"

"I wanted to know if my son had been cut out of his will."

"And has he?"

"Yes, in part. Hentree Farm was to go to Greville Healey, Quentin should still get Ridgeway."

"Did you tell your son this?"

Jessamyn shook her head. "No." She closed her eyes. "Do you think if I had . . .? But I didn't have chance. He was only on leave a very short time, you see."

"Could he have known anyway? Perhaps you weren't the only one to see the will or letter. You said he visited Ridgeway Farm."

Jessamyn bit her lower lip and nodded. "It doesn't matter now though, does it? Quentin will be the next in line. Unless Sheila Beere makes a claim on it. She's Greville's mother. Always was an acquisitive bitch. I bet she told him to come up and work for my father the moment he left school. Wheedle his way in. It was one way of getting back at Josiah Slattery, I suppose. They all hated him for sending Davy away."

"Did you?"

"Oh, heavens, yes."

Bob looked around at the chamber, empty now, measuring his next words. "How much did you hate your father, Jessamyn?"

"Did? Past tense. Not him as well!" Her voice rose with genuine panic. "What has happened to him?"

"We don't know. I saw that he was injured. When I went to find him, to help him later, I couldn't locate him."

Jessamyn frowned. "Tell me. Tell me what happened."

Bob sighed and briefly, as gently as he could, related what he'd seen at Hentree Farm on Friday last. "That's how I came to find the woman we think is your mother."

"I don't understand – what good was killing Greville and my father? You can't possibly suspect me! I don't want Hentree – or Ridgeway – or a single inch of Devonshire land thank you."

"No. But perhaps Quentin does."

Jessamyn gulped and took a deep breath. "I know what you are suggesting, Inspector Drury has come to the same conclusion. It's just that I simply can't believe it, and . . ."

Bob sat for a moment wondering how he would feel if his son was accused of murder. Would he still love and try to protect a boy who'd taken another boy's life? Before he could speak again, Jessamyn put a hand on his arm, "There is someone else you should ask." Bob waited. "Lavinia Baxter-Salmon. She was out on Friday afternoon. She took my car – somewhere."

"Does Mrs Baxter-Salmon know how to use a gun?"

"Shotguns, yes. Her family were part of the county set in Berkshire."

Bob pulled a face; he couldn't see Lavinia hiding among trees then slinking into a farmyard with a nine-millimetre pistol. But then again, after her revelation about what happened to her husband it wasn't impossible. "Why do you think she may be involved?" he asked.

"Because she has always said she would do anything for me. Because she thinks she owes me a special favour, if you like. She knew Quentin was harassing me to ensure Hentree came to him as soon as possible." Jessamyn put a hand to her forehead and took another deep breath, trying to calm herself.

"This must be agony for you. Come on, let's see if we can get a schooner of sherry. If not, it'll have to be the local cider."

"Oh, heavens no, that goes straight to your knees and elbows."

"You're telling me."

They made their way into the comforting atmosphere of the King's Head on the quay and sat facing each other across a tiny round table.

"I do love a morning pub," Jessamyn said. "When it's early and there's the smell of beer and lavender polish. Do you think it might be Estelle who's taking our ornaments?" she asked suddenly.

"Might be."

"What do you think I should do?"

"You've got keys to her room. Have a look."

"Then what?"

"Depends whether you want to take it further. Me, I'd – erm – pinch them back."

Jessamyn nodded. "Might be best."

Conversation petered out and Bob tried to make small talk, but it was evident Jessamyn was badly affected by what had emerged during the inquest. In the end he said, "Would you like me to take you up to Hentree? Be there with you? It might help to put your mind at rest, or at least answer a few questions for you. You might know where to look for your father, too. Places we haven't discovered."

Jessamyn's eyes opened wide in horror. "No. Absolutely not."

"You do realise there may have to be another inquest – the way things are going?"

"I dare say there will. But I shan't be there. The sooner I get away from this cursed town the better."

Bob felt as if she'd refused to marry him. Trying to cover his embarrassment, he said, "In that case, you'd better let me get on with my obligations," and got to his feet. "Can you make your own way back? I have to return to the station to fetch Laurie Oliver."

With infinite grace, Jessamyn Flowers put on her cotton gloves, gathered her handbag and exited the pub as if it were a palace.

Bob followed and waited until she had walked down the quay towards the High Street, then he made his way back to the police station.

Laurie was waiting by the desk and obviously couldn't get out fast enough.

"What happened?" Bob asked as soon as they were in the street, referring to Mr Pots.

"Oh, Sarge, it was awful. The poor man sort of diminished. The moment West said, 'Come with us' he hunkered down on the floor and covered his head. Something terrible must have happened to him during the first war. Terrible."

"I thought that might happen. No fight then?"

"No, but we had to virtually carry him to the car. They're talking to him now – about whether he's got licences for the guns and that. Oh, that reminds me, it's almost certain he couldn't have used any of the pistols. And he says he hasn't got any more, or any ammunition."

"Had any of the guns been used?"

"Not since 1918. There's an automatic nine-millimetre pistol, but it's Italian and empty. A German Luger – also nine-millimetre – ditto, and a French standard issue army revolver. Mementos, nothing more."

"One suspect off the list then, unless Quentin gave him a pistol to use. Our dear Quentin could have spun a yarn about how the boy at Hentree was robbing Mrs Puddicombe or some such taradiddle . . . We can't discount that woman Baxter-

Salmon, either, now. She owes Jessamyn a debt or two, and she does what she's told. Quentin could have got to her, easily."

"Drury's decided the only culprit is Quentin Beere. Who's Mrs Flowers' son apparently. Is that true?"

"Yep. And I rather think she's of the same opinion. She's terrified of him anyway. I reckon she plans to go into hiding so he can't find her again."

"Crikey! Her own son."

"Yeah, well, as you said, families."

Bob unlocked the car and they settled into their seats like an old married couple. Before Bob started the engine, though, Laurie said, "That woman next door at Number Two made a hell of fuss about us fetching the cook. Harold, she called him, you'd think he was her hubby the way she went on."

Bob scratched his chin. "That place gets weirder by the minute. Come on, let's have one final crack at the Lees to see if they're hiding Slattery in among their kidney beans, then we're calling it a day."

"Which place is getting weirder?" Laurie asked vaguely as Bob drove out of town. "They're all weird. Ridgeway, Hentree –"

"And Peony Villas."

"It'll be nearly empty after Monday. The Waywards are moving into Daneman Court."

"And we'll be on our way as well. Yippee."

"Aren't we supposed to locate Mr Slattery first?"

"He doesn't deserve finding, Laurie. The misery that man has caused his family – he deserves to be dropped into hell direct."

"That's a bit harsh. I doubt he was born that way. What do we know about *his* father and *his* family?"

Bob frowned and remained silent apart from the odd expletive while he navigated the busy High Street, got stuck behind a parked lorry then fluffed a hill start. When they were finally out into the country lanes, he said, "Slattery's father, from what I've seen in the drawing room at Ridgeway and picked up along the way, was an educated agnostic who thought living on a farm would be some sort of rural idle."

"Idyll," Laurie corrected.

"That's what I said."

Laurie bit back a grin and turned to look out of the window. "So not prepared for the rigours of agricultural life."

"In short, a failure. And that got passed on to the son Josiah, who took it out on his own kids."

"The sins of the fathers. Wasn't really a sin, though was it? Wanting a healthy country life for his family."

"Healthy! You are joking I hope."

***

# Chapter 35

They found Mr Lee standing on the edge of his neatly planted market garden staring morosely at a row of lettuces. "Nibbled, every one of 'em," he moaned. "Bloody rabbits. We could have sold ten boxes of lettuces this morning, same number of beetroot and carrots, but no, local wildlife makes sure we can't even make ends meet at the end of the month. Where's the fox when you need him, eh?"

Bob made a sympathetic gesture, noting that Jack Lee was in need of a second income, which he had once had at Ridgeway Farm. Did he hold a grudge against Slattery for sacking him?

Laurie began walking down the gravel path towards the end of the row. "You're right," he said. "Every single one. Do you think they do it on purpose?"

Bob gave an inward sigh: was the boy deliberately infantile? Then Laurie said, "You could always lie in wait of an evening and shoot them. Do you have a shotgun?" and Bob revised his opinion. They should have asked this long before.

"No point wasting pellets on those little buggers," Lee whined, "never heard the expression, 'breed like rabbits'?"

"True," Laurie replied. "Perhaps Greville Healey has shot all the foxes."

"More like," Lee said. "Shoot anything on legs that boy would. I told you."

"You did," Laurie continued, "but you didn't tell me if you ever joined him for a bit of sport, with your own gun."

"Sport! Sport, you call it. That's a townie for you." Mrs Lee appeared in the porch at the raised voice. "This boy thinks shotguns are for 'sport' round here," her husband called.

"Well they are, some places. The Carhews have shooting parties," Mrs Lee replied.

"Everybody living on a farm must be able to shoot, surely?" Laurie asked guilelessly.

"Well, I can't." Mrs Lee's tight curls shook left to right twice.

"This ain't no farm! It's a market garden, woman," her husband snapped. Then, turning to Laurie, he added, "But yes, I do have a shotgun, if that's what you're after?"

Mrs Lee took this as dismissal and headed back indoors. Bob managed to intercept her in the porch, "Can I have a word, Mrs Lee?" he asked.

"I'll put the kettle on," she replied, evidently pleased to have an excuse to talk to someone who wouldn't shout her down.

Leaving Laurie to annoy Mr Lee a good deal more and extract details about his weapons and shooting prowess, Bob nipped under a rose-trellis porch and followed her into the kitchen.

"Pretty as a picture, this cottage," he said, noting a large bowl of fresh eggs on the table.

"That's what we thought when we bought it," she said. "Mind you, living in a town has its advantages. I miss my little job at the glove factory, to be honest. I miss having someone to chat with. You know – company."

"You didn't ever chat with Mrs Slattery, then?"

"I did to start with when we first came, then she got bedridden. Or so that evil husband of hers said. I feel that guilty, Mr Robbins. I should have insisted – tried to help her. I believed him, you see, and . . . They were saying such things when we called in at the store this morning. She'd been dead in bed for years and years and we never even suspected. Everyone feels bad. Ethel Hook was crying her eyes out. Vicar's wife says she and her husband deserve to get the sack."

"News travels fast round here," Bob muttered. "Inquest's barely over."

Mrs Lee busied herself with a fancy blue whistling kettle and lit the gas under it, and Bob settled himself unasked at the table. After rinsing out the tea pot she put a plate of home-made biscuits in front of him, saying, "I did say they were a funny lot up at Hentree. Oh, yes, and I wasn't surprised when he told me the stairs would collapse. Although that was to stop me going in and going up them, I know that now. Terrible thing to do, and to his own wife." She shook her curls at the awfulness of it all.

"Did nobody suspect anything at Ridgeway Farm? There must have been people working there."

"No, nor in the village. It was only my husband at Ridgeway. Except – now I think about it," Mrs Lee leaned forward in her characteristic way, "Mrs Slattery lived at Hentree *on her own* even before our time. They say the boy Quentin lived there with her. They were saying this morning that he and his grandfather wouldn't be in the same room together and poor Mrs Slattery couldn't abide all the shouting so she kept to her family's old place as much as she could. They kept it to themselves, though. Well, we knew about her being at Hentree – but as to the rest, I expect people kept quiet because we don't none of us want people asking about our private lives and family matters, do we?"

Bob shook his head then tucked into a biscuit. No, he thought, we've all got something to hide. Joan's family spent years 'not talking' to each other on a rotational basis. He put out a hand and touched the eggs in the bowl on the table, remembering a family Christmas when his own son was still a nipper – they'd had been left with a turkey to feed twelve because Joan's parents had had a row with her sister and they'd all stormed off back home before the pudding was even in the steamer.

Mrs Lee said quietly, "About these eggs, I've got a bit of a confession."

Bob looked up. "Sorry?"

She looked at the eggs, "I don't ack-chew-ally have permission to collect eggs at Hentree. Fact is, I'm not allowed on the property. Neither's Jack. Mr Slattery got angry with us over Jack leaving and, well, truth is, I only get the eggs from the hedgerow. Only," she paused, grimaced, "only sometimes I get through the gate in the woods and get what I can, see."

"So, when we saw you last week – Saturday . . .?"

"I was getting eggs, but I was curious, see. We always go up to Barnstaple of a Friday, take salad and veg to the pannier market, and we stayed there all the day last week because it was our anniversary. Went to the Royal, took Ronnie, our evacuee, with us for a treat and had a proper roast dinner, and we didn't get back till late. Then Saturday morning Mervyn Jeffries came around with the milk and told us 'bout the ambulance and all that and – I was curious, that's all."

"Today's a Friday. Were you in Barnstaple this morning?"

She nodded and smiled, "Sold everything in the first hour. Pity we didn't have more to sell or we'd be celebrating again. Spent it all mostly, now though. Stopped off at the shop for our rations and got in some extras, and well . . . two pounds, four shillings don't go very far these days."

Bob looked at her. "Why did Mr Lee leave Ridgeway?"

"He couldn't stand the way Slattery treated his animals. He told your young detective."

"I certainly did." Jack Lee's voice boomed across the small kitchen. "Unthinking cruelty to animals. Neglected, they were. Cows need milking with a proper routine. Animals have to be fed the same time each day. You can't not get in fodder cuz you've run out of cash, or leave dairy cows out in the pasture twenty-four hours a day cuz you've got other things to do. Ignorant, unthinking, bloody cruelty. That's what I couldn't stand. I reported him, too. That's why he got rid of the cows. That's why I was sacked – and damn glad to leave I was, I can tell you."

Bob turned to look at the wiry market-gardener now standing in the kitchen doorway. He was red in the face and fuming angry.

"But if you think I shot the old devil, you're wrong," Lee continued.

"And you have no idea where we can find him."

"No. I told this streak of bacon that the other day." He pointed a grubby thumb at Laurie standing behind him. "And he hasn't come around asking for a cuppa since then, neither. I wouldn't have his carcase on my land, not as compost nor manure! And now we hear what he did to his wife, I know I was right about him from the start. Self-centred, evil bastard. We haven't spoken to him since June '39 and I'm glad of it."

Bob got to his feet, grabbed a handful of biscuits and said, "In that case, we won't be troubling you any longer, sir. Thank you for the biscuits, Mrs Lee."

Bob and Laurie walked up the lane from the Lee's smallholding in silence. A rabbit scuttled out from under some brambles, making Bob smile.

"You didn't really think the Lees had anything to do with it, did you, Sarge?" Laurie asked.

"Not really, and they've just confirmed everything they told you. It was only an off chance there was something else. Which I reckon there is."

"What?"

"Only that there may be more to why Lee left Ridgeway than he's telling us, but he hasn't got Slattery's body pushing up lettuce leaves, unfortunately."

"Have the Bideford lot been asking as well, do you think? They've been checking up on us. I discovered that today. The desk duty officer this morning is Hester's father. He's a bit of tartar."

"Checking up on our progress, are they?" Bob blew out through his cheeks. "What a blooming nasty farce." Stooping down, he picked up a large snail from the centre of the road and dropped it among damp ferns in the hedge. "What's their analysis, then?"

"DC West says that discounting the Land Girls, there's only two people who could have shot Greville Healey, and Healey must have shot and injured Mr Slattery with the Springfield rifle."

"Oh, yes, he was the one who did for Old Man Slattery, I'd lay my life on it," Bob said. "Question is, where did he hide the body? Have they found an answer to that?"

"There's also the 'why', Sarge. The Healeys needed Mr Slattery's death certificate."

"I know. Greville Healey shot the old man so it would look like an accident though, I'm certain of it. They hoped the old man would die of his injury. There'd be an inquest and it would all be a tragic accident. Then Hentree becomes Healey property, and the Healeys sell it to Hoblin's for a holiday camp."

"Except, Quentin sneaks up on the day arranged and eliminates *his* only rival . . . because he's also heard about the Hoblin offer," Laurie concluded.

As they reached the gate to Hentree, Laurie said, "Why do you think Mrs Healey might have set it up?"

"Revenge for what happened to her brother, and because she liked the idea of the money it would bring in." Bob kicked a small stone into a puddle. “There is, however, one other suspect, two if you count her friend, and I’ve been staring at them for a full week now.”

“Who?”

“Jessamyn Flowers, unfortunately.”

“Oh, you’ve definitely been staring at her, Sarge,” Laurie laughed. Then he went quiet. “What makes you suspect her?”

“Revenge, again. She’s Slattery’s daughter. I think she knew or believed her father was maltreating his wife. She feels guilty enough about it now, anyway. In mental agony I would say this morning, and not just for what she’d heard at the inquest. Second: to get her son off her back. He needed money, I don’t think she has that much of her own, and her husband could have lingered on for years. She must have known about the holiday camp – although she says she didn’t – and seen it as the perfect way to keep Quentin happy.”

“Crikey. Do you think she actually fired the pistol?”

“Not sure. Probably not, but she was a farm girl, she’d be able to use a shotgun so with a bit of practice she could aim a pistol all right.” Bob paused then went on, “To be honest, I think it has all got out of hand and she’s scrabbling to hold the bits together at the moment. She’s planning a runner as soon as the funeral’s over.”

“Did she tell you that?”

“In a manner of speaking.”

“And the other possibility?”

“Her loyal, loving friend Mrs Baxter-Salmon, who in a roundabout sort of way let me know our lovely Mrs Flowers has form.”

“Never! What’s she done?”

“Arranged another tragic accident. Mr Baxter-Salmon was a drunken pest and Jessamyn – known as Pearl Pascoe at the time – found a neat way to get rid of him. Marbles on the stairs, would you believe? It could have gone wrong: he could have just been bruised or broken a leg, but no, he broke his neck. She didn't actually do it with her own hands, of course, but as good as."

"Crikey," Laurie repeated.

"And what about Mr Pots? Is he involved do you think? He could have been up here and done what either Mrs Flowers or Quentin told him to do?"

"I don't think he did, Sarge." Laurie opened the gate into the Hentree farmyard. "Not after the way he behaved this morning."

"No. Poor fellow. Right, let's have one final look and bid this ruin farewell." Bob strolled into the yard, keeping a wary eye open for anything on trotters. "Before we start, remind me what you've found so far."

"Bits of metal; a metal suspender thing for dungarees, a length of cable for an engine; baler twine –"

"There was some green cloth, wasn't there? The dungaree fastener, did it have any cloth on it? I can't remember."

"No, it looks like it's been chewed up in a plough or a harvester or something."

"No harvesters on this property," Bob sniffed. "Hmm. Right then, you start down the field where I showed you I'd seen old man Slattery first, then come back up into the yard and the barn, see if I missed anything. I'll go into the house again, do the privy area and meet you back in the barn."

They split up and Bob headed into the house via the back door. It was all exactly as he'd left it, except now he could see that Mrs Slattery had been living here. The pantry, abandoned even by mice, had once been well-stocked. It had been stripped of anything edible – meaning someone had been into the house to supplement their rations. The dresser held generations of tablecloths and plates belonging to various different services.

The sitting room contained the village fair prize for Mrs Martha Slattery he'd looked at thrice now, but this time he noticed her chair, and – he opened a cupboard beside the fireplace – her knitting.

He wandered into the hall and looked up the stairs. Had she died in her sleep and been ignored? Slattery might not have come here every day, but he must have visited. He would have known she was dead. It was a criminal offence to leave a body unburied. Did he know that, or simply not care? Was he really what everyone – everyone he'd spoken to so far – had said: a miserly, truly unpleasant person, who'd punished his family for his own failures? And why hadn't Greville Healey said or done anything about the absent Mrs Slattery? They'd never know now.

Bob forced himself upstairs again. This was where the baby Quentin must have been born. Misery seeped from the peeling wallpaper. Bob took one final look at the main bedroom and went back downstairs.

Arming himself with a broom that hadn't been used for years, Bob went back outside and checked in the privy. All exactly as he'd last seen it. He gave a deep, heartfelt sigh. "He has to be in the barn somewhere. That's the only place we haven't taken apart," he said to himself and started to walk across the yard. Then he heard Laurie.

"Sarge! Sarge!"

"Bloody Norah!"

Laurie was trapped inside one of the stables, leaning out like a panicking thoroughbred he was yelling at the tops of his lungs over the sound of grunting, greedy, ill-fed pigs. A dozen of them at least. One of the bigger ones was jumping up at the stable door, snapping at him.

"Get them away!" Laurie screamed, seeing his boss.

"How?" Bob started to yell, but too late, some of the back runners had seen him and charged. Bob waved the broom at them and a young boar took the head off it with a single bite. He swept the handle left to right, but it made not the slightest difference.

Scared stiff, Bob turned and ran. The privy was nearest. He got there just in time to shut the wooden-slatted door on three hungry snouts. Shaking in his shoes, he pushed the feeble bolt home, turned his back and leaned against the door, hoping like hell they hadn't got the intelligence to combine their weight and push it open. He wasn't very hopeful. If they did, climbing up on the toilet bowl would be useless, he'd just seen one of the buggers stand on its hind legs to get at Laurie in the stable.

"Jesus, Joseph, Mary *and* the bicycle," Bob blasphemed, groping at his heart. What a way to die: alone in a privy surrounded by pigs.

And then he knew. This was what had happened to Slattery: his pigs had got him. The Healey boy had moved him somewhere, and then the boy had been shot. The shooter had got away, and the pigs had feasted on the farmer who didn't feed them.

"As ye sow, so shall ye reap," Joan said, quoting her Bible.

***

# Chapter 36

How long Bob stayed quivering in the privy he had no idea. It felt like hours. The grunting and snuffling stopped, but he hadn't the courage to even look between the slats to see if the pigs had gone, in case they got the scent of him again. Eventually he heard Laurie call, "Sarge, where are you?"

"In here, in the privy," he tried to reply, his voice a croak.

There was an almighty roar and Laurie charged out of his stable refuge on the Healey boy's motorcycle. Halting at the ramshackle out-house, he leaned off the machine and banged on the door. Bob inched it open to find his rescuer, sweating and red in the face. "Get on!" he screamed.

Bob nipped out of the privy and tried to shimmy onto the pillion end of the bike. It took three goes. The pigs had begun to disperse thanks to the noise and petrol fumes, but Bob's heart was having a panic attack as Laurie swerved the machine round to face the yard and head for the gate, which, Lord be praised, they had left open.

Stopping the bike next to Bob's old Morris down the lane, Laurie was grinning from ear to ear. "That was fun," he chuckled.

"Mad bugger!" Bob grunted, not unlike one of the hungry porkers and nearly fell off in his relief to be back on tarmac. Righting himself, he put a shaking hand on the door to his car and then stopped. "Wait," he said. "Wait."

"What, Sarge? We can get back to Bideford now."

"No, we can't, we've got a nasty little mystery to solve, and I think I finally know where to look." Taking a deep breath, Bob said, "First, you get us back into the barn on this machine. Right inside, if you can manage it. Then, you grab anything that looks like fodder, straw, anything."

"To distract the pigs?"

"You got it."

"I could ride back to Peony Villas and raid the compost heap."

"And leave me here on my own? Not bloody likely."

"All right. I find some sort of fodder – in case the pigs are in our way – then what?"

"We brave the sty," Bob said. Laurie's eyes shot open and he pulled a horrified face. "Got to be done, lad. It's the one place nobody's looked."

Laurie was quiet for a moment then said, "So, Healey shot the old man in the back, either by design or accident, and while he was unconscious or injured . . . That's how you saw him, isn't it, Sarge?" Bob nodded. "While the old man's unconscious he drags him out to the pigsty. Hell's gnashers! The pigs have eaten Mr Slattery."

"Could be. Healey thought he could make it look like the pigs had got him and there'd be no bits of shot gun damage left to examine. Accidental death."

"Except someone with a loaded pistol was waiting for Healey when he came back through the barn. Quentin?"

"Or Lavinia Baxter-Salmon, or potty Mr Pots. But yeah, probably Quentin. Ready?"

"Yes, but one thing, shouldn't we arm ourselves in some way, pitchfork or something – just in case."

"Yes, and that'll help us sift through all that disgusting slurry as well. Good thinking."

Laurie revved the engine, swung the bike around to re-enter Hentree farmyard and Bob struggled back on. There were no pigs in sight but even so Laurie kept revving the engine, making as much noise as possible, and as they entered the barn he yelled at the top of his voice for good measure.

Bob shuffled off, grabbed a sturdy looking pitchfork and waited until Laurie found a usable rake. Armed like this, they strode side by side to the latch-less door leading into the pig yard.

The old sow was still there. But with fewer piglets. Bob didn't want to consider why. "The straw," he whispered, "you've forgotten the straw or hay or – anything."

"Bollocks," Laurie hissed, dropped his rake and raced back into the barn and up into the hay loft, while Bob cowered behind the door.

A bale of dusty old straw suddenly fell from above, followed by two others and a heavy sack of something. Bob scuttled to drag a bale of straw to the door, then pushed it out into the yard with his pitchfork. Returning to floor level, Laurie did the same with his rake, braving the pig yard to push the fodder as far from the door and their single known escape route as possible.

"Ready?" Bob repeated, and the elderly detective and youthful policeman sidled towards the glutinous, black slurry under the collapsed roof of the sty.

It didn't take long, although it did take a strong stomach. First, they found a boot, then a long bone, chewed – probably a femur. Then the upper part of the torso and what had once been a man's head.

Bob grabbed the bone and a length of slimy green shirt material and Laurie picked up a boot, and they retreated slowly, very slowly into the barn and shoved the door shut. The spare bales of straw were used to ram it in place.

With Bob clasping the grisly evidence to his chest, Laurie ferried them back to the Morris, where it was wrapped in Bob's green tartan car rug and stowed in the boot. Then, somewhat reluctantly, Laurie returned to the farmyard and parked Greville Healey's new motorbike beside the ancient tractor and closed the gate.

They drove back to Bideford in something like a state of shock. Only getting the giggles when they opened the boot and squabbled over who was to carry the tartan bundle into Drury's office.

***

# Chapter 37

Drury had the decency to offer them a cup of tea and give them time to get themselves under control before Bob related what had happened in an even, no nonsense tone. It took a while.

Drury glanced at the exhibits wrapped in Bob's car rug lying on the floor, then steepled his hands on his desk and looked at them from one to the other. "So, what you're saying is, Healey dragged the old man out to the pig sty deliberately. He shoved him in the pig pen to look like it was an accident, that he'd fallen or tripped over a piglet, *and they have eaten him?*"

"Yes. That way, if you found pellets in Slattery during a post mortem, Healey could say he'd gone to feed the pigs or look for the old man and he'd used his shotgun to scare them away – and missed – and it was all a tragic accident. The boy knew Slattery wouldn't survive being mauled by the pigs –"

"Or eaten," Laurie whispered. "That's why we couldn't find him."

Drury blinked and with a hand encouraged Laurie to follow through.

Leaning back in his chair, arms crossed in the pose of a Hollywood cowboy icon, acting DC Oliver began a verbal report. "The shooting in the field might have been planned or fortuitous. Either way, Healey had an opportunity and took it. He pulled the old man up the field – which is when Sergeant Robbins saw them – then dragged him through the barn and left him in the pigsty, so he could say to the police and ambulance crew that he'd tried to help his uncle or boss, who was being attacked by the pigs, but he couldn't get near enough so he'd fired his shotgun to scare them away – then, because there was no telephone connection at Hentree Farm, he'd had to ride his motorbike all the way back to Ridgeway Farm to phone for help. Knowing by the time anyone actually arrived it would be too late. It might have all been improvised at the last minute, but Greville Healey had a shotgun with him – and – perhaps he deliberately hadn't fed the pigs for a week or so beforehand."

Laurie paused and said as if to himself, "Heavens, what an awful thing to do."

"Very unpleasant," murmured Drury.

"That was his plan, though, I think," Laurie continued. "What he didn't know was that someone was after *him* as well – with a pistol. Quentin Beere, or someone else, comes right into the farmyard with a gun. Whoever it is has seen that the old man is injured – perhaps a fortunate coincidence for him or her, too. It doesn't matter whether Greville Healey sees them or not, though, because they are almost certainly one of the family. Healey might even have said 'Hello, I wasn't expecting you,' then got it in the chest. Point blank range with an Army pistol – "

"Yet to be located." Drury interrupted. "How did this Quentin – assuming it is Quentin – know his grandfather and/or Healey would be there?"

"Because," Laurie changed his position, eased his shoulders then said in a rush, "Because he'd been up at Ridgeway with the Land Army girls." He turned to Bob, "That's what they weren't telling us, Sarge. You said there was something missing. Quentin and Cilla were still seeing each other."

"You reckon?" Bob queried.

"Yes, Quentin had been going up there on the quiet with a few NAAFI extras they didn't want us to know about, and he'd been keeping tabs on the holiday camp offer and Healey that way. When he finds out he's being posted abroad, he risks Healey getting what he believes is his inheritance unhindered, *and* all the money from the holiday company . . . So, he decides to do something radical or definite to make sure of . . . what, Sarge. What am I missing?"

"Not a lot." Bob grinned with satisfaction at 'his boy'. "Hentree Farm is worth serious money to a holiday company or housing developers. Healey – and his mother – thought they could get Old Man Slattery to change his will – which in fact he had already done, according to Mrs Flowers. Besides, Quentin is in uniform: he might not survive the war. By which time, Healey will have earned his right to the property by helping out all these years."

"So, Greville has to go," Laurie continued. "And Quentin doesn't give a toss what happens to his injured grandfather – assuming he'd seen him like you did, Sarge. And he wouldn't know his grandfather was subsequently missing because he's back on duty or on a troop ship somewhere."

"That's about the size of it, *Detective* Constable Oliver," Bob concluded, and looked at Drury to see his expression.

"It's like Asclepius, the Ancient Greek doctor, and the tale of the two travellers," Laurie muttered.

"Why's that, then?" Bob nudged, having never heard of Asclepius, the Ancient Greek.

"Asclepius's story showed that the things that happen to people are like the people they happen to – more or less."

Drury gave an appreciative nod of the head. "Well, you've more or less solved our case, I'll give you that."

"And can you also give him a decent letter of commendation for our boss in Cready?" Bob asked. "This boy deserves early promotion to my way of thinking."

"Not so fast. I have a few comments first," Drury replied, tapping his desk. "This Quentin Beere, who is the son of Mrs Flowers, also known as Mrs Arthur Puddicombe . . . Quentin goes up to Hentree on his push bike. Leaves it in the woods and goes through the trees to take a pot shot at his rival, knowing he'll be untouchable on a troop ship within days if not hours. But you, DS Robbins, interrupted him as well."

"Was it him, though?" Bob said, trying to square what he had overheard later at Peony Villas with this scenario. "I'm not convinced it was Quentin, to be honest. It could have been a Mrs Lavinia Baxter-Salmon."

"Ah, we know all about her," Drury said.

"You do?" Bob was astonished. Then he remembered Hester's family connections.

"You can discount the Baxter-Salmon woman. She was in here at four-thirty p.m. on Friday last, reporting a suspicious alien – not you, Robbins – at that fancy guest house."

"Hah!" Bob replied, hoping Drury was making an attempt at humour. "Let me guess, Wendell Garamond."

"Otherwise known as Wenzl Goldstein, which rather rules him out as a Nazi spy, much as she'd like to pin it on him."

Bob smiled and shook his head. "No, you're right, I don't see him as a Nazi spy, let alone a sympathiser." He paused, "Her motives might be a bit skewed – I suspect she wants him out of Peony Villas permanently so it may be nothing more than . . ." he stopped before the word 'jealousy' and grimaced. "There's something not right about Mr Garamond-Goldstein, though, I'll give her that."

"Such as."

"Call it 'copper's intuition'. He's far too anxious to partner Mrs Flowers in all matters for a start."

"Maybe he's after a marriage of convenience – to stay in England," Laurie suggested.

"Hasn't her husband just died?" Drury asked.

"Mmm . . ." Bob's mind drifted back to what he'd discounted as absurd accusations by Miss Maud Puddicombe. "Will you follow it up?"

"Haven't had chance, yet." Drury replied. "It's on my list, though. DC West and Policewoman Picket are bringing him down here about now. They've just taken that cook fellow back. You were right about him, by the way. Psychologist job, that one. Seems like he was collecting war mementoes, anyway. Nothing more sinister as far as we can tell."

"That's good," Bob said, and meant it. Then he looked Drury in the eye. "You say Mrs Baxter-Salmon was here on Friday, before I came in to report what I saw at Hentree?"

"Yes."

"Is that why Sergeant Edson gave me the address of Peony Villas?"

"Possibly."

"Ah, right, and Mrs Flowers – you know about her being an actress – and Ada Slattery."

"This is a small town, Robbins. People have good memories when it comes to its more exotic inhabitants."

"Especially one who married a policeman's son from Barnstaple."

Drury's mouth twisted. "You have been digging. Is there anything else you want to tell us about her?"

"Mrs Beere, Mrs Flowers, or Mrs Puddicombe? Not that I can think of, no."

"Well, that's that then," Drury got to his feet. "I'll say thank you for your work here and bon voyage."

"You won't forget to call Inspector Small at Cready, will you, sir?"

"I won't. Ah, you don't want that car rug back, do you?" Drury indicated the gruesome bundle by his desk.

"No, sir, I shan't ever use that again, thank you."

The three men shook hands, then the two visitors to Bideford, one older and dumpier, one every inch the rising star, prepared to leave the police station in companionable silence. Getting to the entrance first, Laurie peered out. "It's tipping down," he said, "we'd better hoof it."

"Unfortunate choice of metaphor," Bob smirked and jogged down the steps to the pavement after his young assistant.

As Bob started the Morris's trusty engine, Laurie said, "Do you think the Bideford lot have swallowed the pig theory? No pun intended."

"Drury didn't like it, but so what?"

Going up the steep High Street, Bob was once more forced to stop behind a lorry, heave on his handbrake then crash into first gear for a jerky hill start.

"I'm getting good at this," he said. "Exmoor will be piece of cake. I'm staying here until Monday, by the way. Thought I might go to the funeral. Seems only right."

They got back to Peony Villas to find Number One in a collective state of panic: there was no Gala Night supper.

Mr Pots had been returned by the police, gone directly to his cubicle and refused to come out, and Wendell had apparently put on quite a performance when asked to accompany them on their return to the station.

Jessamyn and Lavinia had taken over in the kitchen, intending to knock up egg and chips, and found all manner of food items they had never purchased, including various waxed-paper packages in the meat-safe neither could identify.

Bob took in the mayhem and said to Laurie, “Changed my mind. I’m leaving tomorrow morning.” Then, seeing Laurie’s disappointment, he added, “You ought to stay for the weekend, though. In case anything turns up.”

Laurie grinned and gave him a double thumbs up. “Thanks, Sarge, I’ll go back Sunday night on my bike.”

Bob gave him a cheeky wink and headed for the telephone to speak to the landlady at the Stag Hotel on Exmoor.

***

# Chapter 38

**Saturday**

Jessamyn accepted Bob's cheque for his and Laurie's accommodation and wrote out a receipt in virtual silence. Once Bob had folded it and stored it in the pocket of his crumpled linen jacket, she said, "Have you spoken to Detective Inspector Drury?"

"Yesterday."

"Is there anything I should know, about my father – that you might have told him?"

Bob shifted from foot to foot, he really didn't want to tell her how Mr Slattery had died, or by extension get involved in what they believed Quentin had done. Picking up his duffel bag and knapsack, he gave her a lop-sided smile, "DI Drury needs to confirm everything first. He'll tell you what's happening in the next couple of days, I'm sure."

"If I'm here," she muttered. Then in a louder voice said, "In that case, Detective Sergeant Robbins, it has been a pleasure meeting you." She led the way down the black and white chequered hallway, clip-clip on dark green high heels to the front door. Bob tried to keep his eyes on the tiles.

Once in the porch, checking to see who was in hearing distance, ascertaining they were alone, Jessamyn said, "I am genuinely grateful for what you have done," and extended her hand.

Bob frowned, unsure what she thought he had done. He dropped his bags and took her hand in his. "If you need me, I'll be at Cready Police station, near Bodmin in Cornwall. Call there and they'll get me directly. Anything, anything at all."

She leaned towards him and gave him a warm kiss on the cheek. "You are one of the very few genuine and good people I know. Actually, you're the only truly good man I know – after Arthur, my late husband. Perhaps fate will bring us together again."

Bob returned the chaste kiss. Her cheek was as soft as the silk she so favoured, as soft as a petal . . . He felt romantic and silly, and he simply couldn't help it. Choked with emotion, he grabbed his bags and hurried down to his old jalopy.

He waited until the engine was running before turning back to wave to Jessamyn Flowers. She was leaning against the door jamb with her arms crossed, a pale peachy-coloured cardigan cloaking her shoulders. Her expression was . . . Bob searched for a word and settled on 'unreadable', 'enigmatic'. What was she thinking? What had she ever been thinking? Had it all been a performance? Was there anything left of Ada Slattery that was genuine?

"Narrow escape, Bob, me lad," he said to himself, releasing the handbrake. Then he turned to loyal, dependable Joan at his side, "Shall we take the scenic route, love?"

*****

**Author's Note**

Bideford is a historic port town situated on the Torridge estuary, which is on the Atlantic coast of south-west England. People who know the town or who live there will see that I have taken a few liberties with its geography. Larkham Cross is a fictional village somewhere out beyond Abbotsham. Barley Cliff is in the general area of Green Cliff; the two farms, Ridgeway and Hentree, are, fortunately, entirely fictitious. Westward Ho! (the only place name in England with an exclamation mark) played an important role in the preparation for the Normandy landings during World War II, but I have chosen to bypass this as what was happening at the time was very 'hush-hush'. The area did, however, welcome many wartime refugees. Railway enthusiasts will see that I have omitted the train stations of Bideford and Westward Ho! That is because they didn't fit with my story.

If you would like to know more about my books and their settings, drop into www.jgharlond.com and/or my blog 'Reading & Writing', Please feel free to leave a comment.

My author page on Facebook is:
https://www.facebook.com/JaneGHarlond

## The Author

J. G. Harlond (Jane) grew up near Bideford in the south west of England. She studied in Britain and the USA, and for many years worked in European international schools. In 2010, she gave up an enjoyable, safe and successful career to write full-time. After travelling widely, Jane is now settled in rural Andalucía, Spain. She has a large family now living in diverse parts of Europe, an aging horse and a small but demanding garden.

**Novels by J.G. Harlond:**

*The Empress Emerald*
*The Doomsong Sword*

The Chosen Man Trilogy
*Book 1 The Chosen Man*
*Book 2 A Turning Wind*
*Book 3 By Force of Circumstance*

Bob Robbins Home Front Mysteries
*Local Resistance*
*Private Lives*

**Praise for J.G. Harlond**

**The Empress Emerald**
*'Every once in a while, you come across a piece of literature which marks its territory in your heart (...) a brilliant work that is certain to stay with the reader for quite a long time.'* Indian Book Reviews.

**The Chosen Man**
Readers' Favorite 5* and a 'Discovered Diamond'
*'Be prepared to be immersed in this book. A well-written period novel that I highly recommend.'* Historical Novel Society Review.

**A Turning Wind**
Readers Favorite 5* and a 'Discovered Diamond'
*'I was transported back to a time of adventure and swashbuckling action on every page.'* Readers Favorite review.

**By Force of Circumstance**
Reader's Favorite 5* and a 'Discovered Diamond'
*'This is the stuff of good historical fiction: made-up characters adventuring alongside real ones who existed, and undertaking incredible adventures which are written so convincingly you are a little shocked to discover, at the end of the book, that it was all, after all, fiction.'* Amazon Vine Voice.

**Local Resistance: A Bob Robbins Home Front Mystery**
Discovering Diamonds Book of the Month
*'A wonderful story of village shenanigans, war-time racketeering, murder and Nazi spies set in an idyllic Cornish fishing village. Despite the ominous rumble of WW2 in the background, it's a thoroughly enjoyable and humorous read, full of memorable and loveable characters.'* Karen Charlton, best-selling author of the Detective Lavender series.

Printed in Great Britain
by Amazon

54629880R00180